T5-ACP-054

Pray For Mercy

Part One of a Trilogy

To Ms. Sumalingam
Thank you
For the Love
and Kindness

Pray For Mercy

Part One of a Trilogy

Prather Hawkins Jr.

Murcyboy Publishing

Pray for Mercy: Part One of a Trilogy
Copyright © 2009 by Prather Hawkins Jr.
Murcyboy Publishing

All rights reserved. No part of this book may be reproduced (except for inclusion in reviews), disseminated or utilized in any form or by any means, electronic or mechanical, including photocopying, recording, or in any information storage and retrieval system, or the Internet/World Wide Web without written permission from the author or publisher.

Printed in the United States of America

For more information visit:
www. pratherhawkinsjr.com

Pray for Mercy: Part One of a Trilogy
Prather Hawkins Jr.

1. Title 2. Author 3. Fiction

Library of Congress Control Number: 2008911871

ISBN-10: 0-9822897-0-7
ISBN-13: 978-0-9822897-0-9

Thank you.

First: Thank you Lord for loving me and blessing me with the gift of storytelling. Mom, Dad, Momma, Cherish, Jalen, Laila, Mani, my brothers and sisters: Daniel, big sis Phyllis-and that gravy, Rashita aka 'skibo'!, Syreeta (my twin), lil' brothers Ha'neef aka Neef Buck, Hakim...baby girls Jamila and Dionne-learn, take in everything you can from us older ones... in-laws; Marty, Ski stay cool fellas. Nephews and nieces... All the rest of my family-it's too many of y'all I love all of you though. My brothers for life: Original squad, Gerald aka'G' for having such a big heart, Big Tone-thanks for understanding, Big-Jason, Garret, Mike, Chris aka Kools, Ki Ki, Major, Hunter, Tom, Cousin Davie, Chris Dunbar 'for letting me hold your 'Sigma' bike when I didn't have one, Big Bob, Karl stay up, Omar Ortiz, Coach Vince Miller-rip, you took me off the street, Miss Miller 'mom', Elder Derant and Pastor Polin, Faith Assembly of God, Saints Tabernacle-my new home, Oski'locka for the cuts when I was broke in the projects, cousin Jay-G-this D&k H#$%!-Lol!, Tony D, Sheed, Nilzy, Light Foot and the Company, The Comission, Wizza, B. Mavi, Eem and Jordan, Sandman-*Daddy! *96 Frankford Squad-Gooo! Uncle Fletch rip, Chuck, Lee, Phil, M. Brooks, the Welsh family, Oow-Waddy, Jim Jim, O', Ak. Everyone that read the sample chapters: Big-Chuck! Jessica aka 'Gangsta J'—this was* so necessary!

Special thanks to Diamond Depot of the Franklin Mills Mall, Ms. Trina Reid and Lysette Artiss

To everyone I missed, apologies, Love you all though,
Thanks for all the love and support.
This is just the beginning!!!

FOREWORD

Outside of learning how hard life can truly be, there are only three things obtainable from the Ghetto. Those things are Love, Money, and, Respect. When Love is obtained from the Ghetto, it can be gained from many things. If someone comes from a prominent family, just happens to be good looking, or is very good at something that is popular there, like sports or being a hot rapper… they will be loved. This especially applies to males.

When Money is obtained from the Ghetto, it will more than likely be earned illegally…through some source of income outside of this country's economic system. If the dollars are tax-free- they are illegal. And even if a person in the Ghetto is lucky enough to start his or her own business; whether it is a barbershop, dry cleaners, corner store, hair salon, etc, he or she will not always be able to fork over Uncle Sam's complete share at the end of each year.

Respect is the trickiest of all to obtain, because it has another side…and that is DISRESPECT. Respect can easily be tied in with being feared…giving truth to the old saying, "A coward can kill you." Respect can come if someone's family has money, if one is a stylish dresser, or if he or she is deemed as a flat out thorough person because of how he or she does things that people in the Ghetto have an interest in.

The flip side of Respect is "DISRESPECT". It can either cause people to try to be something they are not, or make them react out of anger and land themselves in jail or, worse. They can end up dead or cause the death of someone else. But for some, being Disrespected fuels them…to go out and do great things for themselves. It can lead them to living better lives. While the ones who receive any, or all of D'Evils, are considered to be 'What's up', the ones who are DISRESPECTED are really the fortunate ones, because they have the most drive to do better for themselves and the easiest pathway to possible success.

CHAPTER 1

With the end of the school year just three weeks away, most eighth grade students are well adjusted to the daily routine of waking up early in the morning and being to school on time, but not Randy. For the fifth time, his mother has called his name and he still has not awakened. Randy is in his usual comatose state at this time of the morning. Even when his mother, who is hardly ever around, does send him up to his bed at a decent hour, he still finds it extremely hard to get sleep. He does not find it hard to get to sleep at night because he suffers from insomnia or anything. He just has a fear of what the next day will hold for him. When he wakes up…he is fully aware that during and after school, he will be teased because of his family's misfortune.

A normal school night usually consist of him going into his room, which he shares with his younger brother, turning out his light, and climbing into his bed fully clothed. Once in bed, he lays there watching television until he falls asleep…never getting back up for the rest of the night to brush his teeth or wash-up after a hard day of playing in the projects. He thinks that since he usually has to wear his clothes for two, sometimes three times in a row, he does not have to worry about undressing.

Because of this, he frequently has to fight off reoccurring ringworms.

His parents are not in touch with his life, so they do not see when their child's clothes need cleaning. Almost every night he will lay in bed staring at a broken down, 13-inch black and white television that sits on a milk-crate next to his bed. The milk-crate that the TV sits on is filled with cobwebs and debris. The television is frequently left on all day, because there will not be any electric-bill coming to the house at the end of the month since Randy lives in the projects.

"Randy!" His mother called again as she stood on the other side of his room door…never laying a single finger on the knob.

Randy opened one eye and looked over at her shadow under the door; cast by the sunlight that shined into the hallway from the bathroom window. Then, clinching the lid tight in frustration, he buried his face deep into his pillow. He was bothered because it was morning already, and the thought of not being able to get anymore sleep was enough to make him want to cry. But he was 15, and those days of crying when he could not sleep any longer were over.

"*Yes*?" He finally answered.

"Get up…it's almost eight-fifteen!" She said, sounding annoyed.

But nothing was wrong with her. This was how she usually sounded this early in the morning. She stood in front of his door for a few more seconds listening for the squeaking sound of his old box spring. The sound let her know he was attempting to get up. Then she turned and headed back into her bedroom. Because she stayed up half the night getting high, she was normally as tired as he was at this time of the morning. And like most people who do the same, she would sleep until mid to late afternoon. Randy rolled on to his back, opened one eye, and then closed it back again…clinching it tightly. He knew that once his mother had gone away from his door, she would not be returning to bother him again. He maneuvered his head around on his pillow trying to find a cool spot. Then he exhaled…hard through his nose after finding one. Drifting back into his comfort-zone, he turned his face…moving his left cheek into a puddle of saliva.

"*Ugh*!" He grimaced loudly, popping his face up from the pillow.

With a look of disgust on his face, he wiped his cheek with his left hand and rubbed his wet fingers on his bed sheets. He knew that going back to sleep was pretty much an after-thought. He laid his head back down and began staring at the ceiling. With both his eyes now open and burning from the morning sun, he began what he called his evaluation period. He would start weighing his options of whether or not he should go to school that day. If he could not come up with enough reasons then he would go back to sleep and not re-awaken until most of the school day was over.

He took about 40 seconds to find enough reasons to get up. The main reason was that he did not eat the night before. Deciding he was not about to be late for school, he swung his covers off and jumped up from his bed fully dressed. He knew that if he hurried he might catch breakfast. Scratching a head of hair that desperately needed to be cut, he looked around his room…puzzled. Then he let out a big yawn, rubbed the back of his neck, and made a mad dash over to a big wrinkly green trash-bag sitting in a corner. Randy knew that out of all seven trash-bags that aligned the wall in his room, this particular one was where he usually found something worth wearing. He was fully aware that anything coming out of it would be dirty. But he wasn't worried about that, because he had a quick and easy method of making things look halfway clean.

Randy dropped to his knees in front of the bag and started digging away with total confidence. He pulled dirty clothing piece by piece out of the bag; tossing them over his head until there was a pile in the middle of the floor behind him. He reached in once more and pulled out a pant leg and froze; recognizing the print of those particular jeans, because they were his favorite. Then he stood to his feet, ripping the entire pair from the bag; pulling other pieces of clothing out with it. Both thighs were heavily soiled, but he never allowed himself to feel down about having to wear dirty clothes. He was used to it. He turned and ran out of his room, down the hallway to the bathroom… where he did his cleaning.

As Randy readied himself for school, the FBI was serving an indictment to a major drug dealer just a few blocks away in his Frankford neighborhood. A good-looking, clean-cut, Black FBI agent walked up to the dealer's house and stood on the top step. His name was Rapth. He was in his late 30's and rough edged. He lightly knocked twice, then stepped aside to allow another agent to come forward with a battering ram. The agent moved into position and prepared to ram the door down. But as he reared back, the doorknob jiggled and the front door crept open. Rapth quickly stepped back to the front. Seconds later; the front door opened and the gorgeous face of a four-year-old boy peeked out. With his eyebrows raised, and a clueless expression on his little face, he looked as if he was about to ask the agents a question. Rapth had learned that there was a small child who roamed freely through the house while both of his parents slept, and he figured it was worth knocking first to see if he would answer. The sight of the child brought a smile to his face.

As he walked into the house, Rapth leaned forward, and picked up the boy, then silently directed the other agents where to go as they entered after him. He carried the child through the living room, and sat him down at the dining room table in front of a bowl of cereal. It was clear that the boy had prepared his own breakfast. Fruit-loops and milk were everywhere.

Sitting on the edge of the bathtub, Randy started scrubbing the stains from the thighs of his pants with a light-pink washcloth and a bar of bath soap. He did not know whose washcloth he was using, but it did not matter because he would just deny it later if confronted about it. After scrubbing the thighs until they foamed with soapy water, Randy held the pants up in front of him to check for any food or dirt stains that he may have missed. In Randy's cleaning system; once he could no longer see any stains, it was time to stop scrubbing and go dry them. He tossed the soapy, discolored washcloth and soap into the sink then hustled out of the bathroom…back to his bedroom with his wet pants over his right arm.

He stared down at his ruffled bed. Then, with one big swipe, he cleared everything off…onto the floor. He laid his pants down flat, reached to grab the iron, and plugged it in. After a few seconds, he spat on it to check for heat. His tart morning breath caused a stinky-vapor to rise as he pressed the iron down on his pants. As soon as the iron touched his wet pants steam shot straight up into the air causing him to rear his head back, dodging the cloud.

If someone had entered the room, and did not know any better, they would have thought he was in there warming up leftovers. He watched the soap, water, and dirt crystallize on the fabric. Then he figured it would be impossible to iron the pants until they were completely dry and still catch breakfast, so he decided he shouldn't push it any further and un-plugged the iron. After he removed the clothes he had worn for the past three days, he picked up and put on a gray sweatshirt that he had knocked to the floor. After slowly putting on his wet pants, he grabbed his old dark-gray sneakers and slid his feet into them. His sneakers were white at one time, but now they were nearly nine months old. He dropped to one knee, tied his sneakers up, and then took off from his bended position…running straight out his room…down the stairs and out the front door; slamming it shut behind him.

While searching the downstairs area of the drug dealer's house, one of the FBI Agents came across a cabinet that was a little off-centered… exposing an opening in the counter. The agent looked down into the dark crack, did a double take, and then quickly walked toward the front door. He returned with a sledgehammer. Then raising his arms in a windmill like motion, he reared back, lifted the sledgehammer above his head and brought it straight down crashing through the countertop. The loud noise echoed throughout the lavishly furnished home which woke up a heavy-set man sleeping in the upstairs bedroom. In a panic, he sat straight up in bed. But, as he looked around his room, he could see that the walls were lined with Feds. He was the man they were looking for and they were patiently waiting for him to gain consciousness.

A young, Black, agent named Smith snatched open the blinds, letting sunlight into the dark room…hitting the man in the face. As he adjusted his sight, the man's eyes came to Rapth. He stared in disbelief as Rapth sat on the edge of his dresser, chowing down on a bowl of cereal. The other agents laughed as Rapth, taking notice of the man staring at him, held the bowl out to offer him some.

A small crowd gathered in front of the man's home as they brought him out. They whispered, pointed fingers, and some even found it humorous to see the man in hand-cuffs as he waddled toward the unmarked car wearing only dark-brown khaki shorts, a pair of white low-cut sneakers with no socks, and a thin platinum Cuban-linked chain that dangled around his neck. However, they became silent when the FBI agents emerged from the house carrying automatic machine guns and four big clear plastic bags filled with kilos of cocaine. As the last agent left the house carrying bags of the drug, one of them fell in the doorway. As the bag broke open, a kilo hit the floor causing a crystal cloud to mushroom almost two feet in the air.

"Can you get that for me, please?" The agent playfully asked one of his colleagues.

Moments later, the drug dealer's wife came to the front door and started yelling and screaming. She directed her vulgar comments at both the agents and the small crowd of people.

"Baby, get the kids in the house. Get the kids back in the house!" Her husband pleaded as he slid over to the car window. "And go call Diego. Go call Diego and tell 'em what happened!"

An agent paid her no mind as he hurried and swept up the drugs. Then, he quickly placed the broom against the wall inside the house before rejoining his partners as they prepared to leave.

"He said to call, *Diego*?" Rapth asked Smith, as they stood outside the car window laughing sinisterly.

CHAPTER 2

Randy was now only three blocks away from his school. He could see its big chimney sticking up over some trees ahead of him. Acting like someone crazed about being to school on time, he flew past a group of small children walking with their parents and other students heading in the same direction. As he came to a crosswalk where the crossing guard was holding up students on the corner, some of the students laughed at how Randy looked as he jogged in place. Many of them knew that Randy hardly ever came to school, especially not on time. They also used to say that he only came to school to eat the free lunch, and at lunchtime would watch him eat to see just how hungry he was. Randy, and the other kids watched as a cop car with a flaring siren escorted four unmarked cars carrying federal agents pass the intersection without stopping. Randy caught a glimpse of the drug dealer as the cars went by, but he thought nothing of it.

Once the intersection was clear, Randy took off like a mad man as the crossing guard led everyone across the street. He was so focused on getting to the school that he managed to run right past the gate with the big Rottweiler behind it. The dog was infamous in the neighborhood because he always seemed to jump out of nowhere…scaring the students nearly to death as they passed by heading to school. Before he reached the last crosswalk leading to the school, he darted past an alleyway where his two closest friends, cousins Zac and Tooch, were walking.

"Hey…wasn't that…?" Zac asked as he turned to Tooch with a frown on his face.

Tooch just nodded his head 'yes' and smiled.

"Never mind." Zac said, hunching his shoulders and shaking his head.

Randy ran across the crosswalk through the school's gate. With his pants still noticeably soaked at the thighs, he made a desperate attempt to get to the cafeteria without running into anyone. He made it to the other side of the schoolyard and reached to grab the door handle. But just as he was about to pull the handle, the door flung open and a number of children with refreshed looks on their faces emerged. Breakfast was over, and they were now ready to start enjoying what little time they had left to play in the yard before the bell rang.

"Hey, did anyone see Zac or Tooch?" He asked in an attempt to save himself from embarrassment...although it was written all over his face.

"No!" Some of the students only responded because he was blocking their way.

"Ah, man..." Randy sighed pretending to be tired from looking for them.

"You said you're looking for Zac and Tooch?" A kid named Khalil asked.

"Yeah! Why?"

"Because they're right there." Khalil pointed toward the middle of the schoolyard. Randy looked back.

"Alright...thanks, Lil" Randy said starting over toward them.

Tooch and Zac were now halfway across the schoolyard and heading straight toward him. They knew right where to find Randy after seeing him fly pass the alleyway. Zac hopped over a puddle of water left from the rain the night before, then walked right up to Randy saying...

"What's up, man?"

Zac was a dark brown-skin boy with light brown eyes, perfectly straight teeth and thick wavy jet-black hair. He also had thick eyebrows and eyelashes that complimented his complexion. Almost every girl who knew him adored him. Randy and Tooch were also very attractive. Randy was a tall dark brown –skin bowed-leg boy with sharp facial features and slanted eyes. Zac was only a single shade darker than he was. Older women, old enough to be Randy's mother always complement him by saying '*boy, wait until you get older*'. Tooch's smooth and even brown skin tone and long straight black hair is what made him. Tooch's hair wasn't straight naturally, but being from down south that was his hair style of choice. People made references to him as the boy with the perfect skin. He and Zac had both of their ears pierced and wore earrings. Zac shook Randy's hand showing his bright white smile. He was smiling at Randy as if he knew something. Tooch greeted him with a handshake then turned around to check out a few girls who were walking pass them.

"What's up?" Zac repeated with a toothy grin.

"Nothing..." Randy responded. "I'm cool."

"We saw you *running*."

"Y'all saw me running? Where were y'all?" Randy asked with a puzzled look on his face. He knew if he had run past his best friends without noticing them that would have been really embarrassing.

"You were *movin'*!" Zac said, slowly shaking his head.

But Randy just stood there looking confused.

"Nigga was tryna eat." Tooch said, in his usual calm voice.

"Yeah, whatever" Randy quickly shot back.

Tooch smiled at him saying, "It's cool, though," then patted Randy on the shoulder.

"Fuck you, man!" Randy said as he moved away from him.

Suddenly, there was a big commotion in the schoolyard. All three boys turned to see what was taking place. The loud commotion was over a kid named Omar, who was in the 8th grade like them. He was in a heated football game. The score was close and it was just about time to go inside when Omar caught a short dump-pass and was heading straight toward the defense. They watched as Omar shook the first defender that attempted to tag him...making the boy lose his shoe. Then he shook three more defenders before taking off...untouched...running up the schoolyard like an Olympic track star.

"They're not catching him." Tooch said, showing little emotion as Omar blew pass them.

"*Speed of the Puma*!" Omar yelled as he broke through the crowd toward the other side of the schoolyard where the touchdown was.

The whole play was beautiful to every one except one kid. He was the same kid who tried to catch Omar and lost his shoe. He was a light brown skinned, heavyset boy wearing a tight fitting; pea green hooded sweat suit with no pockets.

"I got him back here!" The kid said, trying to cheat.

He was lying clean through his teeth. He then went and stood in the spot where he supposedly tagged Omar pointing down to the ground.

"This is where I tagged him, right here!"

"Get outta here! You didn't tag him," A second kid who was playing quarterback for Omar's team spoke up.

"Ya 'hon, I did so...I got him back here." The kid defended himself.

"That's a shame...you're a fat damn cheater," The second kid said, still speaking in his calm voice.

"What's wrong?" Omar asked as he trotted back down the schoolyard with his arms extended outward.

"Omar, he said he got you!" The quarterback answered. He remained calm because he was used to seeing this type of stuff happen. If there was a pee-wee football hall of fame in Philadelphia Omar would have been in it on the first ballot. He was an exceptional talent when it came to sports.

"Get out of here with that, man…you didn't touch me!"

"Yes I did! Right here!" The heavyset kid insisted still pointing down at the spot.

"*No you didn't*!" Omar shouted standing directly in the heavyset kid's face.

"*I did so*!"

"You're a *fat* cheat'n *son of a bitch*!"

"Yeah, *whatever…*"

The heavyset kid, known for being a cheat turned and started walking away just as Omar slammed the football down into a puddle of water. The football hit the water and made a big splash, causing some girls who were jumping rope nearby to take cover. The sound of a whistle chirped throughout the schoolyard as a light-skinned man wearing black sweat pants and a scarlet-red short-sleeve t-shirt came running over. It was Mr. Wyble, the school's math teacher. He was also the basketball coach. He ran over and stood directly between the two boys as the first bell sounded.

"*Up*! Time to go…" Zac said, as he, Tooch and Randy turned and started toward the building.

As they started walking Randy could not help but to notice who was rushing straight at them. It was his grade-school crush, LaFonda. Randy looked down and gave himself a quick once-over, but what he saw did not look good. The thighs of his pants were still noticeably damp, and he needed a haircut so bad that the sides of his hair were sticking out pass his ears. Then he remembered that he had forgotten to brush his teeth and wash his face that morning.

"Hey Zac, let me see your brush", Randy said in a panic.

Zac was un-aware of what was happening. He reached inside his book bag and handed over his brush without hesitation.

"Tooch, you have any gum?"

"Nah…I only have this." Tooch said, showing the gum in his mouth.

Tooch knew exactly what was going on. There was not too much that went on around the boys that he did not catch on to. He was one of those kids from the streets. He was always on the look out for things around him.

LaFonda walked past and gave a flirtatious look, but the look was not in Randy's direction.

"*Zachareeey*..." She said, dragging the last vowel in his name with her sweet little voice.

LaFonda was one of the few girls in grade school with a sassy short haircut, and she was mature enough to pull it off. Tooch and Randy looked at her with their mouths hanging open. But Zac just stared at her silently for a few seconds before answering. He was not in any way infatuated with the brown-eyed young goddess with the cocoa complection.

"What's up, lady?"

"*Damn*!" Tooch bellowed in sorrow for Randy.

He knew Randy had a big crush on LaFonda, and that his friend had no chance at getting with her because of her family's prominence in the neighborhood. Tooch tapped Randy on the chest with the back of his left hand. Then, resting it on Randy's shoulder, they continued walking.

"Yo, did y'all see how LaFonda was on me?" Zac asked, walking between Tooch and Randy.

"Yeah, we saw her" Randy smiled.

Tooch looked at Randy but did not say anything. He saw how well Randy was taking it. He knew Randy was a true friend and did not get jealous about anything.

"Yo...I'm going up to class." Tooch said, as he gave Zac and Randy quick handshakes before turning and running off.

"What's up with him wanting to get to class so early?" Randy asked as he and Zac watched Tooch hurry into the building.

"Uh...he wants my pop to buy him some bull crap car he seen over in Jersey." Zac said, flagging his hand in Tooch's direction.

Everyone knew Zac's father had money from being deep in the drug game, but no one knew whom he dealt with.

"Yo... LaFonda's on you..." Randy giggled...changing the subject.

"Yeah, I know...but there's something about her I just don't like."

"*Really*? Like what?" Randy asked...looking at LaFonda as she entered the school through another entrance.

"I don't know what it is yet," Zac said, squinting at Randy, "but when I find out, you'll be the first to know."

"Whatever..." Randy said, laughing lightly to himself.

"Hey Randy!" a voice called out as the boys walked into the building.

"Ah, it's your boy," Zac said, as they stopped.

Mr. Wyble came running up to them. He was carrying the football that had been thrown into the puddle.

"Hey, what's up man?" Mr. Wyble said gleefully...giving Randy a more than happy handshake.

"Nothing. Why, what's up?" Randy answered in a crabby, nonchalant voice.

"Are you ok?" Mr. Wyble asked...noticing Randy standing with his stomach sunk in.

"Yeah, I'm fine."

By the looks on Randy and Zac's faces, Mr. Wyble could clearly tell that they wanted him to get straight to the point.

"Hey, well...I've been meaning to ask...what you are doing this summer."

"I don't know what you mean?"

"I was wondering if you were planning to play ball anywhere."

"Nah, I can't say that I planned to... why?" Randy shrugged...unimpressed with Mr. Wyble's words.

"The reason I'm asking is because I'm putting together a summer league team...and I thought you might be interested in playing, since you plan to play in high school next year."

Randy nodded his head slightly before responding.

"I'll have to think about it for a while...but, I'm not making any promises, though."

Randy then looked at Zac and nodded, signaling for them to start walking again. As Mr. Wyble watched them walk away, he stared at what Randy was wearing; shook his head, then turned and started back toward the schoolyard.

CHAPTER 3

Inside the building, the children were going nuts. They were running, jumping and yelling in the hallways and stairwells, showing that it was almost time for the summer break. The NTAs tried their best to control the ruckus, but only ended up wasting their breath.

"It's definitely time to get outta this joint," Zac said, walking behind Randy.

Grabbing the banister with his right hand, he pulled his way up the staircase.

"These kids are turning this place into a 'kiddy hop.'"

"I feel you, trust me!" Randy agreed moving aside for two students who went racing pass them heading down stairs.

"Hey, I've been meaning to ask you, what's with Mr. Wyble?" Zac asked looking clueless. "Why does he seem to be so interested in you…you think he might be gay?"

"No, man!" Randy laughed looking back at Zac.

"Personally, I think he likes you a little *too* much! I was just telling Tooch that at dinner the other night." Zac said as he looked at Randy.

He then started doing a hump walk…spanking the air as he and Randy walked toward the doors to leave the stairwell.

"Man, get outta here with that…" Randy said reaching back pushing him lightly with his left hand. "Don't even try that shit…"

"You're laughing…so I know you're listening." Zac tried his best to keep a straight face, but then started laughing as well.

"He just wants to see me play on his summer league team, that's all. Why is it that as soon as an adult wants to help out a young kid, it's always, 'watch your ass!'" Randy said, shaking his head.

He let go of the doors and walked out into the hallway.

Zac did not say anything to him at first, but then he looked over at Randy with his face tore up in disgust and said, "But yo, on the real. What you just said, sounded real *nasty*, man. You sound like a chick, yo."

"Yeah, it did sound kind of nasty." Randy agreed.

Zac and Randy made their way down the busy hallway walking along the left side close to the lockers. At first, Zac looked like he had nothing on his mind, but once he noticed the female he had recently lost his virginity too, he put on a serious look saying, "Hold up…I'll be right back," then slid off.

The girl was in eighth grade also and was standing in front of her open locker looking like she was searching for something. Zac smoothly walked over, and stood behind her, placing his hands in the small of her back and gently sniffed her neck. The girl shivered and turned her back to her locker moaning, "Stop, *Zaaach*!"

Zac moved next to her and leaned back against the locker, preparing to engage her in the kind of bull-crap conversation that men give women just to keep the lines open, so they can call every once in a while…out of the clear blue…to still seem interested so they can maybe hit again.

"What's up with you?"

"Nothing, why?" She asked looking at Zac from underneath her curled bangs that fell just above her eyebrows.

"No reason, I was just asking. You said that you were going to call me."

"*What*!?! I thought you were supposed to *call, me*!" The girl shot back.

Zac cut a look across the hallway at Randy as he stood there laughing. Randy knew Zac was trying to fast-talk his way out of something that he created, and, that Zac was very bad at this.

"*Oh*…I was supposed to call *you*?" Zac said, looking at the girl as if confused.

"Uh, hun…" She frowned.

"Oh man, I'm sorry, with all this graduation stuff, I've been mad-busy and I forgot."

The girl noticed that Zac kept looking behind her in Randy's direction and quickly turned around to see if they were trying to clown her. Randy was looking away with a serious expression on his face. He waited for her to turn back around, and then started laughing again.

"I still have your number…I'll give you a call later, alright…*ok*?" Zac said as the girl stared back at him as if she did not believe a single word he was saying.

"*Whatever*." She said slamming the door to her locker shut before pulling her book bag over her shoulder and walking away.

Zac moved aside as she rolled her eyes at him. Then he shook his head and walked back across the hall to Randy.

"*Damn*, I'm losing it," Zac said, exhaling as if exhausted. "It's definitely time for us to get out of here. These girls are getting too use to me…plus, I'm tired of 'em anyway."

As the boys continued down the hall, Randy, walking a few steps ahead of Zac, came to a sudden stop…causing Zac to bump into him.

"What're you doing?"

"There's something you haven't gotten tired of…" Randy said with a smirk.

He tooted his nose in the direction of a girl named Michelle. She was the one whose attention Zac longed for. And once he stepped from behind Randy and saw her, his feelings showed all over his face. All three years they were in middle school he tried his heart out to land her, but never got any closer than a few telephone calls.

Michelle was very headstrong. She believed everything her parents told her about how little boys are. This is a major part of why Zac wants her so badly. He looked on in anger as Michelle stood over by a water fountain talking to Omar. They were very serious, exchanging flirtatious looks as they were conversing. Omar was leaning against a locker enjoying all of what Zac wanted for himself. The two looked like they were not in a hurry to go anywhere any time soon either. Seconds later the late bell sounded and Michelle and Omar parted slowly, going their separate ways.

"What time do you want me to call you tonight?" Zac overheard Omar asking.

"It doesn't matter, but if you can, call before eight…alright…that way my parents won't be able to complain."

"Yeah…I'll do that…" Omar said; squinting his eyes and biting down on his bottom lip as he watched her walk away.

"Bye, *Michelle*…" he bellowed.

"See you, *Omar*…" she said in a soft tone of voice looking back at him.

"She didn't want to talk to me, but she can talk to him though, right…" Zac said with a look of surprise and disgust on his face.

"Yeah, I hear you…" Randy shook his head.

Zac did not like what he had just seen one bit. He was not very good at hiding his emotions, and he wasn't very good at holding his tongue either.

"Whatever happened between you two?" Randy asked as they started walking again.

"She wasn't tryna hear anything I had to say," Zac said, shrugging his shoulders in disbelief.

"Like *that*?" Randy asked as Michelle came near without speaking.

"*Yeah*, just like that..." Zac mumbled. He watched as she walked pass... almost drooling on himself.

"Well, it definitely looks like she is tryna hear something now...a whole lot of something." Randy said shaking his head as she walked further down the hall. "Come on, man...we're gonna be late."

As Randy and Zac walked into the classroom, they could see their classmates acting out. The teacher was not in the room and the students were sitting on top of the desk, playing MASH, flying paper airplanes across the room, and just flat out being young. It appeared that they were all trying to get out the last bit of play left in them before going to high school, where they would become young adults. "Damn, they're acting like we're not going to high school next year," Zac said.

"Yeah, tell me about it," Randy agreed as he stood near Zac's desk.

Zac then sat down in his chair and watched the kids sitting next to him play MASH. Moments later, a stout Black-woman entered the classroom causing the ruckus to settle immediately. She carried a small black roll book filled with yellow sheets of paper in her left hand. As she headed to her desk, Randy started over to his seat where he sat down and began staring out the window to his left. After the teacher, Ms. Avery, got herself situated, the classroom door opened again and in stepped LaFonda holding a small piece of white paper in her right hand.

"Ms. Avery, I'm sorry..." LaFonda said, clearly trying to be extra nice to the teacher. "But the Principal asked me to have you double-check your 'Honor Role' List for the final report."

Ms. Avery took the note and unfolded it. Then she picked up a black-pen from her desk and started writing something next to the list of names on the paper. There were only three names on the list, and Zac's name was one of them. Zac also had perfect attendance for the second half of the year. He worked hard in school because his father told him that if he brought home good grades he could have whatever he wanted. And Zac did infact have everything he could think of. Randy, however, was in a different boat. He would have repeated this year if he had not gotten left back last year.

Randy sat straight up in his chair in one last desperate attempt to be noticed by LaFonda. "*Randy*, do you have a pen!?!" Zac blurted from the opposite side of the room...where the teacher required him to sit whenever Randy came to class. He stood up from his desk clearly unaware of who had just entered the room. But when LaFonda heard his voice, she almost broke her neck turning around to see him.

"Mr. *Young*, you're about to go to high school in a few months..." Ms. Avery said to Zac without raising her eyes up from writing on the note. "Don't you think it's about time you start acting like it?"

The class started laughing.

"Sorry, Ms. Avery," Zac said, in a low voice before taking a pen from a neighboring student.

LaFonda could not do anything but smile as she gazed over her right shoulder at Zac. But once she turned back around, Ms. Avery was waiting to hand the paper back to her. She tried playing it off by rubbing the back of her neck, but Ms. Avery knew exactly what was going on.

"LaFonda..." She changed the subject. "What high school are you going to next year? Have you decided yet?"

"No, I still have no clue..." She exhaled. "But my mother keeps pestering me...so I kind of figure I should know something sometime soon."

"Have you been offered any money for private schools?"

"Not really, but my parents are still discussing that with some of the schools, though." She glanced back at Zac and gave a flirtatious smile, but Zac just looked back at her with no emotion.

As Randy watched LaFonda he noticed how she looked over at him and cut her eyes away...as if she might catch something if she looked at him too long. He put his head down on his desk looking at his clothes...wanting to cry, but he knew that he would never be able to live that down; especially since some of the children from the neighborhood already making up things about him to totally destroy his name. Then he felt his stomach growl and started feeling even worst about himself.

CHAPTER 4

A concerned Mr. Wyble headed to the nurse's office. He knocked on the door three times and stuck his head in saying, "Uh…Ms. Sanchez, how're we doing this morning?" Then he laughed trying to get her to laugh along with him.

"*WE* are *alright*…but what do *YOU* want?" Ms. Sanchez quipped as she tended to the sore knee of a child who was sitting on the patient's bed with his face frowned.

"Come on now…Just because I am being nice to you does *not* mean I want something. Aren't I just a nice guy?"

"*Honestly*? Ah…*no*! And so far, every time you've stuck your face in my door, you've wanted something…so are you looking to continue your streak through graduation?"

Closing the door behind him, Mr. Wyble entered the room laughing.

"I'm *serious*. What is it?" She repeated.

"All jokes aside…this time it's not '*what* is it', it's *who* is it" Mr. Wyble said, trying to become more serious.

"Well then, *who* is it?"

"Randy…Randy Murcy."

"What about him?"

"It's supposed to get hot out there today…*Really* hot! And he has on a heavy sweatshirt. Will you do me a huge favor and keep an eye on him… *Please*? I'd greatly appreciate it."

"*Sure*, I'll do it…without question… It's my job…but I want you to know, it's for *him*." Ms. Sanchez said cracking a smile.

"*Aah…see*? I knew you cared. That's why I love you so much…you're a great woman." He started smiling again.

Ms. Sanchez then flagged at him as he ducked back out the door.

Mr. Wyble walked into his office in the down stairs gym room. It was in desperate need of a paint job. He placed a crate that he was holding in a corner, sat down in his old, beat up leather chair, and started looking over at a calendar hanging on the wall.

"Let's see..." he exhaled. "This weekend..."

He started checking a roster list that he picked up from his desk.

"Sean, Rob, Lil' Chuck..."

But once he got to Randy's name, he leaned back and stared at it before placing a question mark next to it.

CHAPTER 5

Rapth and the other agents were down town at the federal building preparing for their next assignment

"You wanted to see us?" Rapth asked as he and Smith walked into their superior's office.

"Yeah, come in and have a seat. This will only take a few minutes." Their superior said as he sat behind his desk. "I just wanted to let you boys know that you did an excellent job serving the indictment. I was expecting it to be at least another four to five months until we got something solid."

"Thank you, sir." Rapth said, holding a paper cup in his right hand and a coffee pot in his left.

"But, I want to tell you two…" He said, pointing in their direction, "There is still a lot of money over in that section…I want you to keep your eye on that area."

Rapth nodded his head in agreement.

"Since he went down …" Their boss continued, "there is an awful lot of drug business sitting on the table."

"You don't think someone would hop in that quick, do you?" Smith asked.

"*Shit*…I don't see why not." The boss responded.

"Well, who do you have in mind?" Rapth asked, as their superior reached down on his desk and tossed a manila envelope in front of them.

"I'm quite sure you both have heard his name come up in conversations before."

"Oh yeah…Shannon Young? Rapth said after opening the folder. "But isn't he…I thought Narcotics was handling him?"

"Yeah they were, but apparently he's been a little slick with his business as of late…and they're suspecting that he's starting to tie in with some of the heavier suppliers in the city."

"So, what do you want us to do…has he been handed over to us?" Smith asked nonchalantly as he stared into the window of a building across the street…watching a woman as she opened gifts. It appeared her colleagues were giving her some sort of party.

"No…not yet, but it is only a matter of time before he will be."

Just as their superior began to let them in on the rest of the case, another agent, who was searching for the coffee pot, opened the office door.

"Thank you," He said with a playful sarcasm as he lifted the half-full coffee pot out of Rapth's hand. He knew that Rapth had a thing for drinking cold black coffee…Something he apparently started in college to help him get an instant rush before cramming.

Rapth quickly refocused and asked…

"But what about Diego…You think we should keep an eye on him?"

"No… just worry about this guy. Diego will find a way back into prison on his own. He always does."

CHAPTER 6

The phone rang in the classroom, waking Randy from a comfortable snooze. He opened his eyes and quickly started wiping slobber from under his chin before being seen. Ms. Avery, who was already standing in front of the blackboard, hurried over and answered it.

"Ah…ok…no problem. Yes, Randy Murcy is here," Ms. Avery said, staring over at Randy out of the left corner of her eye. "Randy!"

Randy popped his head up.

"The nurse would like to see you," Ms. Avery said, as she hung the phone up and headed back to her desk.

Randy wiped his face again with his sleeve then got up.

"Here, take this and go to her office." Ms. Avery said, extending her right hand out to give Randy the hall pass.

Randy lurched over toward her, took the hall pass, and started for the door. Before he left out Ms. Avery said…

"If you weren't feeling well… I don't see why you just didn't stay home, like you usually do!"

Randy left the classroom as everyone let out a hardy laugh, at his expense. But he figured he'd save face and not get upset with her for what she said. He was use to hearing these kinds of discomforting remarks from his teachers.

"Can I go with him?" Zac blurted out again, purposely trying to get under Ms. Avery's skin.

"*No, Zachary…Sit down*! You can not go with him." She yelled as Zac started walking from behind his desk as if she already told him 'yes'. "And one more out burst like that and you're father will be getting a call from me… And I am *sure* that will give your summer a nice jumpstart."

"*Yeah*, and I'm sure givin my father a call would *jumpstart* your *big-ass...*" Zac spat back at her in a low voice that only the students around him could hear, evoking laughter.

Randy walked down the empty hallway to the nurse's office. He was really in no rush to get back, so he figured he would take as much time as he liked. He came to Tooch's class and peeked inside room 302 to see what was happening. At first, Randy tried getting his attention by waving, but then he just started watching Tooch...who never raised his eyes up. Tooch was leaning all the way back in his chair reading a piece of paper he held in his hands. From the way that he was focusing on his paper, Randy figured he was taking a test. Then he noticed Tooch look up from his paper to say a couple of words to Omar, who was sitting next to him.

Omar was concentrating on his own paper when a boy sitting to his right reached over and tapped him on the shoulder. The boy tried to hand him a small white piece of paper, but Omar looked as if he was being annoyed... refusing to take it. He then turned to Tooch, and shook his head as if to say 'Do you believe this guy?' Randy smiled as he watched Tooch laugh to himself when the boy handed the note back to a girl who sent it to Omar.

As Randy continued down the empty corridor, he watched the school's janitor open windows in the hall. It was going to be sunny, 87-degrees that day. He rolled up the sleeves on his heavy sweatshirt and looked down to see that his pants had finally started to dry. He walked by the Principal's office, noticing a well-dressed boy being reprimanded by his mother. After slapping the boy around, she started for the wood and glass doors. Randy hurried up and moved out of the way...acting as if he was not trying to be nosy.

"I work too damn hard everyday, for you to have me coming up here for this shit!" The mother said, after she smacked her son in the back of the head a few more times.

"I don't know who the *fuck* you think you are, but wait and see what happens when I call your father!"

"Mrs. Johnson, we want to thank you for coming up here so quickly..." A nervous sounding older White woman in a long red dress said as she stepped out from the office door and watched the angry woman and her son walk away.

Randy ended his quest to the nurse's office where he lightly tapped twice on the door before walking in.

"Hey, Ms. Sanchez...you wanted to see me?" Randy asked, giving her a million-dollar smile. "Hey...Randy..." She shot back.

Randy walked over and took a seat in the chair next to her desk.

"So, what's new? Are you ready for graduation?"

"*No*..." Randy answered bluntly. "I'm not going..."

"And why *not*?" Ms. Sanchez asked with concern.

"I just don't feel like going."

Ms. Sanchez had an idea of why he did not want to participate, but she did not want to push it any further. Randy's real reason for not wanting to attend was that his parents probably would not show up. And even though Zac's father had offered to pay for his suit and all other expenses, so that he could graduate with his friends, he still declined. Ms. Sanchez sat there staring at Randy for a moment as he looked around the office. Then she reached inside the top drawer of her desk and slid an inhaler with his name on it across to him.

"Here, and I want you to take this note," She said, grabbing a pen and paper.

"I have a hall pass." Randy said raising up a big brown wooden block with a big number 311 written in black permanent marker on it.

"Well...now you have two." Ms. Sanchez said handing him the note.

"What's this for?" Randy frowned after reading where her note was directing him to go.

"Mr. Wyble said he might have something for you."

Zac's words from earlier that morning began ringing in Randy's head as he came to the bottom of the stairs where the gym room was. As he tiptoed over to the big green metal doors, he paused...then slowly pulled, peeking in as they creaked open. He was looking to see if anyone else would be down there with him when he met with Mr. Wyble. Randy heard a loud squeaking and clanging sound coming from inside the empty gym. But he could not tell what it was. As he moved his head to see what it was, two teachers walked by on the overpass just above him. Hearing their voices, Randy quickly ducked behind a wall, but the two women did not see him and continued on their way. He waited a few seconds then poked his head back inside the gym doors and heard the sound of the school janitor's raspy voice saying, "How's it going, Wyble?" as he pushed a folded lunchroom table on its side wheels.

"Well, things could be better I guess." Mr. Wyble sighed, from a place in his office that Randy could not see.

Randy did his best to gather himself together before opening the door all the way. Then, with confidence, he walked in. As he approached Mr. Wyble's office, he could see the coach leaning over a treasure chest looking trunk that was sitting on his floor. He was sifting through colored t-shirts with white plastic numbers ironed on the backs.

"Mr. Wyble, you asked to see me?" Randy asked as he walked in.

"Yeah," He said, sounding muffled.

Mr. Wyble stood up holding a red t-shirt with a number one on the back of it. He tossed it over to him.

"Go in there and put it on." Mr. Wyble thumbed his right hand over his shoulder toward the bathroom inside his office.

Randy looked down at the shirt then glanced at the bathroom before walking over to it. Minutes later, he came out wearing the short-sleeved shirt and took a seat in a metal folding chair by Mr. Wyble's desk.

"Feel better?" Mr. Wyble asked…sitting behind his desk.

"Yeah…thanks."

Mr. Wyble then placed his hands behind the back of his head and started rocking in his chair.

"So…do you know what high school you want to go to next year?"

"No…I didn't know I had a choice." Randy answered looking around the gloomy office.

"Well…you had a few schools interested in you after last season. But, I told them they would have to wait because I wasn't sure whether or not you were graduating."

"Yeah…" Randy said humbly…slightly nodding his head.

With his extremely poor grades, hearing about a high school selection was something very new for him.

"I thought high schools weren't allowed to recruit?"

"They're not…but who's going to blow the whistle?" Mr. Wyble said, flagging his left hand. "Now, I've already taken the liberty of speaking with your home room teacher, Ms. Avery, about what your grade level will be next year…and she told me you *are* graduating."

"Yeah…"

Randy was not at all surprised by the news. He was well aware of the rule that said he could not repeat the same grade twice.

"Now, there is no need for you to be embarrassed by anything anymore." Mr. Wyble said, trying to bring Randy's spirits up with a few words of encouragement. "The school that you will probably be attending will not have the same kids from around your neighborhood. And you will have the potential to earn yourself a free college education…unlike some of these other kids who run around here making fun of you. Playing in the summer league would also be an excellent opportunity for you…" He added. "But I am not saying that so you could jump right out and say 'yes'. I just think it might be worth some serious thought on your part."

Randy just looked at Mr. Wyble.

"Anyway..." The coach continued; let me give you this note so you can get back up to class."

Mr. Wyble started writing on a piece of paper.

"But, I already have a note!" Randy said, holding up the two hall passes he already had. "Never mind," he exhaled, as Mr. Wyble handed him the paper.

"Now you have another one. Think about what I just said...alright?"

CHAPTER 7

Randy went back into his classroom feeling much cooler and refreshed in his new red t-shirt that smelled like a Halloween costume. Everyone, including Ms. Avery watched as he walked over to his desk, sat down and picked up his work sheet.

"Hey, do you have a pen?" Randy turned and asked a boy sitting directly behind him.

"No…I only have this one." The student answered without even looking up at him…as if Randy was not worth talking to.

"Randy!" Ms. Avery called. "Here, come take this one."

Ms. Avery held out a pen for Randy to get, but as soon as he stood up the recess bell rang.

"Class, leave your things on your desks. We will pick up where we left off once we get back!" Ms. Avery shouted as all the children scurried to their feet.

"*Randy…*" She said, getting the whole classes' attention. "In case you didn't know…it's not supposed to work this way. You come to school in the beginning of the year and do your work, not at the end. But that's alright, though…you'll have all of next year to try and do it again."

The whole class busted out laughing at Randy as they left the room… except for Zac. He never laughed at any jokes about his friend, because he knew what was going on at home. But so did Ms. Avery. She just acted like she did not care.

Zac walked up and stood beside Randy as he stopped in front of her desk. They both stood there staring down at her, causing her to become fidgety. Noticeably uncomfortable, she pretended to go back to her writing.

A few minutes later, Randy and Zac walked out into the hallway and quickly started weaving their way through the crowd. Randy spotted Tooch running up ahead of them and shouted, "*Tooch*, get the *wall ball*!"

"Yo, we can stop running now…" Zac said, after he and Randy continued to run a little more. "He'll get it."

Just as the boys made it to the main part of the schoolyard, a voice called out Randy's name.

"Randy!"

He and Zac shook their heads and looked at each other after seeing who it was.

"*Damn*, I just left this dude!" Randy mumbled as he squinted from the bright sun.

He turned in Mr. Wyble's direction, then said…

"Hey, I'm gonna catch you over by the wall…This shouldn't take long."

"Alright…" Zac said, laughing sarcastically. "Don't be too long, though. You know we only have a few minutes."

"I won't…" Randy smirked.

Mr. Wyble came over and stood in front of him.

"I wanted to know if you made your decision yet." He asked.

"Ah…actually, I did." Randy then started shaking his head 'no', like he was trying to let Mr. Wyble down easy.

"I thought about it, but I don't think I'm gonna be interested in playing anywhere this summer. I think I'm just gonna try and get a job, so I can pay for my school clothes and books and stuff."

Mr. Wyble looked like his heart had dropped to his butt. And given Randy's current home situation, he could not come up with anything to combat what was just laid on him.

"Hey, Mr. Wyble, do you have another football?" A small boy asked… looking up at him like he was pissed off about something.

He looked down at the boy, and then shook his head.

"No, I don't…the boys took my last one." Mr. Wyble said as he looked over at a large gathering of boys playing a rough game of football in the middle of the schoolyard.

"*Man*, that's a *shame*! They always get to play with the football!" The boy said, sucking his teeth as he walked away.

"*Hey*!" Mr. Wyble called, getting him to stop. "Why don't you go over and see if you can play with them?"

The boy paused for a moment and looked over at the crowd. He saw a kid, who was much bigger than he was get slung to the ground…hard. The small boy continued to watch as the kid rolled on to his feet and went charging headfirst…back into the crowd without even dusting himself off.

Randy started laughing to himself when the boy looked back at Mr. Wyble, as if he thought the teacher was trying to be funny.

"*Randy, come on*!" Tooch yelled as he stood with Zac and a few other boys where they played wall ball.

"Alright, Mr. Wyble…I have to go." Randy patted him on his left shoulder before jogging over to go join the boys.

"*We need one more*!" One of the boys waiting with Zac and Tooch yelled in a panic.

"How about him?" Another boy asked, pointing at Omar as he came walking from the building.

"*Aah, man*… Not this clown," Zac said, pushing his way pass Randy and Tooch to watch Omar as he doubled back to speak to Michelle and some of her girlfriends.

"*Zac*…" Tooch said, as they watched Omar stroll toward the girls with total confidence.

"He's the only one out here at least close to our size, who is not already playing football."

Then Tooch shouted to Omar…getting his attention away from Michelle, "*Hey*! O! You wanna play?"

"*Huh*?" Omar responded, hesitant about leaving Michelle. "*Uh*, *yeah*… I'll play!"

He said…playing it cool.

"*Aah, man*…this is *bullshit*!" Zac said, turning toward Randy and Tooch, causing the boys to laugh.

"See…that's what I like! Always down for whatever." Tooch said, giving Omar a firm handshake.

Omar entered the crowd of boys, making it an even match up. Omar was the same size as Zac. Randy and Tooch were both a little taller. As they all stood in front of the wall waiting for Tooch to start the game, Zac walked over and gave Omar a death look. Randy, who was standing next to Omar, laughed at Zac again as Tooch threw the ball against the wall as hard as he could.

The boys began playing a game called Suicide with a sense of urgency. The rules of the game were simple: whoever touched the ball but did not catch it, had to run to the wall and tag it while calling 'Suicide', or 'Suey' for short. Anybody could be beamed anywhere on the body and head, including the face, by whomever ended up with it last. This was one of the most intense and competitive games the boys loved to play with each other. They scrounged around for the ball like madmen every time it bounced off the wall. Then they tried to inflict pain on whomever touched it. Randy, who normally dominated the game, soared through the air…catching at least fifty percent of the balls.

"*Hey*, I didn't touch it!" One of the boys pleaded as Randy reared back and steamed the ball at him…smacking him in the back.

"*Suey*!" The boy shouted as Tooch picked up the ball; hurling it at him.

The boy ducked his head, causing the ball to nip him before it went slamming into the wall. Tooch did not say anything. He just looked at him.

"*Damn, man*!" The boy said, sulking as he went back over and stood with the crowd.

No one seemed to care that he was ticked off, because when someone got angry, it only made the game that much more interesting. Zac touched the ball without catching it. As he attempted to flee for the wall, the ball bounced into Omar's hands. Omar quickly planted his feet, reared back like a pitcher, and leaned into his throw. The ball steamed straight for Zac and hit him dead in the center of his back just before he tagged the wall. Zac turned and stared at him as he made his way to the wall to throw the ball back into play.

Omar threw the ball at the wall. As it bounced high up in the air, both Tooch and Randy went up for it. But neither one of them came down with it. They both sprinted for the wall, leaning forward shoulder to shoulder. But as they both tagged out on time, the same boy that Tooch nipped in the head threw the ball anyway…striking Tooch under his right armpit, as Tooch turned back around facing the game having to put his arm up to block his face.

"*Oh boy*! That's a *free hit*," one of the other boys said laughing.

This was a carnal sin in the game of Suicide.

"*Get that ass up there, boy*!" The others joined in, instigating as Tooch grabbed the ball from Zac after he stopped it from rolling out to the middle of the schoolyard.

They all knew the rule; that whoever caught the ball after somebody else touched it, and threw the ball at the person who touched it…and missed, also had to flee for the wall and tag out before getting beamed. But a person could not, however, get what is considered a 'free shot' on anyone without paying for it.

Tooch watched as the boy slowly walked up to the wall and placed his hands on it.

"*Face* the wall all the way, *man*!" Zac said laughing.

Tooch was given just one shot at hitting the boy, but that was all he needed.

"You already know he doesn't miss..." Randy chuckled as he watched Tooch load up.

Tooch chucked the ball and hit the boy right behind the same ear.

"*Ooh*!"... "*Aah*"! ... "*Man*!" Everyone laughed while gasping for air.

Seconds later the bell sounded, signaling the end of recess.

"*Oh yes*, *ladies* and *gentleman*...still without a single miss on his splendid record, *my man*, *Tooch*!" Randy said, shaking Tooch's hand to show him some love.

And as the boy who was hit started toward the school, Randy, Tooch, Zac and Omar all stood together staring at him.

CHAPTER 8

Randy was now suffering from sharp hunger pains, but he still felt a bit like Hercules after his efforts in the game. Then he turned to Omar and said, "What's up, Omar?"

"Omar..." Omar answered, swinging his hand back to shake Randy's hand.

"O Yeah...," Tooch said jumping in. "This is my best friend right here, Randy."

Tooch wrapped his left arm around Randy's neck.

"Oh...ok." Omar said, looking back to see if Zac would introduce himself next.

Zac cut his eyes away, pretending as if he did not see what was going on.

"Where are you from?" Randy asked.

"North Philly."

"Ah, you used to live down there?"

"Yeah.."

"So, you live up here now right?."

"Yeah."

"Oh..." Randy raised his eyebrows in surprise, "You're mixed, right?"

"Yeah, man..." Omar laughed. "I'm Black and Puerto Rican."

"Who's Puerto Rican...your mom or your pop?"

"My mother is."

Randy continued asking questions getting to know Omar better as Zac walked behind them pretending not to be aware of Omar's presence. He had his head down, looking in the opposite direction. He could not have cared less about who Omar was or where he was from. All he cared about was when he was going back.

"Oh, yeah…this is Zac." Randy said, extending his right arm as Zac walked into it. "He and Tooch are cousins."

Randy introduced them, then stepped back while trying not to smile.

"Hey, what's up man?" Zac said, shaking Omar's hand with a laid back, conceited snarl on his face.

"Yeah…um, I'm sorry, Omar. This is my cousin." Tooch impeded.

The four boys walked to the building together and stepped inside the doors.

"We have health next, right?" Tooch asked Omar while pointing down stairs.

"Yeah" Omar answered moving toward the stairs.

As Zac and Randy headed to class, the boys went their separate ways.

As Randy and Zac walked upstairs, Randy looked down at Tooch and Omar. Then he turned to Zac saying, "Why are you acting like that?"

"*Acting* like *what*?" Zac answered, like he didn't know what was going on.

"You know…"

"*Man*…I'm *cool.* I don't know what you're talking about."

Randy smiled at Zac and shook his head in disbelief.

"I don't believe you. You're actually hate'n over a girl."

"*What*? What are you talk'n bout? I am *not*!" Zac frowned as if he thought Randy was crazy.

"*Yes* you *are*! I know you. Why else are you treat'n him like that?"

"Because I don't *know* him…what am I supposed to do…get down on my knees and service him?"

"Now you're just being a flat out *cockhead*!" Randy said, before becoming silent…creating dead air between he and Zac for a few moments.

Then, Randy began to smile once he looked back up at his friend. Zac tried not to look over at Randy or smile, but ended up smiling anyway.

"You're a *sucka*."

"No I'm not!" Zac chuckled.

"You're gonna act like that over a girl, a *girl*!"

"No, man, I was talking to her first, *hun*."

"You're acting like a baby" Randy pushed Zac lightly. "But let me ask you a question: though…you were talking to her first, *right*?"

"Yeah…" Zac nodded his head.

"But she wasn't talking to *you*, though. So what does *that* mean?"

"*Man, whatever*", was Zac's only come back.

Upon reaching their classroom, Randy and Zac spotted Ms. Avery standing in front of the door handing out papers to students passing by as they went into the room.

"Why did we have to have double periods of this *shit*? *Damn*!" Zac sighed.

"Don't say anything, just go inside, take your seats and get started." Ms. Avery said in an annoyed tone.

After taking a paper Zac and Randy looked at each other, and then went inside…separating as they moved toward their seats. Ms. Avery walked in behind them slamming the door shut and saying, "Do this worksheet. Then, when you are finished, come up here. I have another one for you."

"Ms. Avery, why do we still have so much work to do? Graduation is two and a half weeks away…" Zac asked, straddling his chair.

"Because, I have to teach you this by the time you graduate. Besides, you have to learn it at some point before you get to high school. And, *Zachary*…the next time you have something to say, raise your hand. Don't just call out."

Randy sat at his desk staring down at his worksheet with a blank expression on his face, then raised his hand.

"What is it, Randy?" Ms. Avery answered, sitting at her desk with her hands folded up in front of her face.

"I need another worksheet. I can barely read this one."

"Here then. Come get this one," she said, taking another worksheet from a pile and holding it out for him.

"Not that it'll matter much…" she added, "even if you could read it."

The class laughed at Randy as he walked over and took the paper from her hand. Then he turned up his lips and looked back at Zac. As Zac flagged her, he blew up his cheeks and crossed his eyes to show that he thought she was nothing more than an over-weight woman with a mean attitude.

"We only have a little more than an hour until lunch, so try not to spend too much time on one question. We need to at least get through five of these today."

"*Uuh, man*!" The whole class murmured throughout the room.

"Ms. Avery, How many do we have left? *Dag*!" Zac asked, calling out again.

Ms. Avery quickly looked at Zac like she was getting ready to say something, but then she noticed Zac's hand was in the air.

"That's not important! But like I said, try not to spend too much time answering one question. You have to start cleaning out your desk."

Ms. Avery was clearly behind schedule with her class. She had a bad habit of waiting to teach things. Then she would try to force-feed them information. As Randy tried to concentrate on the worksheet, he found it extremely hard to do so on an empty stomach. He sat there staring down at the worksheet, trying to complete most of the questions he somewhat understood. He got a large portion of them correct before his stomach churned again, causing him to pass gas from being empty. Then he put his head down, resting on his arms.

Randy looked over at Zac and noticed him staring.

"After school…you're coming to my house, *right*?" Zac asked under his breath.

Randy did not understand.

"*What*? I don't understand you." Randy mouthed back, lifting his head up some.

"*After*, *school*, come with me to my house." Zac motioned his lips once more.

Ms. Avery, who was reading an article in a magazine, raised her eyes up to see what was going on. She looked over at Randy, who had already dropped his head back down to his arms, then at Zac. Zac was acting like he was doing his work. After watching the teacher lower her eyes and go back to reading, Randy and Zac peeked at each other laughing silently.

"Never mind, just wait until lunch," Zac said, under his breath, pointing up at the clock above the black board.

Ms. Avery sat the magazine down, then reached across her desk and picked up a list with her students' names on it. She was required to place the grade her students would be going into next to their names. She placed the number nine next to almost everyone's name on the list, but once she came to Randy's, she paused and looked over at him as he was looking down through his arms. She shook her head and wrote the number '9' next to his name.

"It's a *darn* shame." She mumbled to herself as the lunch bell sounded.

CHAPTER 9

The boys arrived down stairs in the lunchroom where Tooch and Omar were already waiting. Randy walked in after Zac, then went over to Tooch and Omar saying, "What's up, *William*?" giving Tooch a cheesy smile.

"*Yeah*, alright, nigga…You know better." Tooch replied, shaking Randy's hand.

Tooch did not like anyone to call him by his real first name. It was also his father's first name, and even though his father was dead, he did not like it because his father denied him at birth.

"You know I'm just kidding, Twin," Randy said, smiling at Omar.

"Yo, Omar, what's up man?" Randy shook Omar's hand.

Zac sat on the other side of Tooch, away from Omar, then turned his head, looking in the opposite direction. This was Omar's first time sitting with the boys.

"*Man*, this isn't going to be over with fast enough," Tooch said, looking around the lunchroom at the crazed students talking loudly.

"Yeah, tell me about it…" Zac agreed just as an NTA went running across the lunchroom to break up two boys slinging milk at each other.

"Didn't I already tell you two to cut this shit out?" A Black middle-aged female shouted, gritting her teeth.

The woman appeared to have a very low tolerance level for bullshit from students. She grabbed the two boys under their underarms and walked them away. They both looked like they really were not too concerned about what she had to say. Randy got up from the lunch table and headed over to get his lunch saying, "I'll be right back…y'all want anything?"

"Nah, I'm cool…" They all answered simultaneously.

Then Zac called over to Randy.

"*Yeah*, bring me a chocolate milk, please? Thank you."

Minutes later, Randy returned with his lunch on a tray and extra chocolate milk in his right hand for Zac. He tossed Zac the milk, and then put his food down on the table before sitting down himself. Omar watched as the three boys discussed everything that they would be doing after school. It was as if he was not even there.

The school day finally ended and Zac and Randy were standing outside in the middle of the schoolyard waiting for Tooch.

"What do you think is taking him so long?" Randy asked.

"I don't know…but hey, did we get homework?" Zac asked.

"No, we just…"

A student yelling cut Randy short.

"*Fight*!" The boy shouted as he raced down the street behind four other boys.

They were chasing a tall skinny Black kid wearing a floppy book bag. A large crowd of students followed the boy who yelled. Tooch and Omar were amongst them.

"There he goes right there," Randy pointed.

"*Come on, let's go get him*," Zac said, taking off running.

"*Nah*…hold up…" Randy said frowning.

He stood in the same spot with his hand on his stomach.

"I'm going home. I have to go to the bathroom."

"Alright then, We'll be pass your house later!" Zac yelled before taking off running again.

"Alright."

Randy turned and started walking in the opposite direction, but before he could take three whole steps, he spotted LaFonda walking out of the schoolyard. Randy picked up his pace, trying to catch up with her. After reaching her, Randy slowed and started walking behind her as they were led across the street by the crossing-guard.

"LaFonda!" Randy called as she reached the sidewalk.

She turned around slowly, noticing who it was. Then she lowered her eyebrows thinking…'What could he want'.

"What's up with you and Zac?" Randy quickly asked, adding his friend's name to save himself from any further embarrassment.

The other students were now looking at what was going on.

"Why?" She asked.

At first, she had a serious look on her face. Then she cracked a smile.

"*What*…He say something to you about me?"

"*Ah…um…nah…*not today, but I do hear him saying stuff about you from time to time."

"Really?"

"Yeah…" Randy said, going along with what he just said.

"What kind of stuff does he say?" She blushed, acting surprised.

"You can't really expect me to tell you that, he'd kill me. Besides, you might get a big head."

"*Please*, Randy…I promise you I won't say anything or get a big head. *Please.* " She then came close to Randy locking her left arm around his.

Randy looked down at her arm wrapped around his and took a few quick sniffs to get a whiff of what she smelled like. He was surprised at how fast a guy like him, with no reputation, could be accepted because of who his friends are.

"*Please…*" She continued, squeezing tighter.

Even though she was not holding onto Randy for his sake, it was still good enough for him to finally have her clinging to him. This was something that Randy could not imagine happening in his wildest dreams.

"I'm surprised he didn't say anything to you about it yet."

"About what? What did he say?" she pleaded.

"You promise you won't say anything?" Randy asked, sneaking a look at her out of the corners of his eyes.

"Yes, *please*. I *promise*, I won't say anything…hope to die. Now tell me what he said!"

"He said that…he thinks you're pretty."

"That's *it*?" LaFonda's facial expression dropped. "I already *knew* that…he told me that back when we were, like, in six grade together…when I first met him."

LaFonda let go of his arm.

"And, he also said that he would like to take you out sometime, to like, dinner or a movie…or something." Randy said, moving his eyes around, trying to think fast.

"Really?" LaFonda said, grabbing his arm again.

Randy started having butterflies because he unmistakably knew that he was feeling LaFonda's left tot-ta pressing up against his arm and make no mistake he had a serious 'woody' in his pants. He looked over to his right at some students walking on the other side of the street. The students were looking at LaFonda clinging to him. They frowned, wondering what the hell a nice girl like her was doing with him. They thought they had surely tarnished his name enough, talking about him being dirty, so he would not have the slightest chance of getting with anybody nice looking.

"He said..." Randy continued, "...he thinks you're not allowed to have a boyfriend, *so*..."

"*Oh*, I can have a boyfriend!" LaFonda blurted. "But he would just have to keep it a secret, that's all. What else did he say?"

"I'd rather not tell you that. When you get the time to talk to him, he'll let you know."

Randy wanted to discontinue his lies and not go any further, because he was afraid that he might be putting his best friend into too tough of a situation. Especially since LaFonda was known to hang out near Zac's house.

"I won't tell him that we talked or anything. But, I'll try to hook the two of you up, ok?"

"Thanks, Randy."

"No problem. Don't worry about it, lady."

Randy now spoke with a much more laid-back expression than he had at first. His butterflies quickly went away after he started realizing how gullible LaFonda was...pressing her tongue up against the roof of her mouth when he was referring to the "something" Zac wanted to do with her. He really liked her when he did not know much about her. However, when he found out something about her that he strongly disliked, he didn't like her anymore.

LaFonda cracked a smile at him, and then walked into the front gate of her house, which was not too far from their school. Even though Randy now had a different frame of mind about her, he still stopped and looked back at her.

"*Damn*! He exhaled, shaking his head. "That girl's *fine*!"

CHAPTER 10

When Randy arrived home, he was surprised to find his front door unlocked. He walked inside finding yet another surprise; the house was clean.

"Hello!" He called, as he placed his bag down on the floor and went straight up stairs to the bathroom, closing the door behind him.

Minutes later, he sat down on his living room couch. The couch was originally white with a flower print, but his family had had it for a while and it was now a little closer to beige. He reached over and turned on the 25-inch television-set that sat on top of a broken floor model Television. But just before he settled into watching his cartoon, he heard a thump coming from up stairs. He quickly turned the television down, and waited to hear another sound before getting up to go investigate. He slowly crept up stairs to the second floor where he opened each door, checking to see where the noise was coming from. He heard the thump sound again. It was coming from his sister V's room. Randy went over and opened the door. His older sister V was laying in bed in a fetal position holding her stomach.

"What's wrong with you?" He asked as he went and sat at the foot of her bed. "You didn't go to school today?"

"No, I went to the doctor's." V moaned.

"What did they say was wrong with you?"

"I have food poisoning."

"*Really*! From *what*?" Randy asked rearing his head back frowning.

"I think it was from the food I ate the other night."

"*Ah*…that's not good…where'd you get it from, down the street?"

"No, Downtown…"

"Did the doctors give you any prescriptions for it?"

"Un'hun. Mommy went to get it."

"Well, Kiddo…I hope you feel better soon." He said as he placed his right hand gently on her foot.

Suddenly, he was startled by three hard knocks on the front door. Seconds later, there were three more hard knocks.

"Hold up. I'll be right back." Randy hopped up from the bed and took off downstairs.

He raced to the front door, opening it without asking who it was.

"Yo, what're you doin'?" Zac asked looking him from head to toe.

"Nothing, why?"

"Come on, then. Come with me to my house."

"Why, y'all ready to leave already?"

"Yeah…We're taking the ride early, so we can stay longer."

"What time do you want us to leave?"

"Not for at least another half-hour."

"Why so long?"

"Because, I still have to fix my tire."

"Alright… I'll meet you around there in a few minutes."

"Alright…just try and hurry up." Zac then turned and jogged off Randy's steps to go catch up with a crowd of students walking down the street.

He went and stood in front of his pantry, looking at his bike buried under what looked like a pile of rubble left over from an explosion. The pile was made up of old shopping-carts, taken from super markets, water hoses, heavy-duty home appliances that his family had no need for since they lived in the projects, and some other stuff that was just stuck in there for the heck of it.

Even though Randy had not seen his bike in a few months, it was still in pretty good condition. A 'far cry' from the way he lived. It was an all white professional trick-bike with black-mag wheels, tires and handlebars. The brake cables and gyro were also black. The only thing that was presently wrong with his bike, however, was that it needed a little air in both tires. He squeezed the back-brake grip on his handlebars, lifted his bike onto its back wheel, then pushed it ticking into the living room, then leaned it up against the front of the couch before going back into the kitchen.

He returned to the kitchen where he opened the refrigerator and pulled out a pitcher. Walking it over to the sink, he grabbed a big plastic cup from the dish rack. The cup had faded cartoon characters from an old movie on it. He took the cup and pitcher over to the wooden table, sat them down, and opened the lid of the container, looking down inside it to see what he was about to drink. It was grape Kool-Aid with lemon slices and a dash of ginger ale soda. This was Randy's favorite drink in the whole world. He filled the cup with as much as it could hold. Then he stood back drinking, everything that was in the cup before taking it down from his mouth.

"*Urp*!" He burped, tossing the empty cup into the sink. "*Oh boy… hew*!"

Randy was now ready to go for a nice long bike ride. He placed the pitcher back in the refrigerator then walked into the living room, grabbing his bike and headed for the front door. Randy closed the door behind him, then hopped on his bike and headed for Zac's house, looking down at his half filled tires.

No more than ten-minutes later, he arrived at Zac's house where he received a more than warm welcome from Zac, Tooch, and their newfound friend Omar. The warm reception was a reminder of why he loved these boys so much. The boys were sitting in front of the house watching Zac attempt to fix his bike.

"You ready?" Zac asked, looking up at him from where he was sitting on the ground in front of his bike.

Zac was dipping his deflated front inner tube into a white bucket of water.

"Yeah, I just need to put some air in my tires." Randy answered looking down at his wheels.

"What's up, Omar?" Randy asked, smiling as he went and picked up the air pump.

"Nothing man, chillin." Omar answered, sitting on the steps watching Zac in boredom.

"What's up, Tooch?" Randy cracked a smile, noticing Tooch's facial expression.

"Nothing man…I'm chillin."

Tooch looked like he was nearing frustration as he stood with his arms folded watching Zac take his precious time. He usually let Zac try to fix his bike himself, but then he would become fed up.

"*Move, man*!" Tooch yelled moments later…charging toward Zac and abruptly pushing him out of the way.

Tooch started trying to push Zac from in front of his bike, and as Tooch shoved him, he almost knocked the bucket of water over. A small amount of water spilled on the ground and onto Zac's sneaker.

"You don't know what the *hell* you're doing. *Watch out*!"

"*Yes* I do. I need a new inner-tube…" *Zac* tried reasoning with Tooch before getting pushed out of the way.

"No you don't, man!"

"I do, now move!"

Tooch and Zac were acting like two toddlers in a crib fighting over a rattle, and it came as a complete surprise to Omar. It was also evident to him that Zac clearly did not know what he was doing. But Zac would not allow Tooch to fix his bike for him without at least putting up a good fight first. This way Tooch could not say that he ever did him a favor.

"Don't worry about it, O'…this always happens." Randy chuckled, looking at Omar who just sat there watching with his eyebrows raised.

Randy remembered that Zac was not too crazy about Omar and looked back down at Zac smiling. Zac quickly caught on to what Randy's facial expression was about and turned up his lips. After winning the push and shove battle, Tooch pulled the inner tube out of the water and dried it with a towel. Then , after inflating it to see where the hole was, he deflated it and put some repair glue over the holes and on a rubber-patch before lighting both the inner tube and patch on fire with a match. Seconds later, Tooch blew out the fire and placed them together…binding them. Randy, Zac and Omar stood in silence as they watched Tooch stuff the inner tube back into the tire and fill it up with air. Once the tire was finished, Tooch stood to his feet. Then, pulling the handlebars from the ground, he turned the bike upright and let it bounce.

"*Ok*?" Tooch said sarcastically, as Zac came over and sat down on his bike…smiling from ear to ear.

Zac had his head down admiring his bike and would not dare bother raising his eyes up to look at him. The tire was now as hard as a rock and sealed airtight.

"*Alright*, *now* are we ready to go?" Tooch asked while looking at Randy and Omar with his face still frowned.

As Tooch turned to go inside the house, two thuggish looking young Black men, in their 20's, came walking up. They stepped onto the front steps and knocked on the door. The young men did not even bother stopping their conversation as they rang the doorbell.

"Is your father home?" One of the men asked Zac only after noticing the boys staring at them.

"Yeah…he's here. Hold on." Zac got off his bike and went over to the basement's window.

"Dad! You have someone here to see you!" He yelled.

"Alright!" His father yelled back from the basement.

A few moments later; a good-looking, well-dressed, well-groomed Black man, in his late 30's stepped to the front door wearing black-framed glasses, a black tank top, khaki colored dress shorts, and a pair of brown leather sandals.

"What's up, gentlemen?" He smiled, with a toothpick in his mouth.

"We wanted to come by and see you about something. Can we holla at you for a minute?"

Zac's father, Mr. Shan, looked both ways up and down his block then said… "Yeah, alright…come in," stepping aside allowing the young men to enter.

"*Zac…*"

"Yeah, pop?"

"I'm gonna need you to hang out for a minute…I'm expecting an important phone call…"

"Yes…I hear you."

"What's up, Randy?" Mr. Shan said, smiling down at Randy.

"Nothing, what's happening?" Randy smiled back.

Mr. Shan then quickly glanced at Omar, who was facing away, before turning and going inside. Tooch caught the door before it closed saying, "Yo…come on…y'all might'as well put y'all bikes in right quick."

The inside of the house was nicely laid out with all modern furniture, including charcoal black coffee tables, black marble statues and lamps, and pictures framed with silver and gold. Zac became quiet and fidgety after seeing his father go down stairs in the basement with the two men, but then after only a few moments he started to calm himself down. It was as if he realized that it was just business as usual and it would be ok.

"Does anybody want anything to drink?" He asked getting up from the chair heading for the kitchen.

"Oh, yeah…me, I do. I'm thirsty," Omar said, getting up from the couch to follow him.

Zac looked back at Randy, but Randy shook his head 'no', and Tooch, who was going upstairs, just simply ignored him. After Randy realized that Omar was about to go into Zac's kitchen for the first time, he quickly hopped up from the couch hustling over to them. Randy wanted to see what Omar's facial expression would be after seeing what was in the kitchen. Randy walked over to the doorway…opening the draping-beads and looked Omar straight in the face. Omar was standing there with his eyebrows raised. Zac's kitchen was filled with surveillance equipment set up on the kitchen's counter. It also caused Omar to become curious about what was going on with Zac's father and the two thug looking gentlemen down stairs in the basement.

"*Whow*! What's all this for?" Omar asked.

"Oh. That's nothing, that's just our security system, that's all." Zac flagged, giving a nonchalant answer.

But Omar looked at the three monitors then gave the entire kitchen a once over with his eyebrows raised.

"What's wrong, O?" Randy asked grinning.

Omar shook his head silently at first then answered, "Nothing..."

Zac turned to Omar and smirked as he opened the refrigerator door.

"What do you want to drink, juice, ice tea or soda?" Zac leaned halfway in the fridge.

"You have any *water*?" Omar asked, frowning as if all of what was offered sounded gross. Zac shrugged his shoulders then reached in for the jug of spring water. Moments later, Zac's father and his company came up from the basement.

"...Thanks for the offer anyway, gentlemen. It truly is a generous gesture, but I don't think I have any interest in exploring those avenues."

"I kind of figured you wouldn't, but then it was still worth a try, you know..." The gentleman said, making a face like he already knew what Mr. Shan's answer would be.

"No problem. It's cool, playboy." Mr. Shan smiled as he turned to Zac, Randy and Omar and asked, "Did anybody call for me?"

"No." Zac answered.

But just as Mr. Shan and the two men turned to walk out of the kitchen Tooch came walking through the living room holding the black cordless telephone as it rang in his right hand.

"Hello? Here, it's for you," Tooch said, answering after the first ring.

Tooch barely raised his eyes up from the floor as he handed the phone to his uncle and continued to the kitchen, looking like he was in deep thought about something.

"Y'all ready?" Tooch asked after walking over to a tall trashcan by the back door and throwing a white envelope he was carrying in it.

"Yeah..." Zac and Omar answered...throwing back their heads to finish off their drinks.

Mr. Shan was standing in the living room watching Tooch closely, but did not say anything.

"Y'all gonna catch cramps, watch..." Randy giggled.

"No we're not." Zac answered, shaking his head.

CHAPTER 11

The boys exited the house with Randy and Zac bringing their bikes down first. Omar rolled his bike down on its back wheel while Tooch stepped out the front door and guided his bike down the steps as Omar held it by the handlebars, allowing it to bounce slightly. Tooch's bike was the same as Randy's and Zac's, but his frame and handlebars were all silver. Omar looked at their three almost identical bikes, and then shook his head with a frown. He had a nice trick-bike of his own, but his bike was red with gold-forks, handlebars and spokes. Tooch locked the front door, then got on his bike. Just as the boys were about to pedal off, Khalil, the boy from school, came riding up.

"Where y'all about to go?" he asked stopping in front of Randy.

"For a ride…" Randy answered as Tooch took to the street.

"Where to?"

"Down South Philly…to the Lakes."

"*Ooh*! Can I come?"

"*Nah*…We're probably not going to be getting back until after it gets dark." Randy giggled as he started pedaling with the boys down the street.

Zac hopped off the pavement a few seconds later and started riding behind Tooch.

"Plus…you know your mom ain't gonna be playing that."

The boys started picking up speed as Tooch lead the way, swinging his bike hard from side to side. Omar hopped off the sidewalk into the street after weaving in between two parked cars. And Randy went charging after them, leaving Khalil riding on the sidewalk, by himself, to admire their speed and formation as they exploded down the street. Just as the boys disappeared from Khalil's view, Zac sat down and looked back at Randy talking to him. Before long, the boys were in what they called the 'no stopping zone'. That was when they were out of their neighborhood and riding through unfamiliar territory. The boys pedaled at a steady pace up and down hills, making left and right turns until they found themselves on south Broad Street.

"What're we supposed to be doing once we get there?" Omar asked.

"We're just going to chill…it's a big nice park." Randy answered.

"A *park*?" Omar said, sounding not too thrilled with the notion.

"*Yeah*…it's a nice park though; it lights up at night and everything. You'll like it." Zac jumped in…to Omar's surprise.

"*Yeah*?" Omar said enlightened.

The two of them continued their conversation finally getting to know one another for most of the ride. Then Zac couldn't resist temptation and asked, "*So*, ah…what's up with you and Michelle?"

"*Ah…nothing*. I think she likes me, but I don't think her parents will allow her to have a boyfriend." Omar responded

"Really? Well, she's about to start high school, and I don't think that that's gonna hold up much longer."

"Yeah…I hope not…because she can't even have phone calls, let alone come out the house. "*Damn*…what's wrong with her parents? Why are they so up-tight…they religious?"

"No, just overprotective…that's all."

"Oh, shit…" Zac exhaled as if he already knew what that was hit'n for.

"She told me before she gave me her phone-number, though…to just be aware that her parent treated her like she was a baby."

"Well then…I guess you can't be too mad. That's what you signed on for," Zac said, standing up and pedaling some, then sitting back down.

"I didn't sign on for *anything* yet…ain't nothing official."

"I know her sister had a baby while she was still young."

"How old was she when she got pregnant?"

"*16…*"

"*Oh…*"

Zac didn't say anything else, but he raised his eyebrows and leaned his head back looking at Omar.

"I guess that's why she told me that she wanted to be a virgin until after she finished high school…" Omar continued, "because she was afraid that she'll get pregnant before she graduates."

"That's messed up…because that's a heck of thing to have on your mind."

Zac then looked over at Omar and started to feel somewhat sorry about how he was treating him earlier. He realized that all along Omar was putting up with some things from a female that he wouldn't have dared ventured into. Randy looked back at them then smiled; happy to see them finally getting along.

"*We*'re *almost there*!" Tooch yelped as the huge park came into view.

"I'm *ghost*!" Randy said, exploding pass Tooch to the front of the pack with the three boys accelerating behind him.

"You got anything left in your tank!?!" Randy shouted to Tooch who was riding behind him but kind of on his right.

"*Hell yeah*! I already told you, kid…I'm a madman on this thing!"

The boys blew down the final block of their quest and jumped off the sidewalk into the street, cutting off cars that were just about to pull out into an intersection at a green light. They ripped into the park, rumbling through the grass and kicking up dust and dirt as they weaved past people who were walking on a trail.

"Last one over to the swings gives *top*!" Tooch shouted laughing and causing the pack to surge forward even faster.

The boys all arrived over at the swings at the same time and quickly hopped off their bikes, running over and grabbing swings.

"Too close to call?" Zac asked after seeing they all made it over at the same time.

"Yeah…" Tooch answered looking to his right at Omar.

For Tooch, this was yet another sign that Omar was not a loaf, but was the kind of kid who could do a lot of the things that the three of them liked to do and keep up. Omar also had all the same qualities as the other three boys. He was confident, good-looking and knew exactly when and when not to take any shit from anybody.

Tooch and Zac truly did enjoy being at this park, but, not as much as Randy. He loved this park because of the ambiance. There were fully green trees and large fields with lakes; also there were professional sports stadiums that sat in the background. Some of the fields were made up of well-kept baseball diamonds and basketball courts. Randy especially loved being at the park at night during professional sports games over at the stadiums. When the stadium lights were on, along with the lights from the fields, it added an extra dimension that made him feel like he was a Professional Athlete.

"Hey, does anyone want to go with me to get something to drink?" Omar asked pointing across the field at a store on an avenue.

"Yeah…" Tooch and Zac both answered.

"Do y'all think that store is open, though?" Omar asked as he stared across the field at the store on the other side.

In their neighborhood, it was very common to go up to a store thinking that it was open for business, only to find it closed down. Surely, that type of thing could ruin a whole day. It was good that Omar asked this question, because Tooch was now looking at him as if he was realizing something. And truth be told; it wouldn't have looked good on Omar's part if on his first day hanging out with the boys he would've rallied up the troops and went charging over to a store that was closed down. This was yet another reason of why Omar would make such a perfect fit as the fourth member of their crew. The four boys sat there on their swings watching the door in silence and looking like they were hoping that someone would either go in or come out. Then suddenly the door opened and a White lady with a little girl dressed in a pink short set came walking out.

"*Oh*…alright, *cool*…It's open." Tooch said, being the first to break the silence.

"Well, come on, O. We can go over together…I'm thirsty too. Does anybody else want anything?" Tooch asked, picking up his bike from the grass.

"After that long ride…*sure*, I'll take something to drink…but I can't stand to ride any further, though." Zac answered, sitting with his shoulders slouched from fatigue.

"Yo…you sound real lazy right now, man!" Tooch said, looking at his cousin bright-eyed.

"Ya' see…that's that same lazy shit I was telling you about."

Even though Randy had filled up on Kool-Aid before leaving home, he really wanted something to drink right about now. But since he had no money, he remained silent.

"Here, get me and Randy two big fruit punches," Zac said, reaching into his right pocket and pealing off a ten-dollar bill from a nice size wad.

Tooch saw Zac reaching into his pocket, then rode off with Omar… leaving Zac sitting there with his money held out in front of him watching them ride off.

"Yo, Randy! Randy, you listening to me?" Zac said, leaning his neck around his swing's chain staring Randy in the face.

Randy was in a deep star gaze, looking across the big field at what looked like a basketball league game taking place.

"*Yeah*, yeah…I hear you…I'm listening…" Randy mumbled, not really paying attention.

"So what do you think…you think I should still try and talk to her?"

"*What*?" Randy said, snapping out of it. "Talk to *who*?...*man*... Would you leave that damn girl alone already...Let *him* have her. And plus...hold up...now that I think about it, you never even really tried talking to her."

"*What*? Yes I did." Zac giggled, trying to hold his smile.

"No you didn't. You were petrified of her."

"No I wasn't..." Zac laughed, looking at Randy who was now staring away from him again.

By the look on Zac's face, one could tell that what Randy was saying was the truth.

"Oh, boy," Zac sighed. "You know what? I'm not gonna try and talk to her anymore...*Ok*?"

"That's *good*, that's real *good*, *Zachary*." Randy mumbled again as he turned his attention back to the game. "...Tryin to make'n it seem like, you're not doing yourself a favor...*Psssh*...*man*, please."

"Go ahead with that, I heard you." Zac jokingly pushed Randy on his left shoulder.

"What's going on over there?" Zac asked after tuning in on where Randy's focus was.

"I don't know, but it looks like some sort of league game or something."

As Randy spoke, a whistle blew and the crowd erupted.

"Let's go over and see what's going on." Randy said, getting up from his swing going and grabbing his bike still in a deep stare.

"Hold on, don't you think we should wait for Tooch and Omar to get back? They might miss us and not know where we went."

Randy looked back at Zac still sitting on his swing, then turned up his lips saying...

"Come on lazy!"

Zac was a bit lazy at times, but it was because he was extremely spoiled.

"We'll walk'em over then. *Alright*? Is that better? They should be able to see us before we get over there?" Randy shook his head as he got up from his bike.

As Randy and Zac walked their bikes over to the game they heard the huge crowd '*oohing*' and '*aahing*'. Zac changed his mind about walking and climbed onto his bike. Randy didn't say anything to him, looking at him silently , and shaking his head.

"What's up with you, man?" Randy asked seconds later.

Zac looked back at Randy and shrugged as he started checking back to see where Omar and Tooch were.

"Here they come," Zac said, stopping to wait for them.

Tooch and Omar came rumbling up with the sounds of tires and metal shaking over dirt and grass.

"Where're y'all goin'?" Omar asked, slightly frowning.

"Over there to check out the game…" Zac answered, taking the bag with his drinks in it from his cousin.

Moments later, all four boys were walking their bikes over and drinking. The closer they got to the game the bigger the crowd got, and the bigger the crowd got, the bigger the players on the basketball court got.

"*Damn*…they're *huge*!" Tooch said aloud.

"They'll *kill* you!" Tooch turned to Randy. "What in the world kind of league is this? *Damn*!"

As Tooch was in the midst of marveling over the size of the players, one of them launched a healthy three point shot high into the air. The ball spun backwards with tight backspin on it then came crashing down through the net '*SWISH*!'

"This is college-ready…" A White man said after hearing part of what the boys were saying. "These are all boys who plan to play in college after they graduate high school and boys who play in college *right* now."

Randy was both overwhelmed and a bit intimidated by the size and apparent skill level of the players out on the court. But he tried his best not to show it, convincing himself to channel his nervousness. He learned to do so when it came to playing against legitimate competition. Then just as Randy started to comment on the smart remark Tooch made, a player put a move on a defender and caused Randy to hold his tongue for a moment. He put the move in his memory bank to use later when it was his time to shine. Randy's motto was…'No good idea should ever go un-stolen, especially basketball moves.' After the player left his man, he went into the lane laying the ball in over two more defenders who were much taller than he was.

"*Hey*…that's Mr. *Wyble*, isn't it?" Zac asked, looking pass Tooch and Omar.

"*Where*?" Randy asked, looking around at the crowd.

"Right there"

"Right *where*, I don't see'em…Where is he sit'n?"

"He's *not* sitting; he's out on the court. He's a ref."

Randy then noticed Mr. Wyble and was stunned, because this was the last person he was expecting to see at his favorite spot. Randy began trying to get Mr. Wyble's attention by waving his hands.

"*Hold up*, wait a second. Here he comes now." Tooch said, waving as he stepped forward a little more.

"*Mr. Wyble*!" He called, just as Mr. Wyble went running by in hot pursuit of a play.

Mr. Wyble looked back with a normal facial expression, but once he noticed Randy standing with the boys, he frowned. He then did a double take and blew his whistle just as the player heaved up a last second shot that clanked off the rim.

'*Tweeet*!' The wistle blew.

"That's the half." Mr. Wyble called, waving his hand in the air in a circular motion.

"What're you boys doing down here?" Mr. Wyble asked, after walking back over to them.

"We're always down here…this is our hangout," Randy said, shaking his hand first.

"How'd y'all get down here?"

"On our bikes…like we always do." Zac answered.

Mr. Wyble became happy once he realized he had another opportunity to speak with Randy about playing on his summer league team.

"*Randy*, this is where the team plays I wanted you to play for…" Mr. Wyble said, opening his hands as if he was presenting something to him.

"You still say you don't plan to play anywhere?"

"*Noo*… I don't want to play against these guys. And besides…" , Randy quickly went into his bag of excuses while still maintaining a level of arrogance in his voice, "I haven't had enough time to practice…"

Mr. Wyble laughed, cutting him off.

"You wouldn't be playing against *these* guys. You would be playing against kids your own age, who are about to go to high school next year like you. This was what I was saying about you having a chance to see what you'll be going up against in high school."

Mr. Wyble looked at Randy and flailed his eyelids. This was one of the many things that Mr. Wyble truly loved about Randy, his confidence in himself and his knowing what he was capable of.

"Ah, I still don't know." Randy said, looking to see what the other boys' reaction would be.

But Tooch just looked at Randy with a straight face and said…

"*Play*."

Then Zac and Omar both gave the same, straight-faced response.

"*Ah*…then I guess…I'll play then." Randy answered, exhaling as he turned back to Mr. Wyble.

"*Great then*. I'll pick you up this Saturday at eight with the rest of the team."

Randy then froze and said, "*Huh…Saturday* at *eight* you said?"

He did not look too sure of the decision he was making.

"*Yeah*…" Mr. Wyble laughed.

Because Randy had not ever played in any summer leagues outside his neighborhood, this was something that was totally new for him.

"Well, ah…guess I'll see you then." Randy shrugged.

Even though Randy tried not to look scared, Mr. Wyble could still tell he was. Mr. Wyble also knew that if he were going to help save Randy and his basketball future, he would have to get him out of his neighborhood and playing against some stronger and better competition. Randy's neighborhood leagues were never really strong enough to help develop his game. Because most of the players in his neighborhood leagues knew each other and/or were related, like in most small leagues in ghettos, they were able to get away with heavy pushing and shoving.

"Alright then, I'll see you Saturday." Mr. Wyble said, shaking Randy's hand again.

Mr. Wyble then turned and happily walked out toward center court where the two other referees were standing and talking. Randy waited for Mr. Wyble to walk away, and then turned to the boys and said,, "*Man*…y'all really think I should play?"

But all three boys stood there staring at him silently, shrugging their shoulders and nodding their heads 'yes'.

"You plan on playin in high school next year, *right*?" Omar asked.

"Yeah…"

"Then you should start off by playing out here against these guys. After all they'll be the ones you'll be facing next year."

Tooch and Zac looked at each other thinking about what Omar just said and nodded their heads 'yes', like they couldn't agree more.

"Are y'all coming down here to watch me then?"

"*Man*, of course we are. My father will bring us down." Zac answered.

CHAPTER 12

The boys stood in the same spot and watched the second half of the game, then the first half of the next game before heading home.

"What time do you have to be in?" Tooch asked Omar, over the whistling sound of oily bike chains and rubber tires treading across the asphalt.

"Around nine-thirty, because my mother isn't coming home tonight. My sister's watching me tonight."

"Yeah?"

"Yeah…she usually lets me stay out late."

Omar's mother was hardly ever home, because she is a regional manager for large retail company and had a very busy work schedule. Her shifts rotated so often that she was only home about two to three days a week. The boys arrived back in the neighborhood after a short while and went straight to Omar's house. Once they got to his house they instantly started scopin the layout; and were very impressed. Even though Tooch and Zac had already seen Omar's house earlier, they were still very impressed.

"Omar, you have a nice house, man…" Randy complimented him with Tooch and Zac both following him up.

"Thanks," Omar said, looking back over his left shoulder as he walked up the steps to go inside.

Omar's house also had a double front staircase making the house sit high above ground level.

"This must be his sister's car." Tooch said, tooting his nose at a midnight-green Toyota Camry with beige leather interior.

It was parked directly in front of the house by the curb and still ticking from recently being driven. After Omar went inside, a car pulled up and parked across the street. A thin young Black man wearing a white sweat suit with a college logo on the front and back got out and walked up saying, "What's up, guys?"

The boys were staring at him as he walked up. Tooch and Zac moved aside clearing a path, showing obvious respect. Randy, however, looked at him and did not move an inch.

"What's up?" Randy spoke in a low voice. "You play for them right there?"

Randy was referring to the college logo on his back. Randy was feeling his ball player juices flowing and was looking to get into some sort of quick competitive spat if he could.

"Yeah…this is my squad." The guy smirked. The guy had the appearance of a college ball player. After watching the guys down at the lakes play, Randy figured this 6-feet-2, 150-pound brittle-framed guy had very little chance of competing at an elite Division-One level. However, these thoughts contradicted the sweatsuit logo.

"He probably doesn't even play for them." Randy mumbled after the guy walked up the steps and started tapping lightly on the screen door.

Randy was much younger, but he was already the guy's same exact weight. Omar was standing in the kitchen with his sister, Taya, getting something to drink when he heard tapping at the front door.

"You have to bring your bike inside, Omar" She said. "And wash your hands next time before you just go into the refrigerator, nasty!"

"Did mommy call?" Omar asked not paying attention to what she just said.

"No, and I'm about to have company…so you need to hurry up."

Omar just turned and gave her a blank stare before walking out the kitchen for the front door. As Omar opened the screen-door he stared the guy straight in the face not saying a word. Then he cut his eyes away and walked pass letting the screen door hiss closed in his face.

"What's wrong, man?" Zac asked, noticing Omar's displeased facial expression.

"Nothing, man." Omar exhaled.

"Are you coming back out?"

"Yeah, I have to put my bike in, though…" Omar answered as he carried his bike up the steps.

Taya held the screen door open for him. Taya's company had also gone inside and made himself comfortable on the couch. Omar rolled his bike through the living room, placing it in a closet; then turned around and quickly left back out. All the while, Taya was still holding the screen-door open for him. She closed and locked the screen door as Omar started down the steps then said, with authority in her voice.

"You can stay out, but you better not get lost…also make sure you stay around the house."

"*Yeah…whatever…*" Omar smirked irritated.

As Omar walked down the steps his sister's friend got up from the couch and came over…wrapping his arms around her waist.

"Cut it out, *Daryl*." she said, nudging him with her right elbow.

Omar glared back at Daryl as he grinned down at him, then looked at his sister before cutting his eyes away.

"*Yo, Omar*…you *cool*?" Tooch asked, frowning as Taya closed the door.

"*Nah*, man…I hate when my mom's not home. My sister always gotta be on some bullshit…like she's somebody's boss and shit."

"Yo, so who was dude?" Randy asked after the boys started walking their bikes down the street.

"That's some dude she met in a parking lot stopping for lunch one day.

The boys walked to the end of the block then made a left at a corner lined with tall bushes.

"*Damn!* I wonder why there are so many people out here tonight." Randy asked frowning at a large group of kids that darted pass them playing 'hide and seek'.

"That's because there's no school tomorrow…" Tooch answered.

"*Really*!"

"*Yeah*, *really*…and your ass would've known that had you came to school any this week."

"Yeah, I know. But that's because your mom…you know how she get's. She didn't wanna let me outta the bedroom." Randy quipped.

"*Whatever, nigga*." Tooch answered as the boys all shared a laugh.

However, Omar was not too sure how hard he should laugh. He did not know whether Tooch would have caught bad feelings about him laughing as hard as he wanted to.

"Where are we going now?" Zac asked, looking at Tooch.

"To the house to put the bikes up." Tooch answered Zac, and then he mumbled to Randy…

"Hey, but dude's gonna knock his sister off?"

Randy broke out laughing.

"What, what he say?" Omar asked, turning to Randy who was still cracking up.

Omar only caught a small part of what Tooch mumbled, but he knew that it was something referring to him.

"*Nothing*, man…I didn't say anything…" Tooch said, waving his hands as if it was nothing.

"What he say?" Omar repeated.

Randy did not want to tell Omar, but at the same time, he did not want him to feel like an outsider.

"He said 'dude's gonna knock your sister off'" Randy chuckled.

"Yeah, *alright…whatever*, man. My sister ain't doing *nothing* with that dude…*Damn clown*!"

"*Ok*." Tooch mumbled, as he turned his face away.

Things had already heated up between Taya and her friend Daryl. They were on the couch fully clothed. They were touching, feeling and kissing like they couldn't wait another second to be alone.

"Yo, I think we should go to my house first." Randy said. "Since, I live the closest."

"Alright, then we'll go pass your house first then." Tooch agreed.

Once the boys got near the Projects, a voice called out Randy's name, again, and for the third time today. Randy had to turn around to see who it was.

"*Randy*!"

The four boys stopped then all turned around.

"*Ah*, it's your boy." Tooch said sarcastically, then giggled as he looked at Zac and Omar who both smirked.

"What's up, Randy? Y'all just gettin back?" Khalil asked as he came jogging over holding a small brown-paper bag in his right hand.

"Yeah…what're you still doing out though?" Randy asked frowning a little.

"My mother let me out to run to the store…want some?" Khalil said offering candy.

"Nah…I'm cool." Randy held up his right hand.

Khalil looked at Zac, Tooch and Omar, who were staring at him and said, "*Hey…Michelle* and them are outside," with his face lighting up.

"*Forreal*?" Zac asked, becoming excited.

Randy quickly turned and looked at him, shaking his head in disbelief.

"Who else is out there with her?" Zac asked now trying to clean up his mess.

"I don't know'em. I do know that they're not from around here, though. They must be her cousins or something. They look good too."

Omar, who had already started running down the street yelled, "*Come on*!" as he galloped side-ways away from them.

"*Whoa*!" Tooch called, waving him back. "Let us go put our bikes up first!"

At first Omar seemed like he did not want to stop, but then he started back with his shoulders slumped. He was well aware of the fact that Michelle was hardly ever allowed outside without her parents, and that this would be a golden-opportunity to spend some time with her. So, he didn't want to miss this for anything in the world.

"*Alright*, then…" Omar tissed.

"Thanks Khalil!" Randy yelled back over his right shoulder as the boys started in a different direction.

"Let's split up," Zac said, as Omar got on the back-pegs of Randy's bike.

"Randy…y'all two go to your house, and we'll go to our house. Then we'll meet back up on the Strip, alright?"

"Alright." The other boys agreed as they separated.

The strip was on Tackawanna Street where Randy lived. However, the 'Strip' was farther down from his house where all the drug dealing went on.

"Randy, do you think they'll still be outside when we get there?" Omar asked with concern in his voice.

"Yeah…they should be. I *mean*…that's if they were really ever out there to begin with…and if he wasn't lying."

"*Ah, man*, don't say that. He'd better not be. I'm *telling* you…"

"Well, we'll soon find out."

Moments later they arrived at Randy's house where he found his front door unlocked again, but closed.

"Hold up…I'll be right back."

He went inside, leaving Omar on his front steps.

"Alright…hurry up."

Randy would have loved to invite Omar inside, but under his current home circumstances, he was too embarrassed to do so. Randy rolled his bike into the kitchen, leaning it up against the wall, then came racing back out in a hurry. He and Omar then ran down Tackawanna Street, heading toward where they were to meet back up with Zac and Tooch. After a few minutes, Randy spotted Zac and Tooch. He instantly noticed that Zac had changed his clothes.

"*You changed your clothes*?" Randy asked curiously.

"*Ah*…yeah, *um*…my pop made me." Zac stuttered as he spoke keeping his eyes to the ground.

He knew his best friend of ten years would have seen straight through him. After hearing him try to feed Randy some bullcrap, Tooch turned his head away from Zac; looking in the opposite direction.

"Come on y'all, let's get around there." Omar said again being the first to take off.

The boys hustled to Michelle's block. She was in front of her house with four other girls her age jumping rope on the sidewalk. The only problem was that her parents were also outside with them.

"*Hold up, wait*!" Omar said, suddenly stopping…causing Zac, who had his head down, to walk into the back of him.

Omar alerted the boys of who her parents were. He was the only one who knew what they looked like.

"Let's wait until her parents leave." He said, ducking into the darkness of some tall bushes down the street from them.

From where the boys were they could clearly see Michelle and her parents. They watched as her mother and father talked to her before getting into their car and pulling off…driving right pass where they were crouched in the bushes.

"*Alright*…come on." Omar announced, exiting the bushes first.

Zac looked Omar from head to toe, and then smirked, as he was still not quite ready to let Michelle go. He was displeased to see how eager Omar was to see her. Randy noticed what Zac did then gave him a quick shove in the back making him move forward.

"*Go*!" Randy grunted playfully, pretending to be aggravated.

As the boys walked down the street, Michelle noticed them and became alarmed. She stepped from behind her cousin, who was turning the rope, and looked in the direction that her parents drove. After seeing that they were far away, she calmed herself and began showing off, trying to be cute.

"It's *payback*." She said, turning up her lips and folding her arms. "*Watch*…"

The girls were playing double-dutch.

"Hey, what's up with you?" Omar announced as he came walking up first.

"*Hey*…" Michelle answered in her sweet little raspy but soft voice.

Michelle's voice always slightly cracked when she spoke, sounding like she was just waking up from a nap.

"How long have y'all been out here?"

"For a while."

"Where did your parents go?" Omar asked looking back at Zac, Randy and Tooch as they walked up and stood behind him.

"To get dinner…y'all can't get caught out here…y'all will get us in trouble." Michelle spoke with her eyes showing the seriousness of the situation.

"No we won't, we'll run." Omar answered, giggling as he looked back at the boys again.

"*Ah*, but I'm sorry…this is my man, *Tooch*, and this is *Randy*, right here, and this is…"

"I know who they are, *silly*." Michelle frowned, cutting him short.

"What's up, *Randy? Hey, Tooch*, What's up, *Zachary*?"

Omar, standing corrected, placed his right hand on his chest, raised his eyebrows, and looked down at the ground. Zac, however, swooned his way in with a very smooth and flirtatious,

"*Hey*...what's up, *lady*?"

Randy quickly turned and glared at him as if he was standing on his foot or something.

"*What*?" Zac asked under his breath.

Randy shook his head and looked at Tooch, who was also shaking his head.

"Who is that...Michelle?" One of her cousins asked...stepping out of the jump rope.

"Ah... that's my boyfriend." Michelle answered softly, and then sucked her teeth like it was no big deal.

Omar's face lit up like a hundred watt light bulb. He was in shock... standing with his shoulders up and his head slightly reared back as Michelle walked past. She looked at him as she grabbed the jump rope from her cousin. She glanced at Omar with her tongue pressed up against the inside of her left cheek before playfully cutting her eyes away. Her little habits like these made Omar, as well as Zac crazy about her. The other boys were also caught off guard by her comment, and it showed on their faces as they stood with their shoulders hunched nearly up to their ears.

"*What* the *hell*..." Zac mumbled, causing Randy to giggle.

Zac could not believe his ears, nor did he want to hear anymore.

"*Fuck*!" Zac turned away, looking down in the street.

Everyone was caught off-guard by what Michelle did except for Tooch. He was expecting her to say something like this eventually. He and Omar often talked in class, and he could not have cared less. Then, without saying anything, he strolled over to check out the other girls.

"Let me see what we're working with here..." He said to himself.

Before he could get a chance to say anything, Randy said, "*Hey, isn't* that..."

"*Oh, that's* my *parents*! *Oh, my goodness*!" Michelle blurted, cutting him off.

Michelle knew the headlights of her parents' car from anywhere. The headlights were all she needed to see. The boys took off, nearly running into each other as they laughed while trying to get from the front of the house.

"*Quick*, in *here*..." Zac said, running into Michelle's front gate.

"*No, don't go in there*!" Michelle pleaded. "*I have a dog*!"

By then it was too late; the boys were already halfway to the back of her house. Her dog heard the sound of voices and quick motion and came out of the darkness from the side of the house. He stood directly in front of them, scaring the day lights out of them.

"*Aah*!" They all yelled.

The huge red-blooded Doberman Pincher stood right in their path.

"*Spread out*!" Tooch cried, hoping to confuse the dog.

The boys weaved pass the dog's snapping jaws as it pulled and tugged, trying to break free of its leash. It managed to give itself enough slack and snagged a piece of Omar's butt and left arm. Tooch, however, was the last person to run by the dog. He was only a few steps behind Omar, so the dog could not bite both of them. The boys made it pass the dog and ran to a red brick wall in the back of Michelle's yard. The eight-foot wall would have posed a problem for the boys on any other day, but since they were so scared, they cleared it with no problem. All four boys landed safely in the alleyway on the other side, and then separated. Randy and Omar ran one way, while Zac and Tooch the other.

Michelle's parents pulled up and parked in their parking spot, hearing nothing but the sound of their dog wailing in the backyard. Michelle's mother got out from the passenger side holding two large white pizza boxes with red lettering on them. She looked at the girls with her face frowned.

"What's all the noise in the back of the house?" She asked, and then looked back at Michelle's father, who was standing up from the driver's seat.

Michelle's father looked straight at her as if he already knew she was behind it somehow. She watched as her father stared straight at her, and then turned her face lowering her eyes to the ground.

"Michelle…why is the dog barking?" He asked calmly as he stepped onto the sidewalk.

"I don't know…somebody must be back in the alleyway or something." She answered, shrugging cluelessly.

The girls all looked at each other after Michelle's parents started for the house and started snickering with their hands over their mouths. After they all entered the house Michelle's father opened the back door and went out to try to silence the dog. The dog never ceased his barking. He was still pulling toward the back wall.

"Shut up, I said!" Her father yelled going over to the wall raising himself up and peeking over. There were also other dogs barking hysterically down the alleyway as well, so her father shrugged as if it was nothing.

CHAPTER 13

At Omar's house, Taya and Daryl were upstairs in her bedroom. She was getting all that she thought was missing from her life; a strong man with a good head on his shoulders and a bright future ahead of him making love to her. Unfortunately, the telephone rang and interrupted them.

"Hold up…wait a second…" She said, pushing Daryl in his chest as he humped away.

"*Nah*…don't worry about it." He insisted, even though he heard the phone ring.

Taya attempted to climb out from under him as he was still humping.

"*Come on*…don't worry about it…" He repeated.

"What do you mean, '*don't worry about it*'…it's probably my mother," She said, giving him one more good shove in his chest…forcing him off her.

Daryl watched her clamber from underneath him in disgust, then watched her take three big stomping strides across the rugged floor picking up the telephone.

"*Hello*?" She answered breathing somewhat heavily.

"*Taya*!" Her mother said sharply into the telephone catching her by surprise.

"*Yes*…"

"What's wrong with you letting the damn phone ring like that?"

"*Hun*, I was…"

"And why are you breathing like that?"

"Ummm…I was outside on the porch, and heard the phone ring, so I hurried up and came running inside."

"Where's your brother?"

"He's outside with his friends…that's who I was just out there looking for."

"Then go find him…and tell him that I said since he doesn't know how to bring his ass in the house when he's supposed to, he's on punishment for a *week*."

"Ok…"

"*Taya*!" Her mother called again, then became silent suddenly.

"Yes?"

"You don't have anybody in my house do you?"

Taya looked over at Daryl as he pulled his pants up and walked out the bedroom then said, "*No, mom…I don't*." She answered, as if she had just been asked an annoying question.

"Go find your brother."

"Alright…Bye."

Taya hung up the telephone then walked out the bedroom. She walked up to the closed bathroom door, and knocked three times.

"Yeah?" Daryl answered in a crabby voice.

"You have to put your clothes on…I have to go look for my brother."

"Alright…"

Taya looked at the door, like she was expecting him to say something smart, but then she cut her eyes away and went back into her bedroom looking surprised.

CHAPTER 14

Zac and Tooch were laughing and running down the street toward their house.

"*Shhh*!" Zac said, trying to get Tooch to quiet down while laughing out loud himself.

"*Alright*, *alright*…stop laughing, before you make us have to go in." Zac said, placing his right hand over Tooch's mouth, "*Zachary*!" Mr. Shan called from inside the house.

The front door was open, but the storm door closed and locked. Mr. Shan was sitting in the living room with different company. Only the light from the television lit the room.

"Yes…" Zac answered.

"Now *see*, I *told* you…" Zac whispered, still trying to stop himself from laughing.

"What're you doin'?"

"Nothing, pop…Tooch and I were just laughing about something that happened around the corner, that's all."

Tooch snickered even louder, causing Zac to laugh and cover his mouth again.

"Alright… Go play. You only have about a half an hour left before you two have to come in. And don't leave off this block…you hear me?"

"Yes…I hear you, pop…But I have to come in anyway." Zac said, walking into the house after un-locking the door, followed by Tooch.

"I have to wash my hands."

As soon as Zac came in, he noticed two young unsavory men sitting and watching television with his father and became curious. As they sat on the couch, on the left of his father, Zac realized he had never seen these guys before. They were now both grinning at him with big superficial smiles and giving him the 'thumbs up.'

"Hey…what's up, big-guy?" The first guy said with a Puerto-Rican accent.

"What's up?" Zac replied, simply nodding his head with a slow jerk.

Tooch stood behind Zac looking at them silently. Then he cut his eyes away and darted up the stairs without saying anything. Zac never stopped staring as he headed for the kitchen. The men went back to conversing with his father. Zac turned and opened the refrigerator door. He reached inside and grabbed a tall, foggy, plastic container filled with ice-tea. He sat the container down on the counter before heading over to the sink to wash his hands. He then poured himself a tall glass of ice tea and drank it as he went back to watching his father and the men. From the looks of things, he could tell that his father really was not trying to hear anything the men had to say, but he would still give a nonchalant nod every now and then.

Zac finished his tea then spun back around to the sink. Just before he could run water on his glass, there were three small taps at the storm door. The light taps caused Mr. Shan and the two men to look at the door suspiciously. They could not see who it was, but could hear voices, as if someone was whispering. Zac looked at the monitors and started smiling as he walked out of the kitchen. His father stood up from his chair cocking back his big black Dessert Eagle 44, with an illegal Israeli attachment. Tooch came flying down the stairs darting pass him out the front door.

"*Haaah*!" Tooch said gleefully as he allowed the door to close behind him.

Mr. Shan shook his head and looked back at the two men. He laughed hurtfully as he realized that Tooch did not seem at all troubled by brushing the same hand in which he was carrying the huge gun. Then, as his father tucked the hand-cannon back into his waistband, Zac walked pass and went outside.

"*Boy*, children these days, I'll tell you…" Mr. Shan said, shaking his head as he sat back down.

Randy, Zac and Tooch were all outside trying their best not to laugh too hard at Omar as he was still in pain.

"That *dog* tore your ass *up*, *didn't he*?" Tooch said.

"*Yeah*…thanks to *Mr*. '*Quick* in here.'" Omar said, nodding at Zac.

Randy suddenly burst out laughing again, and leaned to his left placing his head on Tooch's shoulder.

Omar could only rub his backside and look at him shaking his head.

"I'm sorry, man." Randy apologized, waving his hands out in front of him.

"Are you alright, though?" Tooch asked, resting his elbows back on the steps trying not to laugh.

"I didn't think her parents were gonna come back that quick!" Omar said, showing a look of curiosity.

Zac, Randy and Tooch all agreed with him.

"Yeah, but you know what? I was trying to figure out why they came back so fast. They probably ordered the food before they left, then went and picked it up…" Randy said, gathering himself.

"That does make a lot of sense." Tooch agreed with him.

"I thought I heard her yelling something while we were running back there, but I wasn't too sure about what she was saying…Now that I think about it, she was try'na tell us she had a dog," Tooch said, giggling a little.

"That was a *big* ass *dog*!" Zac said quickly, glancing back at the screen on the storm door to make sure his father didn't hear him.

"I thought I was gonna pass out when I saw how big it was."

"Hey, what time is it?" Randy asked.

"10:14…" Tooch answered, looking down at the watch on his right wrist. Tooch was the only one in the crew who was a lefty.

"Damn, I have to get ready to go in." Randy said.

Randy really did not have to go in this early, because no one would be looking for him, but it sounded good. None of the boys were hungry because they stopped to get something to eat on the way home. Randy turned and looked down the street in the direction that he would be heading in.

"Yeah…my pop should be telling us to come in soon anyway…" Zac added, looking at his cousin who was sitting next to him yawning.

Omar's sister Taya had been looking for him for the past half-hour. She drove pass Zac's block without stopping, but after she saw kids sitting out in front of a house under a light she slammed on breaks. She backed up then drove down the block where she spotted Omar.

"*Omar*!" She called him softly, but still managed to catch him and the rest of the boys by surprise.

The boys all turned to look and see who it was calling Omar's name.

"*Oh, damn*. How'd she find me?" Omar said.

"Come on. You have to come in now…Mommy called!" Taya shouted.

"Alright…" Omar turned and shook the boys' hands. "Hey, I gotta go."

"Alright, O'…But what're you doing tomorrow?" Tooch asked.

"I don't know… I'll give you a call in the morning, alright."

Randy looked over at Zac to see what his response would be, but Zac just sat there quietly and did not show any kind of reaction. After Omar left, Randy stood up and shook Zac and Tooch's hands as they were about to go inside.

"Yeah…it's time to take it on down…how they say…'Back home.'" Tooch said, groaning like an old man after he struggled to stand up.

"Hey, Omar!" Randy called, stopping Omar just before he got into the car.

"Yeah?"

"Michelle said she goes with you!" Randy said, cupping his hands around his mouth and laughing.

"I know!" Omar responded, cracking a huge smile.

After hearing what he said, Taya looked at Randy and flailed her eyes. Randy turned and started walking down the street pretending to dribble a basketball. Even though he had a pretty-nice walk ahead of him, it was a beautiful, breezy June night and he was up for it. On his way home he came to a small park where there were four older guys playing two on two basketball. He stopped for a moment to watch some of the action from the other side of the fence. One of the four guys playing was a 'playground legend'. He was arguing with the guy guarding him.

"You *can't* stick me! I don't even know why you're even try'n," The playground legend said, who was much taller than the guy guarding him.

He dribbled the basketball twice before blowing straight by his defender leaving him standing in one spot. He went to the basket…slapping the backboard hard with two hands shouting…

"*Yeah, and what*?"

Then he turned around looking back at the much shorter defender.

"Yeah, whatever…" The guy said, placing his hands on his hips.

"Yeah '*whatever*'. .*Man*, you're getting *killed* out here." He continued.

"Ain't none of us out here get'n paid to be play'n out this bitch…So why don't you just shut the fuck up and play, man, *damn*!"

"*Yeah…*"

"*Forreal…*" The other two guys agreed.

Randy shook his head then let go of the fence and started walking again. Those words were the same exact words that he never wanted to have thrown up in his face. The threat of being nothing more than a 'Neighborhood Legend' and having himself be put in the same position where those same words would surely be applied to him was enough to make him want to start studying for 9th grade right now. Then he started thinking more positively, remembering that he was scheduled to start playing in the summer league down at the lakes where it counted.

CHAPTER 15

Omar and Taya arrived home where they both found a surprise. "I know he's not still here." Taya said to herself, looking back at Daryl's car.

They got out of the car and walked up to the front door. Taya unlocked it and stepped inside. But as soon as Omar stepped in behind her, Daryl came walking down the stairs pulling his sweatshirt over his head.

"*Daryl*! I thought I told you to leave before I got *back*?" Taya said, nearly in tears from embarrassment. Omar stood there watching Daryl fix his shirt. Disappointed, he shook his head as he quickly walked away. The words that he heard Randy repeating from Tooch's mouth started ringing in his head.

"I know, but I had to use the bathroom." He answered; trying to pretend everything was cool.

"*But I left almost 45 minutes ago*!" Taya exhaled, growing even angrier with him after hearing his dumb excuse.

"*Alright, man…whatever*!" Daryl said after he noticed the look on Taya's face. Daryl then stepped pass her and went out the front door. Taya glanced over at Omar with regret in her eyes, then looked down at the floor and covered her mouth …too embarrassed to speak.

"*Goood night*!" Omar said sarcastically, as he went upstairs never looking back.

CHAPTER 16

Tooch was in the bathroom taking a shower while Zac was knocking on the door trying to get him to hurry up.

"*Tooch*, how much longer are you going to be, *dang*?"

"Man, like another five minutes!" Tooch shouted over the sound of streaming water.

"*Hurry up*!"

"*Damn, man*…let your pop wash his balls now, boy!" Tooch shouted smiling.

Zac turned and walked away from the door shaking his head saying…

"*Stupid ass, Nigga*…I tell you."

Zac stopped at the top of the stairs where he could hear part of his father's conversation. He tried listening in on what was being said, but could not make out much of anything, so he decided to creep downstairs to have a closer listen. Zac slowly crept down stairs, walking close to the wall where he would be undetected. Once he got to the bottom, he was able to hear everything…as if they were talking directly to him.

"The only person I can think of who could help us pull this off, is you." A guy named Diego said as they were still trying to convince Mr. Shan to go into business with them.

"You have all the connects, and you have the long clientele already lined up. So, it's just a matter of whether or not you wanna take up part of *our* clientele. That's all I'm saying."

Zac then peeked around the wall and looked at his father, who was sitting in the mustard yellow leather recliner staring straight into the television set. As Diego leaned close to him drinking from a glass, Mr. Shan still did not respond to Diego. He had already learned from his connect 'downtown', about Diego's part in the earlier arrest of the man by the Feds. Seconds later, Tooch opened the bathroom door.

"*Zac, I'm out now*!" He shouted, causing Zac to jump.

"*Zachary*?" His father called after hearing a small thump over by the stairs.

"Yes?" He answered, peeking his head around the wall.

"What're you doin'?"

"Nothing..."

"Take your ass back upstairs and get yourself ready for bed!"

"Alright dad. But I had to ask you something."

"What is it?"

"Randy's playing in a summer league down South Philly this Saturday. I wanted to know if you would take us down there to watch him?"

"Yes...now get your ass back upstairs and get ready for bed, like I said."

"Yes."

Zac did not even bother standing up...crawling back upstairs like a cat.

CHAPTER 17

When Saturday morning came Mr. Shan, Zac, Tooch, and Omar arrived at Randy's first summer league game in South Philly.

"There's Randy right there." Omar said, pointing as the boys found seats in the metal bleachers.

"Where?" Zac asked, moving his head from side to side trying to see him. "I don't see him."

"Randy, do you have your permission slip?" Mr. Wyble asked, as he picked up a yellow jersey from inside a box he was standing over, throwing it around his neck and letting it hang.

"Yes." Randy replied, then handed him his permission slip.

"He's right there, standing in the grass with Mr. Wyble... *see*?"

"*Ah...yeah*. Now I see 'em."

Mr. Wyble took the paper from Randy and opened it to make sure everything was filled out and signed correctly, then nodded his head giving him a jersey winking his right eye at him saying, "I'm start'n you today." Randy again became nervous.

"But...I...I...I don't know any of the plays, and I'm not in shape to run that much. Are you sure?"

Mr. Wyble cracked a smile and placed his hand on Randy's shoulder saying, "Boy, you're young. You do not need to be in any kind of shape to run. You're still a kid; you should be able to run all day if you had to."

Randy looked over at the game that was already in progress on the court before looking down at the ground speechless.

"*Relax, man*...you're much better than most of these boys out here... they're the ones that should be nervous about playing against you." Mr. Wyble said, laughing lightly.

"But, just wait until the game starts...you'll see. You'll be fine."

Out on the court a skinny dark-skinned boy put a move on a defender and sent the crowd into a frenzy.

"*Damn*, you see that?" Tooch asked, standing to his feet.

"*Nah*, what, what happened?" Zac asked, quickly turning his head to watch the rest of the play.

"The boy with the ball just crossed the *hell*…I mean, *heck* out of that dude sticking him." Tooch corrected himself only after seeing how his uncle looked at him.

"Yeah, that's Tridane…" A man sitting next to the boys impeded. "He's *real* good…he's probably by far the best player out here."

"Yeah…well we'll just have to see about that." Zac mumbled, looking over at Randy.

Tridane continued to show off his highly skilled dribbling ability by penetrating to the basket and being fouled on almost every trip down court. But, what was most impressive about what he was now doing was that there were only a few seconds remaining in the game and his team had been trailing. On Tridane's last basket, he tied the game at 46, and now stood at the foul line about to shoot a free throw. After making the basket, Tridane stared into the crowd gritting his teeth to show how confidant he was. His team now led by one, and was trying to get back on defense before the other team could try to throw the ball in over their heads. But the last foul shot that Tridane sank proved to be the game winner, because there were only four seconds remaining and the other team did not have any timeouts left.

Randy looked away from the court into the stands as Tridane's team started celebrating. He spotted the boys and waved at them.

"*Look*! Randy looks *shook*, doesn't he?" Tooch said smiling.

After a few minutes, the two teams shook hands and cleared the court to make way for the next game to begin. Randy and his teammates were all dressed in white mesh shorts and yellow-jerseys with white lettering and numbers on their chest and backs. They walked out onto the court and began their warm-up drills on the basket in front of the boys. After warming up for a modest five minutes the two teams went to the sidelines and sent their starting five back out to center court. Zac and Tooch looked at each other and raised their eyebrows in surprise, as Randy walked out onto the court with the starters.

"What's Randy think he's doin?" Tooch said.

"I know. Check 'em out." Zac said, breaking into a chuckle.

"I guess we're not going to have to wait to see him play after all, huh? *Ok, Randy*!" Tooch cheered aloud.

Randy heard Tooch's cheer, but tried not to crack a smile as he moved around getting himself into better position for the tap. Randy was very nervous, because he was now playing in one of the better, well-known leagues in the city. It had a list of seriously talented young players that were highly skilled. Randy, like his friends, was pretty tall for his age, but even with him being a little older than some of the kids on the court, he was not the tallest person out there. So, by Randy doing well he would surely be making a serious statement for *his* skill level as well.

"Randy, come here!" Mr. Wyble called after seeing the referee walk back over to the scorers' table to handle a number situation with the other team.

Randy turned and quickly hurried over to see what he wanted.

"There're a few high school coaches out here today…so try and show off your stuff, alright?"

"Ok." Randy responded in a simple voice nodding his head and scanning the crowd.

The ref blew his whistle and Randy quickly jogged back over to center court where the ball went up. Mr. Wyble's team lost the opening tap, but a tall White kid, Sean, on his team stopped it from going out of bounds. Sean passed the ball to another White kid, Rob, who was starting at point guard. He passed it to Randy on the left wing. Randy quickly stutter stepped his defender with his left foot; freezing him. Then, he dribbled past him; going right. Randy paced smoothly toward the basket, and then pulled up for a 'stop and pop' jump shot that fell straight through.

"*Twang*!" Zac shouted, standing to his feet as soon as the ball left Randy's hands.

Mr. Shan, Tooch and Omar cheered along with Zac, but remained in their seats. Mr. Shan had never seen Randy play before, and was very impressed.

"*Man*…it doesn't take him long to find his shot, does it?" Mr. Shan asked, looking at Tooch smiling.

"*Nah*. He said that's like going to work and not knowing where to start." Zac said, jumping in.

As the game went on, Randy continued his solid offensive assault by hustling to every one of the spots he felt comfortable shooting from. He hit one mid-range jumper after another. By the end of the game, He had racked up 31 points on only 12 of 17 shooting. He also contributed to his team's win by collecting eight rebounds, six defensively, and four steals. Randy's efforts helped his team earn their first victory of the summer league. As Mr. Wyble had expected, Randy led his team in almost every category.

"Good game, Randy." Mr. Wyble said, walking up shaking his hand.

"I'm not going to say I didn't think you had it in you, but, I was shocked to see how much you had in you."

"Hey, Wyble!" A voice called out from the large crowd.

It was a middle-aged Black man with a full salt and pepper beard heading toward him.

"How are you doing, man? I haven't seen you around in a while. How are things going?" The man said, *taking* a handshake from Mr. Wyble.

"*Ah…good*, I *guess*. And *you*?" Mr. Wyble answered, pulling his hand away.

"How's the family?"

"They're all doing well, thank you for asking."

Mr. Wyble was now standing with his eyes squinted, because he knew the man, but just not well enough for him to be inquiring about his family.

"*Sooo*…who's the talent?" The man asked, feasting his eyes on Randy with a deep stare.

Since Randy had repeated a couple of grades, many high school coaches had not seen him play for more than a year now.

Mr. Wyble then let off a cunning grin and commenced to get rid of this man; like one would do a 'cheapskate used car salesman'.

"Ah huum…" He cleared his throat. "This is Murcy…Randy Murcy, one of my kids that came up for the camp."

"So he's not from the City then, I take it… Where's he from?"

"*Ah…yeah*, yeah, he's only in town for the first part of this here camp, then he's outta here!" Mr. Wyble smiled.

"Gone outta here just like that?" The man asked, looking Randy from head to toe as Randy stood beside Mr. Wyble.

"Yeah, you know…These types of things happen. They only seem to be here to tease us, *right*?"

Randy looked up at Mr. Wyble as if he was trying to figure out why he would be telling this man such a bold face lie.

"Yeah, that's a shame… I could use a kid like him in the off guard spot this fall."

"Ah, yeah, that's right; you did lose your guard to graduation."

"Yup."

"You guys had a pretty rough year this past season, too."

"Yeah, it was rough… believe me."

"What you guys lose like 12, 14 straight before the end of the season?"

"Yeah, and it's definitely not something I'm proud of or want to talk about, for that matter."

The only reason Mr. Wyble was repeating everything the man's team had done the previous year was because he wanted Randy to hear how bad the team was for himself…so he would be able to get a much clearer understanding of what type of coach he was.

"Man that had to have been rough."

"Yeah, it was. But that was last year. This year, we're gonna be looking to do a lot better for ourselves."

"You know, that's a really good way to look at it…No need in dwelling on the past, right?"

"Hey, well…What's your name again kid?"

The coach asked Randy extending his hand out to him.

"I'd like to have a chance to check up on you someday in the future, you know… looks like there might be something special about you kid." The coach said, smiling and winking his right eye at Randy.

"I'd like to see how things are going for you; since you're just starting high school this fall. I'm Joe Gibson, head coach over at Town Ivory High School, home of the Fighting Knights. Hopefully we'll even get a chance to face each other in a tournament or something someday."

"Yeah, that would be something." Randy smiled.

"But where did you say he was from again?" The coach asked, looking back at Mr. Wyble.

"*New York*!"

"*Florida*!"

Randy and Mr. Wyble both answered simultaneously, but gave different answers.

"*Ah*…I mean *Florida*! *Yeah*…that's right…I keep forgetting." Mr. Wyble said, looking at Randy while trying not to let the coach see his face.

"Alright, *Florida*…" Coach Gibson shrugged.

"That's pretty far. But who knows, you're here now, *right*?"

"*Yup*…you got it." Randy agreed.

"Well, then I guess I'm going to be running now… I'll see you two next weekend."

Coach Gibson spoke with some hesitation in his voice because he was feeling somewhat un-welcomed. He took another handshake from Mr. Wyble before turning and walking off. After watching Coach Gibson walk away, Mr. Wyble looked at Randy and said, "And what did you just call yourself doing?"

"The same thing you were, only I figured since I was the one you were talking about, I'd spruce myself up a bit."

Randy and Mr. Wyble stood there for a moment in silence then broke out into a soft laugh together.

"*Florida*? *Yeah right*!" Mr. Wyble repeated, shaking his head.

"Mr. Wyble, I don't understand why you told that coach a lie?"

"Randy, like I told you before, there are a lot of high school coaches out here, and many of them aren't good coaches for players like yourself. That makes for a world of difference when you are playing in high school. But none of them are willing to tell you that before you come to their school."

"Oh..." Randy said, raising his eyebrows.

"But have patience young one. You'll have more than your fair share of coaches wanting you...and trust me; *he's* not one of them."

CHAPTER 18

Tooch, Zac and Omar came walking across the basketball court to meet Randy.

"Yo, are you ready?" Zac asked, trying not to look Mr. Wyble in the face so he would not have to speak to him.

"Yeah, I'm ready. Alright then, Mr. Wyble, I'll catch up with you later."

Randy turned and shook Mr. Wyble's hand. Mr. Wyble looked at Randy and the three boys, then glared across the court at Mr. Shan, who was standing over in the grass talking on his cell phone. Mr. Wyble had already known of Mr. Shan's drug dealing business for some years now. So did many other teachers at their school. But he also knew that he would not be able to stop Randy from riding with Mr. Shan without causing some sort of scene.

"Are you going to be alright?" Mr. Wyble asked, looking at him strangely.

"*Yeah. Why wouldn't I be*? That's my uncle, you know?" Randy said with a slight smirk.

"Alright…Well then, I guess I'll see you on Monday in school. Oh yeah, before I forget…next Saturday, we have the first game…we play the team that won before we played."

Randy did not say anything. He nodded his head, then turned around and hurried off to catch up with the boys as they walked over to Mr. Shan.

"Wait a sec…" Mr. Shan said, signaling for them to wait a moment before coming any closer.

They quickly stopped on the basketball court, as he continued his conversation on the phone.

While the boys were waiting, they looked to the left and noticed the skinny, dark-skinned kid named Tridane standing with his father and talking with four men who were high school basketball coaches.

"He's good." Zac mumbled.

"Yeah, he is…" Tooch agreed.

"My team plays his team next weekend." Randy added.

"*Really*?" Tooch asked, becoming excited.

"Yeah."

"I *definitely* wanna see that. But, you think you can take 'em?" Tooch asked with a snide grin on his face…after thinking to himself first.

"Yeah, I think my team is better than his. We should be able to take 'em."

"I'm not talking about *your* team against *his*…I'm talking about *you* against *him*, one on one."

Randy waited a few seconds before he looked at Tooch. Then, with his lips turned up, he nodded his head 'yes' saying, "*Hell yeah, man*!"

"Randy, who was that man you and Mr. Wyble were talking to after the game?" Zac asked, butting in.

"Oh, he was just some bum high school basketball coach wanting to know where I plan to play next year."

"*Well*…what did you tell him?"

"I didn't tell him anything. Me and Mr. Wyble told him that I wasn't from Philly." Randy said smiling.

"Hey, *Omar*! What high school is your mother planning to send you to next year?" Tooch asked, switching the conversation to Omar.

"I don't even know that yet. But that's a good question though, Tooch."

The look on Omar's face showed that he had not given the school thing much thought.

"That's a damn good question." Omar continued. "In fact, I think that's what I'm gonna ask my mom as soon as I get home. But, what school are all y'all planning to go to next year?" Omar shot back.

"My uncle said he wants us to go to a private school." Tooch said, tooting his nose in Zac's direction.

"Yeah? Where at?"

"Somewhere around here."

"Really?" Randy jumped in, becoming alarmed.

"But from what we understand, we're both gonna be able to come home everyday…so it shouldn't be that bad."

"Omar, when you go home, you should really try and see if your mom would let you come to the same school with us." Tooch said, placing his hand on Omar's shoulder. "Plus, that way, we can still all be together."

"What about, *Randy*…he coming to the same school too?" Omar asked, now looking at Randy, who was standing to his left.

Tooch and Zac already knew about Randy's parents not having any money. And with Randy's GPA being a negative point something, it was a no-brainer that he wouldn't be able to attend a private school.

"*Um*…Randy's gotta go to a different school so he can play ball and get some exposure…so some big colleges can see him." Zac said, trying not to disclose the real reason why Randy could not go to school with them.

"Are you fellas ready?" Mr. Shan asked, as he walked over, tucking his cell phone into the pocket of his beige khaki shorts.

"Yes, pop." Zac answered.

"Then come on. Good game out there, Randy. You really showed off." Mr. Shan said smiling.

"Thanks, Unc."

"Ididn'tknowyoucouldplaylikethat…boy…Damn!Youmademeproud."

"Yeah…I tried." Randy said blushing as he turned his face away from Tooch, who was looking at him about to say something sarcastic.

Mr. Wyble watched, with a look of concern on his face, as the four boys walked over to Mr. Shan's car, got in and took off. He noticed that as soon as they pulled off, they were followed by what looked like an un-marked police car.

"Hey, dad…What is the name of the private school we're going to again?" Zac asked sitting in the front passenger seat.

"Philadelphia Private Technical School."

"Yeah…that's it, *Tech*. So, Omar…when you go home, you can tell your mom that's the school you want to go to next year."

"Alright." Omar agreed.

Mr. Shan started to say something about the price of tuition at Tech, but then he remembered he did not know anything about Omar's family or their finances, and just remained quiet.

"You boys all graduate in less than two weeks. Are you all *excited*?" Mr. Shan asked, looking in his rearview mirror at Tooch, Randy and Omar.

"*Uh…Kind of…*" They all answered nonchalantly, at different times.

"What kind of answer is that? You boys should be proud of yourselves. You only have four more years left… for those of you who don't plan on going to college." Mr. Shan spoke, looking in the rearview mirror straight at Tooch.

CHAPTER 19

Mr. Wyble was still standing in the same spot near the court thinking about what he could have done to prevent Randy from riding with Mr. Shan when another voice called out getting him to snap out of his trance.

"Hey, *Wyble*!"

"Hey, what's up?"

Mr. Wyble greeted the man with a handshake as he walked over and stood next to him.

"See that right there? That's *greatness*!" The man said, pointing to Tridane.

Tridane was still standing with his father talking to even more basketball coaches.

"That's your boy for the future, isn't it? So I guess you should consider yourself lucky then, hah?" Mr. Wyble smiled.

"*Nah*…not any more." The man answered shaking his head 'no' slowly.

"*What*? What're you talking about, 'not any more'?"

Mr. Wyble's eyes got big as he listened to the shocking news. This man, like the other man, was a high school basketball coach.

"I thought you told everyone that you already had him wrapped up since he was in the 6th grade?"

"*Yeah*, that's what I was told…but that was before daddy over there started talking with schools across the bridge."

"So, what does that mean? That shouldn't have meant anything dealing with you?"

"What that meant…or what that means is all the same thing…and that *means* he'll be playing his high school ball over the bridge come next fall… that's what that meant, and that's for *damn* sure."

"Get outta here. You're *shit'n* me, *right*?"

"Nope…" The coach sighed. "I wish I was…believe me."

"But, I hear he was supposed to be attending summer school though."

"*Yeah*, he was…but he's not."

"*What*…if he doesn't, wouldn't that disqualify him or make him ineligible for any scholarships or institutional money?"

"Yeah, it should, but like I said, that's why his father started talking with schools across the bridge."

"But I still don't get it…I don't see how that's gonna work?"

"*Come on*, *Wyble*…we've all seen him play…what did he score, like 27 midway through the 2nd half today? Who wouldn't cut a few corners to get him.? *Shit*, how do you think I came so close." The coach said, in a sudden low mumble after he noticed the look on Mr. Wyble's face.

Mr. Wyble was surprised to hear those words coming from this coach's mouth.

"I mean, I wasn't just going to *give* him the money…" The coach continued, trying to clean up his mess. "It was a partial; along with some other institutional money."

"But that adds up to about the same as a full-ride…wouldn't it?" Mr. Wyble asked, still frowning slightly.

"Yeah, it would. But they gave it to him straight out…and I'm talking *straight out*! The way I see it, it is a completely different story from what I was willing to do…so give me some kind of credit, *damn*! And another thing, I just overheard his father saying that he's going to be taking the family on vacation within the next few weeks…for the rest of the summer."

"You're telling me he's not gonna be around for the playoffs? But, that's what these kids play for out here?" Mr. Wyble said, laughing lightly in disbelief.

"Nope…" The coach answered sarcastically, smiling back.

"Does Frank know about any of this?"

"Not that I know of…" Frank was Tridane's summer league coach. "But his father just said it only a few minutes ago, so I seriously doubt it. I wouldn't be surprised if his father comes up with some sort of excuse that gets him out of the playoffs this year without looking like a darn snake in the grass, *again*…Now *watch* what I tell you."

"That's a *damn* shame…*poor kid*," Mr. Wyble said, shaking his head.

"Poor *kid*? *Poor kid*? You mean *poor*, *me*! He was my only hope for the future…*shit*! And what about *you*, you *bastard*? You have all of your boys going over to Tech in the fall…you asshole. You could've at least saw to it that I got one of them…*at least* one." The coach raised his voice as he spoke to Mr. Wyble in a serious, yet playful tone.

"What am I supposed to do now...huh? Where is my frig'n sympathy? My job's up for evaluation after this year, and the worst part about it is, all I was asking for, in addition to getting this kid..." The coach said, bobbing his head at Tridane. "was to land at least a half decent swingman. But now, even that's starting to seem like it was asking too much."

The coach then paused for a moment.

"But, hey..." He continued. "What about the kid you had out on the court today? What's his name? Where's he going?"

"Randy...Randy Murcy."

"Ah! And where did you get him? He is good? Where's he from...he from Philly?"

Mr. Wyble nodded his head 'yes'.

"What did he have...like 19, 20 points today? He'll be a freshman this fall, right?"

"Yeah, ah... He's gonna be a freshman."

Mr. Wyble was reluctant to talk to the man about Randy because he coached for a private school.

"He dropped in 31..." Mr. Wyble added in a low voice.

Mr. Wyble then turned his attention to two police cars that were driving pass the park, heading in the same direction that Mr. Shan and the boys went in.

"But, he wouldn't be eligible to play for you this season."

"And why not?" The coach asked, folding his arms, as if waiting to hear an excuse. "What would make him ineligible to play for me? He's about to graduate middle school, isn't he?"

"Yeah...but he would've gotten left back this year had he not repeated last year."

Mr. Wyble spoke without even looking away from the patrol cars that stopped at a red light behind some other cars.

"*Damn*!" The coach said, rearing his head back with his shoulders hunched.

"He's playing with ineligibility already...he's not even in high school yet...*damn*!"

"Yeah, I know. He's what I call one of my 'special-cases'. I'm dealing with him *personally*."

"Hey, well, *good luck* with that one...*sheesh*...because heaven only knows, you're gonna need it. You've got your work cut out for you young man."

Mr. Wyble watched the two police cars flip on their sirens and take off in the same direction that the boys and Mr. Shan went in. An unmarked patrol car parked on the other side of the street made a u-turn and also went racing through a newly changed green light…holding up traffic. Mr. Wyble tossed the last bit of his equipment into a box and took off, leaving the coach standing there looking clueless.

"*I'll talk to you later*!" Mr. Wyble shouted, running across the grass.

CHAPTER 20

"You boys hungry?" Mr. Shan asked, as he slowed down in front of a fast-food restaurant parking lot. All four boys answered 'yes' at the same time.

"You boys have the choice of either McDonalds or Burger King."

"Damn, that doesn't sound like much of a choice anymore…that's always the only selection," Tooch mumbled as he got out of the car, causing Randy and Omar to laugh.

Mr. Shan parked right in front of the McDonalds' window with his back turned to Burger king. Omar and Touch both headed for McDonalds while Zac and Randy started for Burger King. Mr. Shan then pulled his cell phone from his pocket and started dialing. Just as he held it up to his left ear, the two patrol cars flew pass. He quickly lowered the phone and watched them breeze by. Randy and Zac walked into Burger King and went straight up to the counter ordering. Minutes later, they received their food in small brown-paper bags and walked out. As they strolled across the parking lot toward McDonald's, Mr. Wyble spotted them and slammed on the breaks, causing his tires to screech. He quickly whipped the wheel, turning left into the parking lot…barely eluding on coming cars on the other side of the four lane two-way street.

"It's Mr. Wyble. *Look*, he's doing it *again*…" Zac said, appearing noticeably annoyed and surprised.

"He's acting weird again…*Now* I'm really starting to think he's gay."

"*Nah, man, chill.* Be cool." Randy chuckled.

"Hey Mr. Wyble, What's up. What, you forget to tell me something?" Randy asked smiling.

"No…I was just driving by and saw the two of you." Mr. Wyble said, looking over at Mr. Shan.

"*See*, I *told* you." Zac whispered, covering his mouth with his cup as he held his straw in his teeth.

"Oh, yeah…Mr. Wyble, do you know anything about *Tech*?"

"Yeah…it's a private school…why?" Mr. Wyble asked frowning as if he was hoping Randy wouldn't mention anything about wanting to attend that school in the fall.

"Because I was wondering if it was possible for me to go there next year?"

"*Ah*, well, Randy…that *is* a private school. And like I already told you, some high schools are going to want to see your grades from middle school…and if they are not what they expect, they won't let you come in. Besides, that school carries one of the highest tuitions in the tri-state area."

Mr. Wyble tried his best to let Randy down easy, but there just were not enough nice things to say about his situation. Randy did not bother asking any more questions either. He just stood there looking down at Mr. Wyble as he sat in his car.

"But don't worry about it, though…like I told you, there are still a few coaches I haven't had a chance to speak with yet. Don't worry about it…alright?"

"Alright…" Randy replied, shrugging his shoulders.

Randy shook Mr. Wyble's hand and stepped back, letting him leave.

"But, I should definitely know something by tonight…so, don't worry about it, *ok*?" Mr. Wyble said, putting his car in reverse, backing out of the parking lot.

Randy and Zac looked at each other in silence, and then looked at Mr. Shan, who was still sitting in his car talking on his cell phone.

"Welcome to McDonalds. May I take your order?" A young Black girl with a nametag that read 'Tamika' said. Omar and Tooch both stepped toward the counter at the same time and Omar looked straight up at the food-menu rubbing his chin.

"Do y'all still have that triple cheeseburger meal?" Tooch asked.

"No, we don't have it anymore, but I can have them make you one."

"Alright…cool, then I'll take that…thanks."

Tooch then looked at Omar who was standing on his right as Tamika quickly punched his order in.

"Is this going to be on the same bill?"

"Ah…it doesn't matter…which ever's easier for you." Tooch nodded.

Omar still had not made up his mind yet, and, it did not help any that there was a long line forming behind them.

"*Aaah…aah…*I'll have…*aaaah…aaah…*a numberrr…*five*." He said, nodding slowly as he finally lowered his eyes from the food-menu.

Tamika got a good look at Omar and appeared surprised by how good-looking he was. She quickly cut her eyes away and punched his order in.

"Tooch, what did you get?"

"I got a triple cheese-burger meal."

"I didn't see that up there." Omar said, quickly raising his eyes back up to the menu-board.

"I had her make me one." Tooch said smiling.

"*Yeah* man? That's what *I* want. You know what…never mind…you can give me the same thing he's get'n." Omar said, now drawing a much less friendly look from Tamika.

Tamika looked at Omar for about five seconds not moving a muscle, then lowered her eyes back to the key-pad before leaning her head back yelling, "I need the *keeey*!" She yelled as she tapped her long French manicured fingernails on the metal counter in frustration.

"I think you just pissed her off, O'." Tooch snickered.

"*So*!" Omar shot back, shrugging his shoulders. "I don't care, let her get pissed off."

Omar spoke loud enough for Tamika to hear him, but she had just turned her attention to the guy walking up behind her. Randy and Zac walked over and stood with Tooch and Omar. They immediately noticed the girl behind the counter looking bothered.

"What's up…what's wrong?" Zac asked.

"O' wanted to change his order." Tooch said, giggling as he turned his face away from Tamika.

Randy looked down inside his bag to check his order. Then he raised his eyes up, noticing the young Black man coming toward the counter. He froze…looking like he was seeing a ghost. Randy then stepped close to Tooch and started tapping him. Tooch did not see the young man's face as he walked to the counter with his head down and placed a partially opened bag of straws next to the register. Stepping in front of Tamika, he stuck the key into the register and turned it, causing a beep. When the young man raised his head, Randy looked at Tooch with his mouth hanging wide opened and bumped him once more to get his attention. Tooch looked at Randy curiously, then at the young man. His bottom lip then fell almost to the floor also. He next started nudging Zac to get his attention. At first, Tooch pulling on his right arm annoyed Zac. But when Tooch nodded his head at the young man behind the counter. Zac froze. Tooch and Zac both looked at each other with the same facial expression then looked at Randy. Randy just shrugged, as if to say 'don't look at me'. Tooch closed his eyes then nudged Omar in his back. Omar smiled, thinking that one of the boys was joking around with him. Then he caught a glimpse of what Tooch was trying to show him.

The young man standing across the counter was Daryl, and to Randy, Zac and Tooch this was something to get a good laugh out of later. But to Omar, this was far more serious.

"I thought you told my sister you played college basketball in *Maryland…pussy*!" Omar said loudly, catching Daryl completely by surprise.

"You're a fuck'n liar, you *dickhead*!" Omar growled.

Daryl slowly looked up from the register with a blank stare not recognizing Omar or any of the other three boys standing with him. But then something clicked in his head and he remembered.

"You play basketball in college now, huh, Daryl?" Tamika said sarcastically, as she placed the boys' two bags of food on the counter in front of the boys with a smile.

"*Shut up, Tamika…*" Daryl said, as he looked at her with a straight face and sucked his teeth.

"You told my sister a lie. *I should beat you the fuck up*!"

Omar was clearly smaller than Daryl, but threatened him anyway as he snatched his food from the counter. Daryl frowned after hearing Omar's threat then cracked a sinister grin.

"*Oh*, you think we're joking with you…*Calvin*?" Tooch said, jumping in with his eyes popping wide open.

He took a half-swing at Daryl causing him to hop to the side to avoid being hit. Then Zac, swung and caused him to jump away from the counter. Tooch laughed and bit down on his bottom lip.

"*Ew*!" He exhaled in anger.

Mr. Shan was still in his car talking on his cell phone. He watched the whole thing and couldn't believe his eyes.

"*What* the *heck* are those boys in there *doing*?" He said, honking his horn frantically.

"*Hey*…I'm gonna have to hit you back later." Mr. Shan told the person on the phone before disconnecting.

Tooch, Randy, Zac and Omar all heard the car horn. They all turned and looked out the window at Mr. Shan, who was waving for them to come out.

"We're going to get you…*watch…pussy*!" Omar threatened, taking the bag of straws from the counter and throwing it in Daryl's face.

Straws flew everywhere as the boys hurried out of the McDonalds' and got into the car where Mr. Shan backed out of the parking space and took off in a hurry.

"Hey, dude was a faggot, yo. Did you see him...*flinch-mob, flinch-mob*?" Tooch said, laughing and mocking Daryl's motions.

Tooch leaned over placing his head on Randy's left shoulder with his eyes closed and lost it.

"What did you boys just call yourselves doing back there?" Mr. Shan asked getting the noise to calm instantly.

"Nothing, dad...That dude back there told Omar's sister a lie. He told her he played college basketball in Maryland."

By the sound of Zac's voice, he was trying to add some humor to the situation for his father.

"So, he lied to her...what does *that* mean?"

"*That* means he should catch a nice beat-down...that's what *that* means." Tooch happily replied.

"So none of you boys have ever told a female a lie before...is that what you're telling me?"

The car became completely silent again.

"*Ah*...I thought so. Y'all boys can't just go into a place of business like that and call yourselves harassing people. If the police would have been around they could have locked all four of your little asses up for starting with an employee at their work place." Mr. Shan said, looking in his rear-view mirror at his cowboy of a nephew.

Mr. Shan also noticed that through all of what just happened Omar's facial expression had never changed from being serious.

"You boys have to learn that you can't just go around doing things like that to people; especially to people you don't know."

Tooch rolled his eyes around the back of the car and started staring up at the roof before saying, "But *Unc*, he works at *Mickey-D's*! Don't anybody care about what happens in a place like that...*for-real, for-real*."

By the sound of Tooch's voice, his uncle could tell that he was strongly standing by what he said.

"*Tooch*, It doesn't matter." Mr. Shan said, cutting him short. "It doesn't matter if that boy was work'n in a *God* damn *trash-site*!"

Mr. Shan started checking his mirrors again.

"You know what, *Tooch*... I'm really disappointed in you the most. Out of everyone here, you should've been the one to know better." Mr. Shan said, referring to the reason Tooch came to Philly to live with him.

"Boys...what I'm about to tell you, I hope you'll carry it for the rest of your lives, because it might just save you someday. If you don't know a person, who you've seen around where you live, you don't do anything to them, because you don't know who they know or *what* they're capable of."

After a few minutes of silence, Mr. Shan looked in his rear-view mirror at Randy, who was staring straight at him, and winked his right eye.

CHAPTER 21

Mr. Wyble came out his bathroom fresh from the shower. He walked into his cherry-wood furnished home-office wearing nothing but a white-bath-towel around his waist and another draped around his neck like a boxer. He stuck his finger into his left ear to remove the water, and then sat down in his office-chair behind his desk. He grabbed his black cordless telephone and started dialing.

"Hello, is agent *Tom Rapth* around by any chance?" He asked the female on the other end.

"Oh, he's not? *Well*, is…*ah*, agent *Doug Smith* around?"

"Hold on," The lady said. "I'll connect you."

Mr. Wyble sat there waiting patiently as the phone rang. Then, a few moments later a male voice picked up saying, "Agent Smith…"

"Hey *Doug*…what's up, *buddy*?" Mr. Wyble spoke, sounding happy to hear the guy's voice.

"Who is this, *Wyble*?" Agent Smith asked.

"*Yeah*…"

"*Hey*, long time no hear from. *Damn*, man… I thought you forgot about us or something."

"Nah… I've just been really busy with graduation and placing these kids, that's all."

"Ah, that's good. How are things going anyway?"

"They're not bad…but hey, that's what I was calling to talk to you about."

"And what's that, what's up?"

"I know you guys aren't really allowed to discuss your cases, but…"

"*Nah*…go ahead, *shoot*." Agent Smith said, cutting him short.

"Aah…does a guy by the name *Shannon Young* ring a bell or mean anything to you?"

"Not, that I can say. *Why*?" Agent Smith thought hard, trying to remember if he had ever heard the name before.

"He was down to pick up one of my kids from the summer league today, and I thought I saw some of your boys following him when he left."

"What's this guy in…some kind of trouble or something? What's he into?"

"You know…the usual stuff…guns, drugs, violence…nothing un-heard of. But no, he's a drug dealer from around one of my kid's neighborhood."

"Well, *aah*… I could not tell you anything off-hand, I mean, not right now any way. But we did have a briefing earlier this week, and if I'm not mistaken, that name does sound a bit familiar…at least I *think* it does."

"You said it does?"

"*Yeah*…but don't quote me on that, I wasn't really paying too much attention to what was going on…Tom would know better than I would, to be totally honest with you."

"Where's Tom now? I just called and they said he wasn't around."

"He's gone out of town for the weekend, but he should be back on Monday."

"Oh, ok…then I'll give you a call back later. I have to check something, alright?"

"Alright, *cool*. Maybe we can step out for drinks or something…get bent."

"*Sounds good to me*…Sounds like a plan I could go for."

After they hung up. Mr. Wyble sat with his elbows resting on his desk for a moment …with the phone still in his left hand before he started dialing again.

"What? No one's around this afternoon?" He asked himself after listening to the telephone ring about seven times.

"Damn!"

Mr. Wyble started to pull the phone away from his ear. But just as he did, a voice picked up and Mr. Wyble quickly placed it back up to his ear.

"Hello, *Scott*?"

"*Hello*?" The man said. "Who's calling?"

"It's me, *Wyble*."

"*Oh*! *Hey*…what's happening, man…how's it going?"

"That's the same thing I was calling to ask you!"

"*Uh oh*, what is it now?" Scott said, causing the two of them to share a laugh.

"But, no…I'm hanging in there, how about you?" Scott said now laughing lighter.

"Ah…I'm good…but I think I'm gonna need to ask you for a *huge* favor."

"And what's that?"

"It's the type of situation that could definitely benefit you in the future, though."

"Well, I'm listening."

"I'm in desperate need of placing a kid…but not just any kid. He's special, and can play…plays his ass off. And he's got heart too. He's from the projects."

"*Yeah*…what part, where's he from?"

"He's from Frankford…and he's about to graduate middle school."

"Oh, ok." Scott said, trying to recall if he had ever seen anyone out there worth remembering.

"Remember the kid I was telling you about a few years back?"

"*Um…yeah*, if I'm not mistaken, his name was Randy, *right*?"

"Yeah, yeah, that's him…*Randy Murcy*."

"Oh, ok…but what about him?"

"He's finally coming out."

"*Damn*… Wyble, its been a while. How many years has he been in there?"

"*Four*…but you make it seem like he's been in prison."

"It seemed a little longer, actually."

"Yeah, I know…then you should already know what I'm about to ask."

"Then I'm asking, 'why me'?"

"Come on, man…you already know the answer to that. Your school is closer to me than anyone else's. And I can keep a close eye on him. Besides, we have known each other since the 4th grade. Come on, *please*…besides, I know I can trust you."

"*Ah*…now *see*, that's *dirty*, bringing up the 4th grade."

"I know. I have too. It would truly mean that much to me, Scott. And besides, I know your ass should already be sweat'n over that Grant situation."

"What *Grant* situation?"

"The situation with him having to attend summer school for the third straight year. That's what '*Grant situation*'… three in a row now?"

"*Ah, well*, that's *nothing*." Scott sighed, sounding exhausted with the thought of it alone.

"*He's* an *off-guard...*" Mr. Wyble snickered in an enticing voice.

"Oh, *really*?"

"*Yeah...now* do I have your attention?"

"He's still playing the two, huh?" Coach Scott was now really thinking of the possibility.

"Is he *short*?" Scott asked, as if he was expecting something to be wrong with Randy. "I haven't seen him in a while."

"He's a good height. He's already somewhere around 6-feet, and besides, he could be like an insurance policy for you guys next season."

Mr. Wyble sat there listening to the coach breath into the telephone for almost 10 seconds before he finally spoke again.

"*Alright*. But I want to come and see what he looks like first. I already made somewhat of a promise to someone else's kid...and this might mean that I will have to break that promise."

"No problem." Mr. Wyble said, as he pumped his right fist.

"So, when will I be able to come take a look at him?"

"Next Saturday at nine o'clock. And you know what; he's playing against Tridane Spencer."

"*Oh' really*?" The coach got excited.

"Yeah. And I have a funny feeling that after this game a lot of people are going to want to know who he is."

"He's like that, huh?"

"*Yup*, but you'll see. You're getting a steal on this one, trust me."

"Hey, well...I look forward to getting away with a little something every now and then. I call it a blessing."

"Then I'll see you on Saturday. Thanks a bunch, Scott."

"No problem." Mr. Wyble and the coach then hung up. Mr. Wyble sat the phone down on his desk, leaned back, and swung his chair around facing a window.

"*Oh boy*!" He exhaled, stretching his arms outward.

He snatched his arms in and started rubbing his face, and then looked at the telephone as if he was thinking about something, before reaching over and picking it up again.

CHAPTER 22

The next Saturday, Mr. Shan, Zac, Omar, Tooch and his brother –who they call Twin, sat in the stands together as Randy and his team prepared themselves to play.

"Here, hand these to him." Tooch said, tapping Zac on his right arm with a closed can of orange soda.

Zac looked over his right shoulder at Tooch, who was sitting one step above him, then took the soda from him.

"Twin…here." Zac said, getting Twin's attention.

Tooch's brother was a fair skin boy. His mother was Italian and his father, of course, was Black, but his features took mostly after his mother's side.

"Thank you" Twin replied, opening the soda.

Twin then went back to the conversation he was having with his mother, on his left, and who was also sitting one level down from him with her legs crossed. Out on the court, Randy was now standing at center court with his teammates bouncing up and down lightly on his tiptoes.

"Hey Randy!" Mr. Wyble called, getting him to trot over to the sideline.

"Play your game today, alright?" He whispered into his right ear.

"Make sure you keep your focus…if these boys start to get a little timid, don't be afraid to take the ball from 'em, ok?"

Randy nodded his head 'yes' with a serious look on his face then hustled back out to center court for the tap. At that instance, the bad blood between Randy and Tridane began. As soon as Randy stood next to him, Tridane nudged him. Randy shouldered him back, then swung his right leg around in front of Tridane and moved him out of his way with his hip. Mr. Wyble saw this, looked back over his right shoulder at Scott, and nodded his head, as if to say 'I told you so'. The age difference between Randy and

Tridane was also only one year, because Tridane had started school late. Coach Scott nodded his head back at Mr. Wyble then slid to the edge of his white beach chair. Mr. Wyble looked across the court at Tridane's father, who appeared to be curious about the kid who was on the court banging with his son, and smiled.

"Cool it, you two!" The ref said, looking at them as he held the ball ready to lob it up for the tap.

The ref then lobbed the ball up into the air to start the game, and the ball was tapped to Tridane by his teammate. Tridane started dribbling through his legs as he brought the ball up court in front of Randy. Randy was backpedaling. Even though Randy was defending him well, he was still able to find one of his teammates, cutting back door to the basket for an easy lay up.

Hurry up! Get it up! Get it up!" Mr. Wyble yelled, ordering his team to inbound the ball quickly.

The ball was in-bounded to Rob who dribbled twice and passed it up court to Sean. Rob's pass geared two more quick-passes that landed the ball in Randy's hands. Randy, standing just at the top key, caught the pass then dribbled once stepping into a mid-range jumper that fell straight through. The ball fell into the hands of a player on Tridane's team. Their team's point guard, a short, heavy-set, brown skin kid with big calf-muscles, then jogged over and took the ball from his teammate…passing it back to Tridane. With control of the ball and again, Tridane caught the defense by surprise. This time he gave Sean a hard stutter step—to the right, and dropped the ball back through his legs…going left.

After easily getting by Sean, Tridane galloped into the lane for an easy lay-up. Sean ran over and caught the ball as it fell from the net. He then took a step out of bounds…throwing a long in bounds pass to Rob at half court. Rob caught the ball out of the air and dribbled up court with Randy racing along side him on his left and another kid on his right. But and as soon as Rob saw that the defense had already retreated, and was in perfect position to defend the play, he slowed down and grunted under his breath, then dribbled back to the top of the key and held his right hand up in the air yelling, "Set it up, set it up!"

He was looking directly at Randy. But Randy turned and looked at Mr. Wyble with his shoulders hunched and his palms up mouthing…

"Set *what* up…what the *heck* is he talking about?"

Before Mr. Wyble could say anything, Rob snapped a fake, one-handed pass at Randy, causing him to flinch and quickly turned his attention back to the play. Seconds later, Rob dropped a pass right in front of Sean just as Sean went flying pass him to the basket. Sean drew Randy's man away from him as he went pass, then turned back around and dished the ball back out to Randy. Randy was still standing on the left wing. He saw that the defense was way out of position to defend him but looked down on the low post to Chuck, who was busy muscling a defender.

"Bring it here!" Chuck called, with his man trapped behind him.

Randy faked as if he was going to pass the ball back to Rob, but he passed it down to Chuck. All in one motion, Chuck grabbed the ball out of the air, dropped his left foot behind his man… into the paint, and rolled him out of his way to make a strong lay-up. He completed his move just before the defense could collapse on him.

"Yeah, Chuck!" Randy said after coming over to make sure that there would not be any rebounds coming off.

Mr. Shan cheered for the play along with the four boys.

"Yeah, that's right…Yeah, Randy!" Zac yelled.

After the lay up, Tridane took off down court again. This time *his* team was trying to in -bound the ball in a hurry. Randy gave chase, but the ball went sailing over his head. And even though Randy jumped up and tried to deflect the pass, Tridane still caught it and drove to the basket with Randy a few steps behind him. As he continued toward the basket, Tridane pulled two defenders away from their men just before dishing a pass to his teammate, who stood alone…for an uncontested lay-up.

"*Damn*…these boys are playing today!" An older White man said, sitting close to Coach Scott with a smile on his face.

"Yeah, I know…" Coach Scott replied as he turned back to the game and refocused his attention on Randy

"I like watching this type of stuff from these young guys…it's beautiful."

Rob, whose man scored on the last play, grabbed the ball, stepped out of bounds, and passed it back to Randy. Randy caught the ball just above the foul line, then turned around and took three hard dribbles before giving a long, one-handed bounce pass up court to Sean who was cutting to the basket. Sean ducked under the extended arms of Tridane's teammate and laid the ball up for a basket…and the foul.

"*Yes*!" Randy exhaled, pumping his right fist once, and then pulling it back close to him.

Sean sank the one foul shot and the tempo of the game took off. The two teams raced back and forth, trading baskets all the way to halftime. And at the half, Randy's team lead by nine-points.

"Alright everybody…huddle up!" Mr. Wyble said, getting his team to crowd around him.

"Listen guys, I'm not too concerned with how we're playing on offense, but *damn* it…would somebody please attempt to play some darn defense, *geees*! We cannot keep allowing them to catch us out of position every time we score a basket. What good does it do us, if no one is back on defense… It's pointless! If you see three or four of our guys going down court on a break…*stay, back*! There is no need for all of you to run up court. That is not supposed to happen. Do you boys hear me?"

"Yes!" The whole team answered at once.

"Anyway…look guys, we all have to show some hustle on every play, ok? Quit japing! That means you are not getting back on defense. OK?"

"Randy, Sean, Chuck…" Mr. Wyble turned his attention to his starters. "I see what you're doing, and I'm gonna tell you…it's not gonna fly come this second half, alright?"

"My stomach is cramping though, coach." Chuck said, placing his hand on his belly.

"Well, hopefully you'll feel better by the start of the second half."

Chuck saw Mr. Wyble was not about to give him any sympathy. He then took his hand off his stomach and started listening again. Seconds later, the referees blew their whistles and walked back onto the court.

"And one more thing guys…" Mr. Wyble continued, "Let's try and see if we can force some of the other players on their team to make some of the decisions with the ball, alright?"

The team all answered in one sound. Mr. Wyble then turned and looked at Randy and Sean, who were standing off to the side of the team talking, and said…

"Boys, you two are going to have to put up some numbers this second half."

Randy and Sean silently looked at each other, then at Mr. Wyble, and nodded 'yes'. They had not known each other for longer than a week, but they had already formed a strong chemistry. The refs blew their whistles again, and told the coaches to send their teams back onto the court.

"Let's go coaches…" A Black ref in his mid 40's said. "Half time's over!

"And guys…*please*…*please* try not to forget about what this team did last week! Team, on three!"

"*One, two, three, team*!" Mr. Wyble's team shouted, then broke off… running out onto the court.

The second half started very rough for Mr. Wyble's bunch, but fortunately Randy was able to restore order by bringing his team's game plan together perfectly. He prevented Tridane from catching any passes within his striking distance, on either side of the three-point line, by roughing him up a bit. This also helped the other players on his team better defend their men as well; forcing some ill advised passes which resulted in turnovers that lead to some easy baskets. Mr. Wyble's team held a nine-point lead up until there were only three minutes and a few seconds remaining in the game. But when the three-minute mark came, Tridane started to break free of Randy…causing problems. Tridane broke free by running around solid picks, slicing through the defense, with Randy trailing him on almost every play, and by using his silky smooth, yo-yo like dribble. He went down court to the basket two straight times in a row, and each time he drew fouls that sent him to the foul line…plus the basket. Tridane's last three points had also cut the lead to three. And after two misses by both Sean and Randy, the momentum had clearly shifted.

"He's doing it *again*! Look at him!" Zac said as he grabbed the top of his head in disbelief and stood up with the rest of the crowd.

Rob came down court and passed the ball to Randy who was rolling off a pick set by Chuck. Then Tridane, who was moving to Chuck's right, fell to the ground, causing Chuck to pick up an offensive foul.

'*Tweet*'…The ref blew his whistle.

"*Offensive*!" He shouted as he threw his hip to the side, mimicking what Chuck just did.

Randy stopped after getting to the basket, then turned around and looked to see what the ref had just called. But then he quickly became animated and shouted, "*Damn, man*!"

"*Randy, Randy*, calm down!" Mr. Wyble pleaded, stepping halfway onto the court.

"Tweet!" The referee blew his whistle again and jogged over to the scorers-table saying, "I have a tech, *here. One, yellow*…two shots, *gray*."

"*What*?" Mr. Wyble shouted in disbelief. "Let 'em play, Joe. Let 'em play!"

As the crowd reacted, sending a loud murmur throughout the beautiful park, Mr. Wyble just stood and folded his arms.

"*Randy*! Shut up, *man*!" Zac yelled as Chuck led Randy away from the ref.

"Ran…you gotta chill baby!" Chuck said, smiling at Randy. "He already made the call. We don't need that. We don't want you to get tossed."

Mr. Wyble looked over at Coach Scott to see his reaction, but Scott just sat there quietly with a blank stare on his face, watching Randy act out.

"Oh, man." Mr. Wyble sighed under his breath with concern.

He knew that it was these types of things that made coaches reject the notion of working with certain players. And it also made them give scouting reports to other coaches that were not so good.

"Man, I don't believe this!" Zac said, rubbing his right hand over his thick, wavy black hair.

Tooch and Mr. Shan looked at each other, then at Zac and smiled. Mr. Shan was smiling because his son was so emotionally caught up in the game, Tooch, however, was smiling because he and Zac had placed a bet on the game. Tooch was not against Randy, he just saw a perfect opportunity to pick up a few extra bucks if his friend slipped up.

Tridane went to the foul line and sank both of his shots, and with only 57 seconds left on the game clock, his team in-bounded the ball and passed it right back to him. As soon as Tridane touched the ball defenders immediately surrounded him. He faked the crowd…going left, and was able to slither his way around Rob's right leg. He found another open man on his team; who went coasting into the basket for a smiling and easy two handed lay up. Tridane's team now led by one.

"*Jesus Christmas*…what the *heck* are you boys doing? He doesn't need any help!" Mr. Wyble shouted nearly pulling his curly red hair out of his head.

"*Call time out*! *Call time out*!" Mr. Wyble pleaded.

"*42 seconds*!" A young White girl yelled from her seat behind the scorers-table.

Her legs bounced under the table from anticipation as she held the orange game-clock up in the air. .Mr. Wyble gathered his team around him again then started trying to rework his team's game plan by saying, "Rob, when we come out from the stack on the in bounds play, I need you to go three-spread.

But if they decide they just wanna try and pressure us man to man, then go into our five motion play."

"*What*!" Randy said frowning. "What the heck is *five-motion, man*?"

"Randy, you still remember box-high from last year, right?" Mr. Wyble asked.

"Yeah…"

"Well, that's the same play, except only you're not the ball handler."

Mr. Wyble then placed his left hand on Randy's shoulder trying to calm him down some.

"We're just feeding them the same play that they've been running on us all game." Sean said, tapping Randy gently on his right arm.

"Oh, ok…I didn't notice…" Randy agreed, shaking his head…still looking a bit confused.

"Randy, you're on the right elbow. Sean, you are on the left. Chuck, you set the screen for Sean. Sean, you fake as if you are cutting for the basket, then sprint over and set a pick for Randy. Sean…Randy, the two of you run a pick and roll…alright? Now let's get it in and get rid of these boys!"

'Tweet!' The referee blew his whistle again saying, "Timeout's over coaches…Send 'em back out!"

After the two teams got back on the court, Tridane jogged over to Randy and stood in between him and Chuck.

"*Stack*!" A kid on Randy's team said, before starting the inbounds play.

Randy started jogging in place then took off running, after grabbing a hand full of Tridane's jersey and shoving him away to create space. The inbounds pass went to Rob, who faked a pass to a cutting Sean. Then Rob started dribbling back out toward the middle of the court. Sean, doing as told, turned and charged back out to set a screen for Randy. After waiting patiently for the screen, Randy received the pass from Rob then started to dribble as he looked at Sean to start the pick and roll play.

"*Fifteen seconds*!" The girl behind the scorers-table shouted.

Randy dribbled to the top of the key where Sean set the pick and never took his eyes away from Sean as they rolled toward the basket together. In his effort to defend, Sean's man was caught between he and Randy, while Tridane trailed the play trying to get back in front of it. Randy took another step away from the defender as he was still caught between he and Sean, then faked a pass to Sean causing him to back away even further. Randy then went up for a two handed lay-up and was fouled by a third defender who rushed over…colliding into him.

"*That's game*! Give me my money, *man*." Zac said while standing and watching as Randy made the basket and received praise from his teammates.

The referee, who called Randy for the technical earlier in the game, was the same one who blew his whistle on the foul made by the other team's point guard. Randy made the foul shot then turned and raced back up court on defense. Tridane's team did not have any timeouts left, so they were left to try to rush the inbound pass in. But as soon as the ball was put into play, the ref blew his whistle saying, "*That's out*!"

The ref pointed at the left foot of the point guard on Tridane's team. He had stepped in bounds just as he was throwing the ball in play.

"*Aaah*!" The crowd reacted over the call.

After Sean passed the ball inbounds to Rob, who avoided being fouled during the last couple of seconds, Mr. Wyble's team cleared the bench and went racing out onto the court celebrating. Zac, Omar, Tooch and Twin also raced out onto the court to celebrate with them. Even Tooch was out there on the court jumping around and giving hugs and high fives to Randy and his teammates. Mr. Wyble congratulated his players then looked over at Coach Scott…who nodded his head 'yes' in agreement before turning and walking away with a huge smile on his face. Tridane finished with a game high 28 points, and had five rebounds and seven assist. Randy posted 26 points, eight rebounds and four assists.

"Randy! Randy!" Mr. Wyble called, jogging over to him.

"You did it…you did it!"

"Did *what*?" Randy asked, turning and looking at him as the four boys crowded around him.

"We found you a school…and it's a good one!"

"*Really*?"

"Yeah…*Prescott*!"

After realizing Mr. Wyble was talking about one of the perennial high schools in the city for public league basketball, the boys all started to celebrate even harder.

"Yeah, man…that's what I'm talking about!" Tooch yelled as they jumped on Randy, causing Mr. Wyble to laugh.

CHAPTER 23

By Randy's junior year, he was a tremendously athletic 6-feet-6, 215-pound shooting guard. He had made vast improvements over the years, averaging 15.5 points as a freshman, 18.0 points as a sophomore, and 30.1 points in his first four games as a junior . His ability to handle the ball was something that made almost every college scout that had ever seen him play crazy about him. Randy was also considered as one of the top juniors in the Tri-State area. The only down side to this was that Randy had not taken his SATs. He had not even scheduled to take them. This was something that kept him from getting the same national exposure as some of the players he faced on the court.

Randy's fifth game of the season for the Prescott High Tigers was at one of the city's major Universities in front of nearly ten thousand fans. This was the type of crowd he looked forward to playing in front of. But if his team was not playing at a major venue, he would not get to see this type of turn out. A 6-feet-1, 175-pound, dark-skin kid named Pooh dribbled across half court for Prescott and stopped at the top of the key. Pooh was Prescott's starting point guard. He pumped faked a one-handed pass with his left hand, snapping it back to himself, and got his defender to jump out of his defensive-stance. Then he dribbled the ball through his legs from left to right and took off…momentarily leaving his defender standing flat-footed. The crowd cheered and laughed as Pooh dribbled into the lane and rose up getting ready to launch a shot. But he dropped a pass just over a defender's head; into Randy's hands as he was slicing to the basket. Without dribbling, Randy took two big strides and took off for the basket…pulling his right hand back as far as he could, ramming the ball home. After coming down from the rim he looked up at Zac, Tooch, and Omar who were standing in the crowd, and pointed up at them as he back-pedaled down court.

Randy dazzled the crowd scoring 33 points on 11 for 17 shooting, and pulled down 11 rebounds to go along with 7 assist and 3 steals…all without committing a single turnover. When the final horn sounded, Prescott did not seem at all impressed with their 17-point victory. After finishing last season with a losing record, one might have expected them to charge onto the floor going nuts, because they were starting the season with a perfect 5-0 record. But Prescott appeared poised and relaxed as they shook the other team's hands before casually strolling off the court toward their locker room.

"Good game, man." Randy said to the top player on the opposing team, giving him a hug and handshake.

In the locker room, 20 minutes later, Randy stepped to the door of the shower room with a towel wrapped around his waist. He exhaled deeply as he listened to Coach Scott talk to the team.

"*Guys*, we played an almost perfect game out there tonight…and I'm really glad to see that we're finally looking like a team that wants to play together."

He turned his head and looked at Khalil, who had already showered and dressed. Khalil was the same boy that Randy knew since he was younger.

"I have to truly say, I love the way the starters came out and responded early. This was one of those games that let us know whether or not we belong out there playing with the big-boys or not."

Coach Scott's assistant then walked into the locker room, leaned over his shoulder and whispered into his ear.

"Oh, ok." Coach Scott responded, looking at his watch.

"But, anyway guys…" He continued. "It's getting late, and I want you all to hurry up and get home. I will finish up with the rest of what I have to say tomorrow at practice. Coach just told me that the snow we were expecting is finally starting to come down, so finish up and hit the bricks. Oh, and before I forget, that's everyone except for Randy!" Coach Scott said, getting Randy's attention away from Khalil.

"Randy, you hang out a little while longer."

As Randy started to ask Coach Scott why he had to stay, Khalil cut him short.

"*Yeah*, not everyone gets to talk to the media after a big-game." Khalil said as he smiled and pulled the bottom of Randy's towel.

"Knock it off, Khalil. Is your *mother* here yet?" Coach Scott said.

"Yes…she was at the game."

"Who else is riding with you?"

"The six of us right here." Khalil said, pointing to five other players who were all dressed and ready to go.

"Then *take off*!"

"*Yes*, sir."

Khalil got up from the bench and led the five players out the locker room.

"Randy, these came for you today." Coach Scott said, walking over placing a stack of college recruitment letters on a bench in front of him.

"Some of them came yesterday, and the rest I have back at school in my desk. I'll give those to you tomorrow."

"Alright." Randy said as he walked over and sat down on the bench.

"Did you sign up to take your SATs yet?" Coach Scott asked.

Randy, sitting with his shoulders slouched, watched the rest of his teammates and the assistant coach leave the locker-room.

"Nah…" He answered, leaning forward from fatigue.

"Well, what're you waiting for…you should've at least signed up to take them by now. That's something you really need to be on top of."

"I know. I planned to take'em as soon as we got back from Christmas vacation."

Coach Scott tilted his head to the side, frowned his face then said, "Alright… just finish up here and I'll talk to you tomorrow."

He shook Randy's hand, turned and walked out the locker room. As he exited, he met Tooch, Zac, and Omar, who nearly brushed him as they passed by. None of the boys even bothered to stop and apologize. Tooch and Zac were both wearing very expensive looking black lambskin jackets, while Omar had on a thick white sweatshirt with a blue stripe running across his shoulders and down the sleeves. Omar was also talking on a cell phone.

"Randy!" Tooch yelled after they entered the locker room but before they turned a corner where they could see him.

"What's up, cat daddy?" Randy smiled; still sitting with his shoulders slouched.

He reached out and gave them all loud slapping handshakes.

"What's up with you…You tired?" Zac asked.

"Yeah."

"You look it. Good game though, scrap."

"Thanks."

"Are these letters for you?" Zac asked as he picked the stack of letters up from the bench and fanned through them.

"Yo, how many points you drop?" Omar asked, as he broke from his phone conversation and leaned back against the lockers.

"I couldn't tell you. And to tell you the truth, I don't even care right now"

"I hear you."

"But, I'll find out tomorrow."

Randy then took a deep breath and exhaled as he placed his hands behind his head and leaned back on the bench.

"*Yo man, get up*. Let's *roll*." Tooch said, getting him to perk up. "We gotta get outta here…we gotta get over to this party. What you forget?"

"I damn sure did." Randy said with a sluggish voice.

He reached into his locker, grabbed his pants and shirt, and got dressed quickly. Then he and the boys headed out the locker room laughing and joking loudly. They walked pass a crowd of men standing by a security-desk, and then dipped out a side door that led to the parking lot, where they were met by a fresh snowfall..

"Hey Tooch, we have to make a quick stop somewhere, so I can get something to eat. My stomach is growling like crazy." Randy said, as they got into Tooch's late model car.

The pea green station wagon with wood panels on the sides left a huge cloud of smoke in the air as it pulled from its parking space.

"There's going to be food at the party. You don't want to eat there?" Tooch asked.

"*Man*, the last thing I want to do is trust my hunger to a *greedy-ass* party crowd."

"Shit…I know that's right." Omar added, taking a quick break from his phone conversation.

"*Yo*…this nigga is still on the phone!" Zac said as he turned around and looked at Omar…who was sitting directly behind him. Zac was sitting in the front passenger seat.

"You've been gas'n up the horn since *fuck'n* halftime. That better not be a *female*…or I'ma say you are sweat'n the *shit* outta her!"

"Look at *you*. *See*…*now*, it's not even a female. I'm trying to take care of some business." Omar said as he shook his head and looked up at Zac. "And besides…this is my phone. I pay the bill for it. So if I wanna gas up my horn, or use up my minutes, I can…"

"*Bill*…*Bill*! *Nigga,what Bill*?" Tooch asked, cutting him off.

"Don't even try to that bullshit in this car…nigga. That's a burn-out, and you know it!"

By the age of 16 Omar was a hood legend in Frankford. He was a pretty boy so all of the women adored him, but because he did not act like one all of the men loved him. Omar could get his hands on just about anything you could think of just by making one simple phone call. He was best described in the neighborhood as a very attractive guy that was exceptional in sports and family had money. People often wondered why he never played any sports in high school, but it was only because he was having so much fun being in the street game he never had the urge.

"We know you. .How you gonna tell us a lie like that."

"Yeah, whatever, man." Omar smiled. "You just turn back around and make sure this moving block-party gets us to where we need to be."

"*Oh*...you ain't gotta worry about that...that's for damn sure. We're gonna make it." Tooch said as he checked his rear-view mirror, looking back at the cloud of smoke trailing them.

When the boys arrived at the party, they noticed a crowd standing outside of Tooch's girlfriend Phyllis' house. Phyllis was Tooch's girlfriend of two years. They were the same age, but she was in her freshmen year in college. She was also still living at home with her parents. He parked halfway up on the pavement—down the street from the house.

"Good game tonight, man." A guy sitting on the front steps said to Randy, giving him a handshake as the boys walked by.

The guy that shook Randy's hand was also talking to a female that was standing directly in front of him at the bottom of the steps.

"Thanks, dawg." Randy was last up the steps.

"*Hey*, yo, my man...Do me a favor?" Tooch said to a guy who was sitting on the railing of the darkened porch. "Hop down off of there for me please?"

"*Oh*, my bad, *Tooch*...no problem."

The guy promptly placed his feet back down on the porch and stood up.

Zac was the first to enter the house, and Phyllis, who was across the room filled with people dancing, spotted him as soon as he stepped in the door. After making her way over to them she said...

"Excuse me... come here." Pulling Tooch away from the boys by his left arm.

"I got him from here, y'all...You three can take the rest of the night off."

"*It's* like *that*, *Phil*?" Zac said smiling. "I didn't even get to wish you a happy birthday, *damn*."

"Yeah, I know."

"That's *crazy*." Randy and Omar both agreed with him.

"Thank you…but, *yup*!"

"Yo…go ahead, do ya'll thing…dance with somebody." Tooch said, scooting at the boys with the back of his right hand as he was being lead away.

"*Nigga*, we don't need you to tell us what to do. You just worry about your damn self tonight." Zac said, rising up to his tiptoes looking over the crowd at Tooch.

The boys made their way toward the back of the party. As Omar walked in between Zac and Randy, he spotted Michelle, who looked like she was standing directly in the middle of the party. He pulled his right arm away from a couple females who asked him to dance…blocking out everything else around him.

"Hey lady." Omar grinned, embracing her with a big hug.

"I was waiting for you." She whispered into his left ear as she rubbed her hands through his curly blowout and landed a wet one flush on his lips.

"That nigga's in love." Zac said, smiling and shaking his head.

Randy and Zac both laughed as they continued on their way to the back of the party. But before they could reach the rear wall, a girl dancing with her backside turned to a young-man who was up against a wall, spotted Zac. She reached down, unwrapped the guy's arms from around her waist, and went over to Zac. She gently backed him up against the wall, turned her butt to him and started dancing to the music. Randy smiled as he watched the action. Then the girl looked up at Randy and pulled him close to the front of her, staring him straight in the eyes as she grinded her mid-section up against his until he started dancing also. Zac pointed down at the girl's butt so that Randy could see how phat it was, and then bit down on his bottom-lip as if in lust. The guy who she left hanging just shook his head and headed for the door.

CHAPTER 24

Randy stood in front of his locker taking his shirt and shorts out for his next period gym-class when he heard his name being called.

"Randy!"

He squinted his eyes as he turned and looked down the hallway. Then he slammed his locker shut saying, "Yo, what's up?"

He then clicked his combination lock shut and turned his tumbler to the left.

"Yo, did you see today's paper?" Khalil asked, sounding almost out of breath.

"Nah…why?" Randy answered, shaking his head with a nonchalant but curious look on his face.

"Look!"

Khalil opened the newspaper wide enough for both he and Randy to see. Inside there was a half page sized color photo of Randy dunking with one hand during last night's game.

"*Yo*…that thing is *ill*!" Randy gloated.

"*Yeah*?" Khalil asked, looking at Randy strangely.

"*Read* the *headlines*."

"'*Prescott has their's…but where's our Mercy*?' "

Khalil continued reading, "'Randy Murcy torched the night with 33 points, 10 rebounds and 7 assist without a single turnover, but was unavailable for comment after the game'"

"*Aaah*!" Randy exhaled, closing his eyes.

Randy felt like he could have melted right where he stood.

"*Damn…damn…damn*!" Randy said as he turned around and banged his head up against his red-painted locker.

"Good game last night, Randy." A male student said as he walked past with his left arm wrapped around a female student.

"It says here…" Khalil commenced to reading. 'Reports say that Randy Murcy left the arena immediately after last night's contest surrounded by an entourage of friends who were laughing and joking loudly. They were in such a hurry that they even exited the arena through an emergency exit, but the reason for his quick exit is still unknown.'"

CHAPTER 25

Over at the Federal Building; agent Rapth was also reading the very same article.

"...Needless to say, Randy Murcy, skipped all interviews after putting on one of the best performances of his high school career, and some recruiters in attendance even took the liberty of hanging around after the game to try and hear a few questions answered by the youngster. But unfortunately they too shared in the misfortune and will have to wait until Randy Murcy either reaches a maturity level high enough where he is willing to speak with more than just his closest friends after a big game, or is wise enough to respect his role in the sports world. Message to Randy; stunts like these will do little more than guarantee you one of the two following things: A full ride to the City Community College of your choice, or, a first class ticket to your very own living room couch, promptly after you graduate your senior year..."

"*Damn*, this guy ripped him pretty hard, don't you think?" Smith asked briefly interrupting Rapth's reading.

"*But hold up...*" Rapth said, putting his finger up. "*There's more.*"

"Randy Murcy must also learn to exercise better sportsmanship if he plans to prove that he can play with the big boys at the next level."

Agent Rapth then sat the newspaper down on his desk in front of him and smiled.

"You think these were our friends?" Smith asked, nodding his head like Rapth already knew who he was referring to.

"Why do we continue to ask questions we already know the answers to?" Rapth said, getting up and putting his brown sports-jacket on that was hanging on the back of his chair.

"Yeah...that's right...the girlfriend's party *was* last night, wasn't it."

"Sure was…that's what the rush was about." Rapth said as he and Smith left the office.

Rapth and Smith drove out from an underground parking garage at the Federal building in a black Lincoln Town car and made a sharp right-turn out into traffic.

"I think it's only a matter a time, though, when you're dealing with a kid like this one." Smith said, looking at the on-coming cars that Rapth had just cut off, as they slammed on breaks to avoid hitting them.

The snowfall from last night had covered the ground outside, and the streets were still a bit messy.

"*It's* a matter of *time*…? A matter of time for *what*… before this kid wakes the hell up, or a person loses all of their patience with him?" Rapth responded in a hard voice as he turned the steering wheel to his left trying to avoid a spinout.

"Yeah…but I guess you could say that that's the key thing. I'm just curious about what Wyble's take is on all of this."

CHAPTER 26

Randy came walking down the ramp out of the locker room wearing his high school's gym uniform. He tied up his baggy, royal blue shorts as he held his shirt tucked up under his chin. Then heard Khali's voice say, "Randy, hurry up!"

Randy also had on a red t-shirt with gold lettering written across the chest and a pair of black and white Tmac basketball sneakers with his socks pulled up to his knees. As Randy walked out onto the crowded gym room floor, he noticed Khalil and their teammate Taj, standing with three pretty girls at the three-point line. Two of the girls had their shirts tied in the front showing off their flat stomachs.

"Alright y'all bums…lets get this thing started…We got first ball." The girl without her shirt knotted said, reaching to take the ball from Khalil.

"*Hold up* girl…wait a *second*. When you are out here on the floor, you are a ball player." Khalil said, hopping forward taking a shot that fell straight through. "You're gonna shoot for it like everybody else."

The girl squinted her eyes at him saying, "But I'm a *girl…*"

"*So*…and what does *that* mean…girls can get it too." Khalil said nodding his head at her.

The girl shook her head as she watched one of her teammates go over to retrieve the ball from rolling off the court.

"That's messed up…" The other girl with her shirt knotted said.

"What's messed up?' Randy asked as he came over standing beside the 6-foot-7 Khalil, and the 6-foot-6 and a half Taj who both were taller than he was. Khalil and Taj, both belonged a grade higher than what they were placed.

"Chick didn't wanna shoot for it…Taj smirked.

"She just wanted to give us first ball?" Randy asked as he watched the girl that went and got the ball's shot fall off the side of the rim.

"*See*...last year, they would've let us have first ball." The second of the two girls with her shirt knotted said.

"Why can't y'all do the same thing for us...y'all all bigger than us and stuff."

"That's because this ain't last year...we take pity on nobody." Taj said, pointing down to the court as he went down low and turned his back to one of the girls posting her up.

Randy got the check ball from the first girl to complain then passed it to Khalil, and Khalil passed it right back to him as he went into a triple threat position. He looked at the girl from head to toe as she crouched into a defensive-position in front of him...gathering her shorts up her thick golden-brown thighs. They were both athletic and flawless. He closed his eyes to calm himself down.

"*Damn*..." He said before opening his eyes back up.

He looked away from her and sighed.

Minutes later Mr. Wyble stormed in from the snow-covered parking lot with a newspaper tucked under his arm. He gave the crowded gym room a quick once over, then turned to walked into the office on his right. Still breathing somewhat heavily, Randy looked over, saw Mr. Wyble, and quickly ducked for cover behind the girl that was sticking him.

"*Ah, shit...stay still, stay still!*" He whispered as he grabbed the back of her gold gym-shirt...to block Mr. Wyble's view. "What...you think he's mad?" Khalil asked as he also breathed heavily.

"*Nah*...ya think?" Randy quipped. "But you know what...It's cool, man...fuck it."

He then flagged the air before going back to playing, but before he could start dribbling the ball, he heard his coach's voice call out.

"Randy!"

Coach Scott's voice halted Randy's motion. The Coach stood in front of his office with his hands on his hips. Randy looked at him with his eyebrows raised then lowered his head and started over toward him saying, "*Oh*, boy...here we go..."

Randy placed his right hand on his hip as he approached him ...then said, "Hey, what's up coach?"

He was trying to wear a facial expression as if he did not already know what was going on.

"In my office..." Coach Scott said stepping aside shaking his head as he walked pass him with his head down.

"Hey, what's up, Mr. Wyble?" Randy said, after seeing how Mr. Wyble was standing over in front of an office window with his arms folded.

Mr. Wyble's demeanor looked somewhat of a two-year-old child's who did not get his way.

"What's up?" Mr. Wyble said, turning back quickly and giving a nod without looking at him.

"Sit down..." Coach Scott told him as he stepped inside the office closing the door behind him.

"What happened last night?" Coach Scott asked after standing behind his desk.

"*What*?" Randy's face looked like he was clueless.

"*Hold up, hold up*...wait a second...before we even go any farther...I'll say this, ok..."

Coach Scott threw his left leg around the back of his chair and sat down.

"I *saw* Khalil out in the hallway earlier...and he had a newspaper... *Now*, I see the two of you out in the gym playing basketball together... I *know*, *you* know, what's going on. And I know you've seen the newspaper."

After a few moments of silence, Coach Scott looked over to his right at Mr. Wyble who was still standing with his back turned.

"Wyble, you have anything?" Mr. Wyble peeked back over his left shoulder at the newspaper sitting on his desk then answered, "No...I don't have anything..."

"Well...ok...Randy...do you have anything?"

"*Nah*...I don't have anything... I just forgot...that's all...*my bad*." Randy said, shrugging his shoulders as he fixed his shirt around his waist like it was 'nothing'.

Coach Scott then looked back over at Mr. Wyble, who chuckled lightly while shaking his head.

"Well, there's no point in us dwelling on something that we can't change right now...so, let's try and forget about it and move on. Randy, I just wanted to let you know that I *was* able to re-schedule your interview for today during practice. So, make sure that you are not late. Ok? And that means no *detentions* or anything *else* that you might come up with between now and then, alright?"

"Yes..." Randy nodded his head breathing a sigh of relief within.

"We don't need you giving yourself another black-eye dealing with the media...now get yourself back out there and finish up with your class... before you get marked as cutting."

"Yes, sir." Randy stood up and darted out the office without saying anything else.

Once he left, Mr. Wyble dropped his head and laughed tirelessly.

"You think I should still give him these, then?" Coach Scott asked, sliding open his desk's top drawer and taking out another stack of college recruitment letters that came for him.

Mr. Wyble looked at the letters over his left shoulder and did a double take before saying, "Nah…I'll hold on to these…he shouldn't see anymore until he knows how to get his act together."

Mr. Wyble then went and scooped the letters up from the desk and tucked them up under his right arm.

"Everything I need in here?" Mr. Wyble asked, referring to a sealed white envelope that he also picked up from the desk.

"Yeah…transcript and class roster, right…that's all you need?"

"Yeah…"

"What time do you think you'll be getting back?"

"I'm not sure, but I shouldn't be too long…I'll try to be back by the time practice starts."

"Alright."

Coach Scott then watched Mr. Wyble walk out of his office and gently close the door behind himself.

CHAPTER 27

FBI agents Smith and Rapth parked around the corner from Mr. Shan's house and got out of their car.

"Hey, oh, yeah…before I forget…did you hear that they're bringing someone else in on this one?" Smith asked Rapth as they walked down the street wearing Philadelphia Water Department jackets and hard hats.

"No…I didn't hear…when did they decide this?" Rapth asked looking surprised.

"Just thee other day…I thought you heard about it before I did."

"No one told me anything. But, I do plan to speak with someone about me being the last to know. Did they say who it was?"

"Oh yeah…*Flent*."

"*Flent*? You mean *Flent* who is about to retire?"

"*Yeah*…that's what I heard."

"So, I'm figuring they're only bringing him in because they figure it's not much movement?"

"That's what it's starting to look like."

"Bring him in and let him…"

"…**RETIRE** with low risk!" Both men concluded—simultaneously.

"Must be how it works when you have money."

The agents then stepped up into the back of one of two PGW trucks parked one behind the other. The truck that the two agents stepped inside was parked with the two driver's side tires up on the pavement where the agents inside could see Mr. Shan's house perfectly.

"*Shhhh*!" One of the agents already inside said as they opened the gate and pulled back a gray curtain.

Rapth and Smith both quickly shut up and allowed the White FBI agent that was listening in on a phone conversation with one of the speakers from the headset to his right-ear, to finish listening. The agent then reached over and turned up the volume.

"Around what time do you think you'll be getting back?" A male voice on the other end of the phone asked Mr. Shan.

"Um… that all depends on how fast we can get in and out of there. You know how kids are these days…it depends on how fast my son chooses what truck he wants."

"Well, ok then. I'll be giving you a ring back later."

"Alright." Mr. Shan replied as he and the man both disconnected.

"So what's new?" Rapth asked, taking a small white-foam cup of coffee from another agent that poured it for him.

"Nothing much…but they're about to go take the son to get his Christmas present."

"No movement today…no visits from anyone, no females coming over?" Smith asked as he went and started skimming through a few stacks of paper work sitting on a counter.

"Nope…only one call made…and that call went out at, *ah*…around seven thirty this morning."

"Who made it?" Rapth asked with his face hidden behind the cup.

"The son…he called Omar."

"What they talk about?"

"Something about some plans they've made for today…nothing big."

"Hold up, somebody's coming to the front door." The second of the three agents said, peeking through the huge lens of a black 35-millimeter camera.

"It's the nephew, William." The agent whispered, adjusting his sight as he snapped shots.

Tooch came to the front door wearing a navy blue insolated jacket that read 'Valto's cycle center' with his name 'Tooch' stitched in the name space. It was a mechanics jacket. Because he had been pulling out his cornrows, the right side of his hair was sticking straight up in the air. He stuck his right hand, palm up, out the storm door, and then looked down the street at the water department trucks parked at the end of the block. There were also several PGW workers digging a hole in the street, so he thought nothing of it…turned and went back inside; closing only the storm door.

"Are you boys ready?" Mr. Shan asked as he walked from the kitchen with a tall brown-skinned fella wearing an expensive, multi colored knitted sweater.

"Yeah, but princess *Zacharella* is still up stairs fixing her make up." Tooch said, looking up stairs. "Zac…Come on man. We're leaving without you!"

Tooch then turned and headed out the darkened house behind his uncle and the man. Mr. Shan had on a long mustard color trench coat with the belt tied around his waist and was carrying a small leather handbag that matched it perfectly. The FBI agent snapped shots as Mr. Shan went and got in the driver's seat of his car, and his friend got into the front-passenger side. The agent also snapped several shots of Tooch as he held the back car door open, looked at the house, and then got inside the car. Zac was still inside the house standing in front of the mirror. As he wiped his face with his hands, he heard the telephone ring. Moments later, Zac came walking down the stairs wearing his black leather-jacket and looking like he was in no real rush to go anywhere.

"I hope this is her…" He said as he paced over to answer the phone…praying it was the person whose call he had been waiting for.

"Hello?"

"Hello, Zac?" A soft female voice asked.

"Yeah…Trina?"

"Yeah.."

"Ah, what's up… did you get' em?"

"Uh, huh…I got'em."

"Ah, that's what's up. Can you get'em to me later?"

"No…I can't…I'm not going to be able to."

"Why not?"

"Because my family and I are leaving to go visit my grandparents."

"Oh, well, where do they live?"

"They live in Delaware."

"*Damn*…but, I wanted to see you too." Zac moaned playfully.

"*Aw*…I'll try to make it back up to see you before I leave to go back to school, alright…I promise."

"Alright… You sure?" Zac said with a cunning smile.

"Yeah, I'm sure…I told you *I promise*…"

Zac started to speak again, but paused when he heard his father's car horn.

"But, when can you bring them by?" Zac said…still conversing.

"I could come by in a couple of minutes, before we leave."

"Yeah, well, drop'em in the mail slot…I'll have to get'em when we come back."

"Alright..."

"And, hey!"

"Huh..." Trina answered softly.

"You be careful, you hear me? And have a safe and happy holiday... sense I'm not gonna be able to see you... Alright?"

"Alright...You do the same." Trina said before she hung up.

Zac stood there and held the cordless phone in his right hand as he listened to his father's car horn honking. He shook his head because he knew exactly who was outside acting like an ass. Tooch was in the car; reaching over his uncle, pressing the car horn from the back seat.

"*Knock it off, Tooch.*" Mr. Shan said as he pushed him back.

"She ain't gonna call...?" Tooch said to himself...as he looked back at the house through the rear windshield.

Zac placed the phone back on its charger and headed for the front door saying,

"*Alright, alright*!"

"*Damn*, you took long enough!" Tooch said as he got in the back of the car. But Zac just glared at him as he picked his teeth with his tongue. He then looked at his father, who was looking back at him through the rear-view mirror.

"You have everything?" Mr. Shan asked.

"Yes..."

Tooch then gave Zac a nice nudge as Mr. Shan pulled off.

"We'll handle that as soon as we get back, alright?" Mr. Shan told his friend, who just gave him a silent nod.

CHAPTER 28

"**That's our cue**." Rapth said to Smith as he put his foam cup down on the counter and got ready to follow Mr. Shan and the boys.

"You boys are gonna be out of here by the time we get back, aren't you?" Rapth asked.

"Yeah, our work is done here. They're all yours now." The oldest of the three White agents said as Rapth and Smith left the truck to return to their car.

Tooch stared out the window for a couple seconds, then raised and lowered it a couple of times. He then turned to Zac without saying anything, and stared at him with a straight face.

"Did she call?" He asked…after several seconds of silence.

Zac cut a look at him from the corners of his eyes and slowly nodded his head 'yes'.

"Oh, she did…so what she say… she get them?"

Zac nodded his head 'yes' again.

"Did she say anything else…did she say anything about me?"

Zac leaned forward without saying anything and grabbed his father's cell phone from near the armrest.

"What she say…she ask about me…Did she mention if any of her cousins were coming down with her?" Tooch asked as Zac ignored him and started dialing on the cell phone.

"Alright then, *fuck you*!" He said, as he rested his head back and started to play with the window again.

"*Tooch*, watch your mouth…And leave that *damn* window alone." Mr. Shan said sharply, without taking his attention away from the slippery road.

Zac listened as the phone rang twice before a voice picked up.

"Hello?"

"Yo, *Bogotá*…What's up, man? Zac said gleefully.

"Nothin'…What the deal, my nigga…where you at?" Omar asked as he laid on his living room couch with a silver pot filled with Applejacks on the coffee table in front of him. Omar had on a black G-Unit tank top, gray sweat pants and a pair of thick white ankle socks that had black covering the heels and toes.

"We're about to pick up the truck…then we're gonna swing by and scoop you before we go grip Randy from practice, alright?"

"Don't go anywhere."

"Man, come on…where am I going?" Omar laughed as he looked down at himself in relax mode.

"And hey, O'…you know we're definitely on for today, right?"

"*Oh*, you got 'em? That's major!"

"Yeah… she's bringin'em by as we speak. She's gonna drop'em off in my door."

"Cool…then I'll see you when y'all get here."

As Omar hung up, his mother, Ms. Gayle, was in the kitchen talking on the house phone when she heard her other line click.

"Jackie, hold on, girl…" She said before she clicked over to the other line. "Hello?"

"Hi, can I speak to Omar, please?" A small raspy female voice asked.

"Hold on…" She told the girl, and then clicked back over. "Jackie…I'm gonna give you a call back. One of my son's little girlfriends is on the other line…and I have my hands in this food right now. I'll give you a call back later?"

Ms. Gayle then turned the water on, rinsed her hands, and dried them before she clicked back over and headed out the kitchen.

"Here, it's for you." She said as she walked into the living room and handed Omar the phone.

"Who is it?" Omar asked as he looked up from his pot.

"*I* don't know, *boy*. All those girls have crazy names. Talika, Shadeema, Lazaara… I get tired of asking. I don't know what the hell their parents were thinking when they named them anyway."

"Hello?" Omar answered with a curious look on his face.

"*Oh' boy…Now* come on, *Michelle*. Don't no girls be calling me, *man*," He protested "I don't know why my mom would say that. *Look*, I told you… I told you already, man!"

Omar exhaled, then plopped his spoon into his cereal…splashing milk onto his mother's beautiful, white marble and glass coffee table.

CHAPTER 29

Back at school; Randy and Khalil were leaving the locker room carrying their black team bags with their last names and numbers on them.

"You heard we're not having a Christmas tournament this year, right?" Khalil asked as they made their way through the crowded hallway and into the stairwell.

"Yeah, I heard…why?" Randy smiled, expecting Khalil to have a major problem with not being able to play during the holiday.

"That's messed up…I mean…I really wanted to travel somewhere this year, man."

"Yeah?"

"*Seriously*, man…that's *whack*"

"But, I don't think anybody else in the country is having one either." Randy said, getting Khalil's full and undivided attention.

"When did you hear that?"

"I read it, like back in the summertime, in one of those magazines."

"I remember *coach* mentioning something to us about it a little while back, but I didn't take him too serious. I thought he was just trying to pull a bullshit surprise on us or something."

"*Nah*…he was serious…but, you shouldn't sweat it…You should just do what I plan to do."

"And what's that?"

"Forget about playing basketball for a while, or at least until after the Christmas break. Enjoy the time away from the game. It's the best way to do it. And besides, you know that once we get back, it's right back to the grind."

At first Khalil didn't say anything as he stood outside Randy's classroom staring at the floor, but then he lifted his eyes back up saying, "I guess you're right."

Khalil next gave Randy a handshake and a hug.

"Of course I am…" Randy said smiling again, before going inside his second floor class.

CHAPTER 30

At the same time, Mr. Wyble was taking care of some business of his own. He was at a local Division-1 college plugging for Randy to participate in the basketball camp up in the mountains during the Christmas break. This was the same camp Randy and Khalil were just talking about. Mr. Wyble knew that all of the top players were invited to the camp, and would play in front of thousands of college coaches and scouts. While the team was practicing, Mr. Wyble walked along the sideline of the basketball court and went straight up to the head coach.

"Hey, man, how's it going?" Mr. Wyble said as he smiled and shook his hand.

"Not too bad. How about you?"

"You know me. If life is not doing what it's supposed to, things are alright."

"I hear that."

After the coach and Mr. Wyble spoke, they turned and watched as a play developed out on the basketball court. The teams' starting point guard, a short muscular fella, stole a pass out of mid air at half-court and started a hard drive—through traffic—to the basket. He faked a pass to one of his teammates on his left. He then rose up over a 7-feet tall center, for a high floating teardrop lay-up that hit high off the glass and dropped in. The much taller center swung at the ball but missed it. He then chopped the point guard and sent him falling hard to the floor. The coach blew his whistle and pumped his fist.

"*And one*! Now go get something to drink!" He yelled as he turned and went back to rap with Mr. Wyble.

"It seems like some players never get it." He said, looking directly at the 7-feet center as he walked by and went to the water fountain.

"So, how do you think your guys are looking for the rest of the season?"

"Not too bad, but it's still too early to tell."

"I was able to catch a little of your game last weekend…while you were up in New York. Things didn't look all that bad to me." Mr. Wyble added.

"That was pretty much how I expected us to do…early in the season. The latter part of the season is what worries me. The teams we'll be facing will be much tougher, and none of these guys seem to act like they want to play together."

"What do you think your guys are lacking?"

"Ah…I'd probably have to say toughness, more than anything else. They have to have toughness in order to beat people…nobody is going to let us just come into their home court and beat them."

"Most of your games must be away—to finish out the rest of the year then?" Mr. Wyble said with his eyebrows raised.

The coach didn't say anything. He just nodded his head 'yes'.

"But, anyway how's the kid doing?"

"Ah, well…he's doing pretty good for himself thus far this season… grades are all o.k, He's getting to practice on time and staying out of trouble. You know, everything a good kid is supposed to do, I guess."

Mr. Wyble then handed the coach the white envelope.

"That's good, but I'm going to give this to the administrator. I should have something for you by tomorrow…or as soon as she gets back to me."

"Ok. So, I'll be expecting a call from you tomorrow then."

"Yeah…but no promises." The coach said, shaking Mr. Wyble's hand before they went their separate ways.

CHAPTER 31

Some time later, Zac pulled up in front of Omar's house in his gold, pre-owned SUV, which was in excellent condition. Omar heard the horn blow, and ran to the window wearing a big smile. Omar signaled for them to wait, then went to put his Timberland boots on. But just as he was about to charge out the door, Ms. Gayle, who was in the kitchen still talking on the telephone, called him.

"*Omar*!"

"Yeah, mom?" Omar asked freezing in his tracks holding the front door open.

"You put a coat on!"

Omar's mother did not have to bother looking at him, because she knew her son. He was wearing a pair of denim jeans, a thick beige sweater and a pair of wheat colored Timberland boots.

"Mom, I'm gonna be in a car!"

"I don't care. Put a damn *jacket* on, *boy*!"

Omar lowered his head and sucked his teeth as he went over to the living room closet, and pulled out a thin jacket with a gray hat that had a little ball on top of it. Omar's hat also had earflaps to cover his ears.

"*Yeah*, girl..." She continued as he went out the door. "That damn boy, run'n around here with no coat on...like it's the middle of June out there."

Omar ran down the front steps and went and got into the back seat of the truck saying, "Yo, this thing is tough," smiling from ear to ear checking out the Gingerbread.

"Thanks." Zac replied as he reached back and handed Omar a white envelope.

"What's this...the tickets for the ski trip?"

"Yeah.." Zac laughed as he pulled off.

A short time later, an older Black man drove by a McDonalds in a silver Benz coupe. A gay man, sitting in the restaurant, looked out of the window at the car as he drove by.

"*Oooh girl…* that's what *I'm* talking about. We need a man that's driving something like that."

He was talking to Taya, who was also looking out at the car. Taya then looked over at Daryl, who was kneeling down in front of a beautiful, one and a half year old little boy. She closed her eyes and thought back to that fateful night she told him to leave while she went to look for Omar. That same night Daryl found out that his condom had broken, and loss track of time when he sat on the edge of the tub in disbelief.

CHAPTER 32

As Randy was about to start his interview, he sat on a metal folding chair in his practice uniform, with white thermals under it.

"You were in a bit of a hurry the last time I saw you?" The reporter said, laughing as he reached down inside his duffle bag and pulled out a pen.

"Yeah, I had something I had to take care of." Randy smiled.

The reporter was not the same one who ripped him in the newspaper.

"Well, I don't think we should have any problems today... *right*"

"*Naaah...*"

"Here's how we're going to run this...I'm going to ask you some questions, and you just relax and answer them the best way you know how, ok? The same way it's always done."

Randy nodded his head 'yes' and looked over at his teammates as they ran suicides

"Are you ready?" The reporter asked.

"Shoot..." Randy replied, turning his attention back to him.

"So, what do you think goes through the minds of some of the players you have faced...or have had your way with...especially, those who have been, and are still being touted as top players?"

Randy inhaled deeply, and slowly exhaled through his nostrils. Then, he laughed lightly and answered.

"*Ah*, well...I'm not too sure about that one. That's actually a pretty good question. But, if I had to truly pick a response, I would have to say, '*wow*'." Randy flailed his eyes as he spoke.

"Oh, ok..." The reporter said as he jotted down something in his notebook and clamped a microphone to the end of his clipboard.

"So, do you feel that playing your third straight year in the public league has helped you…or made it easier for you…going into other schools and playing in front of their crowds? I know that that can be pretty tough for some players the first few years. How did the past two years help you?"

"*Ah*…it helped. But I think the toughness has to come from within…it has to already be in you."

The reporter turned and looked at Mr. Wyble, who had just stepped into the gym from outside.

"You have improved statistically in every category this season." He continued. "You now average 12 more points a game, at 30.5. Was this something you planned or expected this season? Do you think you can keep this up, for the rest of the year?"

Randy looked at the reporter in disbelief and laughed. Then he leaned forward and said, "I don't know that, man…but I darn sure hope so."

Mr. Wyble cracked a smile as he looked over at Randy, who appeared to be having fun. Then he walked over and stood next to Coach Scott.

"How'd it go?" Coach Scott asked, standing with his arms folded.

"He said he would be giving us a call sometime today or tomorrow… depending on whenever his administrator gets through with what she has to do."

The whole time Mr. Wyble spoke to the Coach, he never took his eyes away from Randy. But coach Scott looked back and forth at the teams as they ran drills. As Randy sat with the reporter, the gym room door opened again and this time the boys stepped in. Tooch, the first to come in, looked over at Randy talking with the reporter and smiled.

"*Randy*!" Omar shouted, cupping both his of hands around his mouth.

"*Oh, goodness…*" Mr. Wyble sighed.

"Should I get rid of them?" Coach Scott asked.

"No…it doesn't matter. Either he's gonna be with them while he's here, or he's gonna be with them while he's out there."

"I guess those are some of your friends coming in now?" The reporter asked as Randy smiled at them.

"Yeah… that's my family." Randy responded.

"And what kind of support factor are they… because the last time we talked, you said that you lived with your mother, and, she had a drug addiction. Correct? Has her situation changed?"

"Nah…" Randy answered quickly, shaking his head 'no.' "It's still the same."

"Have you recently tried to seek any kind of help for her…like, within the last couple of months?"

"Yeah…of *course*, man."

"And what have you done to try and help her?" The reporter asked, jotting down everything Randy said.

"I stopped pass one of the churches in my neighborhood, and I talked with one of the Pastors about putting her in a rehab."

"So, everything's all ready to go for her then…right?"

"I guess…" Randy said shrugging his shoulders.

He did care for and love his mother despite her shortcomings, because he felt that she was his sister in the lord and she needed help.

"She's scheduled to go into rehab one day soon."

"Do you have an exact date?"

"No…"

"And why not?" The reporter asked with his head still down writing.

"Because, I still have to find her and let her know."

The reporter stopped writing and lifted up his eyes from his clipboard. He then scooted back in his chair and looked at him. But Randy had turned and faced the boys in the bleachers, who were laughing at something Tooch said.

"It's *true*…" Tooch continued, with a deeply bothered looked on his face. Who the *fuck* does this nigga think he is…He still ain't won *shit* yet!"

Zac and Omar were both laughing hard, but had their faces covered because they were embarrassed.

"Hey, Randy…" The reporter said in a serious voice; momentarily regaining his attention.

"Yo, what'sup?" He answered, sliding back around in his chair.

"If you want, we can leave this part out of the article and just stick with what you did in the game."

"*Nah, man*…It's cool." Randy chuckled. "You think I'm the only kid in the city going through this?"

Randy then turned back around and listened to what else Tooch had to say.

"Ask him what has he won yet…There's a good damn question… We all would like to know the answer to that one…and *personally*, I think that it deserves an answer right now."

"*Man*, you're *stupid*" Omar laughed with his face still covered.

"And they got this nigga sit'n up in this bitch doing interviews like he Labron or somebody." Neither Coach Scott nor Mr. Wyble could hear what Tooch was saying, but they could clearly tell that he had Randy's attention.

"Alright then, Randy…that was good. You're free to go." The reporter said after he asked a few more questions and shook his hand. "I'm ready to speak with your coach now."

The reporter raised his right hand and waved for Coach Scott to come over.

"I guess that means it's my turn. Excuse me." Coach Scott said before he jogged over.

Tooch saw Randy's coach taking strides in his direction, then silenced his remarks.

"He's done, right?" Coach Scott asked as soon as he arrived near Randy and the reporter.

"Yeah…he's good." The reporter said, nodding his head.

"Then you can go join the team and finish up with the rest of the work-outs." Coach Scott said as he thumbed Randy away, then straddled and plopped down on the metal folding chair.

Randy hustled over and joined his team…quickly finishing off the last of the drills without breaking a sweat.

"All right boys… since you all played so well last night, we're going to wrap this one up early today." The assistant coach said, catching them all by surprise.

The entire team cheered.

"I see *Mr. Superstar* over here still managed to find a way to get off easy *again…Damn*! Even when he's wrong, things still work out for him." Khalil said, turning to Randy with both of his hands placed on top of his head trying to catch his breath. "Boy, your *good*…How do you do it?"

Randy gave him a nudge in his right side as the team was forming a huddle to break practice.

"Bring it in!" The assistant shouted before sending them to the locker-room.

"Hey! I'll be right out." Randy exhaled as he walked pass the boys with his left hand placed on his hip.

Tooch was talking to Zac and Omar. He cut his eyes away from them and said, "*Nooo*…take your time…"

"Scrub them balls, nigga!" Omar added, giggling heavily as he mimicked a scrubbing motion down between his legs.

Randy looked at his friends and shook his head, then lowered his head and went up the ramp to the locker room.

"So, coach…" The reporter said, continuing with his interview. "How do you think this season has been working out for you guys thus far? I'm sure you've got to be happy with your team's play."

"Yeah, I can say that I am…especially after the season we had last year."

Coach Scott answered, referring to how Randy had to carry the team as a sophomore, through a losing season.

"And what about Murcy? Has he emerged as the star and leader that you were hoping for? I'm talking both *on* and *off* the floor?"

Coach Scott took a deep breath, then reluctantly said, "*Uh*, *well*, I honestly can say that he has…in *some* ways."

CHAPTER 33

The boys were in Center City, shopping at the Gallery mall. Zac, Tooch and Randy were all standing beside a clothing rack waiting for Omar to come back out of a fitting-stall. Omar stepped out, in an all white, full body ski-suit. Judging by the insulation, he could tell that the suit was strictly for serious skiiers.

"Nooo..." Tooch said, as he shook his head and frowned. "It's too much."

"What's wrong with it?" Omar asked, fixing the ski goggles on his forehead while looking down at himself. "It's the one I was telling you about."

"When are you gonna have the time to wear it? You're not leaving the hotel."

Even though Omar looked exceptionally good in the all white outfit, Tooch made a good point...which was proven within the next couple of seconds.

"I wonder if they have this one in a size smaller...you think?" A gorgeous, athletically built, Black girl said as she and her equally beautiful girlfriend walked by.

"I don't know... we can go check." The girl friend answered. "Hey cutie..." The girl said, turning to Omar.

Omar looked back over his left shoulder and watched the girls' butts. Then he looked back at Tooch, Randy and Zac, before quickly nodding his head 'yes'.

"I'm gonna take it off."

Tooch didn't say anything, but he closed his eyes and nodded his head 'yes' slowly.

Minutes later, Randy and Zac were standing with a pretty, White female sales associate near a pants rack in another store. She was thuggishly clad in the latest urban apparel, wearing a long sleeve white Mark Ecko shirt, a pair of tight blue jeans and a pair of Timberland boats. She also had her long dirty-blond hair, with blond highlights, hanging off her shoulders.

"You might as well get three pair..." Zac said as he looked at some expensive, brand name pants.

"Nah, it's cool...I'll just take one." Randy said, only taking up the pair that he already had his hand on.

"You know what...then again...can you give us the last seven pair we looked at in a 38-34."

"No...*nah, man*...it's *cool*..." Randy pleaded, trying to block Zac from the counter.

The sales associate laughed as she watched the two best friends argue, then placed all seven pair of pants on the counter as Zac requested.

"*Ah, man*, You're killing me..." Randy said as he stood there scratching his head.

"Chill out...I got it."

Over by the front of the store, Tooch and Omar were now doing their own thing. Tooch was wearing a pair of skis and goggles taken off a mannequin posted by the window.

"I don't know, man...the more I think about it, the more this skiing thing doesn't look like it's gonna happen." Tooch said while leaning forward in a skier's position.

"What, what do you mean?" Omar frowned.

"All I keep seeing on this trip is trees in front of me."

"*Nonsense*..." Omar said as he stepped beside him and assumed the same leaning position.

"All you got to do is bend at your knees, like you getting ready to sit on a toilet. You just lean, keep your balance, and focus on where you're going." Omar spoke as if he had a deep passion for skiing.

"It's that simple, huh?" Tooch asked staring straight out in front of him.

"Yeah...it's that simple."

"But I don't know, man...I still can't see past the trees."

"Really?" Omar said with a look of concern.

"Yeah..."

"Well, maybe you have some sort of phobia or something...you never know."

"You think so?" Tooch said, looking at Omar with two 10-dollar bags of marijuana stuffed in the goggles.

"You're stupid, man" He said as he did a double take and pushed Tooch gently. "Come on; let's go see if they're ready."

As Tooch pulled the goggles from his face, he caught the bags of skunk and followed behind him smiling.

"Y'all ready?" Omar asked, as he and Tooch approached Zac and Randy.

"Yeah, we're ready?" Zac answered, as he pulled two large plain-white carrying bags from the counter.

"Where to, then?" Omar asked.

"Let's go grab a bite to eat…I'm hungry."

"I'm wit it." Omar agreed as they all left the retail store.

CHAPTER 34

The next day after practice, Khalil was sitting in the gym on the bottom of the stands reading Randy's article. Randy sat to the left of Khalil, bouncing a basketball between his legs. Except for the usual humming sound, the gym was completely silent. After Khalil read the entire article, he took a deep breath and said, "Yo…I don't believe you let this dude put this stuff in here about your mother."

Khalil folded up the newspaper and placed it beside him on the stands.

"And why not? It's the truth." Randy said with his head down, shifting the basketball in his hands.

"*Ah…*" Khalil softly gestured.

"Excuse me, but it just doesn't seem like a smart thing to do…with regard to your mother and all."

"So, if I kept it bottled up inside me, and never spoke of it, would that make my situation change any?" Randy asked, dropping the ball back to the floor once more and catching it.

"Let the people know…That's how I see it…I didn't necessarily have him put that in there for people to see it and pass judgment on me either. I did it…because I might be able to help some other kid who is going through the same thing." Randy said as he rotated the ball before dropping it to the floor again.

"Well…" Khalil said as he leaned back on his elbows. "Did you…"

"Man, that's nothing." Randy exhaled…dribbling the basketball fast with his left hand.

Inside Coach Scott's office, he and Mr. Wyble were going back and forth, about who was going to be the one to deliver Randy the news about him having to go away to the camp up in the mountains.

"*You* should do it, because *I'm* his coach, and some of the other kids on the team might start to feel like I'm giving him too much attention." Coach Scott said, as he peeked at Randy and Khalil through the blinds on his office window.

"Alright then... *Fuck it*!" Mr. Wyble chuckled, as he sat on the coach's desk with his arms folded. "I'm the grown up in the situation...I'll do it. What do I have to be scared of?"

He stood up from the desk, grabbed a white envelope sitting next to him, and went out to the gym. Coach Scott did not say anything at first. Then he smiled and said...

"Ok tough guy, go ahead and do it then."

Randy and Khalil were still having their conversation when Mr. Wyble and Coach Scott approached them. By the looks on their faces, the boys could tell that something they might not like was about to be said, and instantly stopped talking.

"What can we do for you fellas?" Randy asked, holding the basketball with his fingertips.

"Here, this came for you today." Mr. Wyble said, handing Randy the envelope.

"What is it?" Randy asked, cradling the ball with his right hand, and reaching out to take the envelope with his left.

"It's an invitation."

"*Invitation*...For *what*?"

"To the basketball camp they're having this weekend, up in the mountains."

"Who are *they*? What *camp*?"

Then Randy remembered the camp he was talking about, from the magazine.

"*I* can't *go*!" He said as he hunched his shoulders...surprised.

"What do you mean you '*can't go*'? All of the top high school players in the country are going to be there. That is why no one is having a tournament this year. Besides, this is the first year that they are attempting something like this. It might be a once in a life time opportunity for you."

"But *still*...like I said, I *can't* go."

Randy shrugged again, and then lowered his eyes to the basketball in his lap. Mr. Wyble looked at Coach Scott then shook his head in disgust after seeing how Randy reacted to the news.

"*I'll go*!" Khalil interjected, with a look of wonder, as if he was being viewed as chopped liver.

"You can't go! It's for juniors and seniors only. And besides, you would need a sponsor!" Coach Scott said sharply, as he glared down at Khalil , standing with his arms folded and legs spread wide apart.

"Oh... *Wup*, takes care of me." Khalil gestured, nodding his head.

"So what do you have to do that's *sooo* important?" Mr. Wyble asked, frowning folding his arms.

"Does it matter?" Randy shot back, as he looked up at the two men... wanting to say 'fuck outta here!'

Coach Scott and Mr. Wyble then looked at each other in silence for a few seconds.

"*Un, believable...*" Mr. Wyble muttered under his breath.

"Well, then, can you at least try to see if you can break those plans for this weekend?" Mr. Wyble asked now attempting to sound a bit nicer.

"Whatever, man...I'll see...But I can't guarantee you anything." Randy said as he lowered his eyelids...bothered by Mr. Wyble's first reaction to hearing him say that he already had important plans.

"Randy, if there is a possibility...I think you should strongly consider going to the camp this weekend. They are having it at a newly built hotel. It has a basketball arena connected to it that is supposed to be really nice." Coach Scott said, breaking his silence.

"You guys can go swimming while you're up there. And they'll give you all new bags, sneakers...the whole nine."

Khalil and Randy turned looked at each other at the same time. Khalil mulled his lip looking like it didn't sound like such a bad idea. But Randy quickly cut his eyes away from Khalil and sat there, speechless...dribbling the basketball.

CHAPTER 35

Later that night, the boys were down stairs in the basement silently pondering what Randy should do about the coming weekend. Zac was on the couch, laying flat on his stomach with two pillows tucked underneath his face. Tooch sat right by his head, and Omar was sprawled out on the love seat with his head hanging off the edge near the floor…clutching a pillow. Randy, however, was the only one standing, staring down at the rugged floor, resting his back against the wall. The only noises that could be heard in the plush basement was that of throats being cleared and sniffling noses. A few moments later, Mr. Shan came down the steps singing and stopped halfway to the bottom, breaking the silence.

"I got heaven right *here* on *earth*… Why the long faces? Are you boys going to funeral?"

The boys all looked up at him, and then turned back to watching television…with the volume turned all the way down.

"So what's happening?" Mr. Shan asked again, taking a deep breath as he sat down.

"Randy can't go with us on the ski-trip." Tooch spoke, despite the blank stares he received from the three other boys."

"And why not?" Mr. Shan asked, turning to Randy.

"*Because, he…*" Tooch spoke again, but shut up after seeing the look his uncle gave him.

"Why not?" Mr. Shan repeated, looking at Randy again.

"I was invited up to a camp this weekend…and if I go, I'll miss the ski trip." Randy said, barely lifting his eyes.

"So, what's the problem?" Mr. Shan asked giving a toothy grin.

"I don't know what I should do."

"You don't know what 'you should do'? Boy, that decision was made already…once you started calling yourself 'a Ballplayer.'"

"And how is that?" Randy asked, looking curiously at Mr. Shan.

"If you consider yourself a ballplayer, then you play ball whenever you're supposed to. That's a commitment you've made, and you're supposed to keep. What I don't understand is how you can call yourself a ballplayer… when a decision about playing is still up in the air. That doesn't make any sense, now does it…?"

Randy shook his head 'no', and then lowered his eyes back to the floor.

"Is that the phone I'm hearing?" Mr. Shan asked, turning his ear to the stairs.

"Yes, I think so…" Zac mumbled with his face still stuffed down into the pillow.

"Boy, I tell you…you young guys these days act like there's plenty of time to do *everything*; especially when it comes to your futures."

Mr. Shan then got up and casually strolled back up the stairs—motioning with his hands as if he was running.

"He's always talking *shit*." Tooch groveled after watching him go completely up stairs. "Like he always did what the hell he was supposed to do"

As Tooch was talking, Zac pulled the pillow from under his head and hit him in the face with it saying…"*SHUD UPP*!"

"*Ill man*! This *fuck'n pillow*'s *wet*!" Tooch shouted as he quickly wiped the right side of face. "*You fuck'n slobbed on it*…you *cockhead*!"

Tooch slung the pillow back at Zac, hitting him in the back of his head as Zac tucked his face down in the couch.

When Friday night came, Randy's team was playing in their final game before the Christmas vacation. Prescott lead Shadewood highschool, 75-64, late in the 4th quarter, and was now playing defense. Shadewood's star player launched a desperate three-pointer that clanked off the side of the rim, and landed in Khalil's hands. Khalil dribbled up the court and passed the ball to Pooh…who spotted Randy running from underneath the basket and zipped him a one-handed bounce pass. Randy caught the pass as he came out into the clear freeing himself of a defender. Then, standing behind the three-point line, he fired up a healthy three of his own.

'Swissh!' the ball touched nothing but the bottom of the net.

The crowd of 800 cheering Prescott fans got even louder as their team now led by 14. Shadewood in bounded the ball in a hurry and went right back down court. They missed another lofty shot with only two minutes left in the game. Pooh brought the ball back up the court again, and passed it straight to Randy as he was already standing in position behind the three-point line. Randy caught the pass, and quickly launched his second straight three-pointer in less than 30 seconds.

"*Damn*!" Zac said, shaking his head looking at Tooch and Omar after the shot went down.

Shadewood in-bounded the ball in a hurry and went racing up the court, where they made their desperation shot. Randy received the inbound pass and was heavily guarded as he brought the ball up court, holding his right hand up in the air as if he was calling a play. He looked around like he was getting ready to pass it to someone…then squeezed from deep and nailed another three point shot from NBA range. As the net cried, the fans cheered even louder. Prescott had pushed their lead to 18 in less than a minute, with under a minute left in the game.

"*Yeah*, he's *pissed*!" Omar said smiling at Zac.

They both started nodding their heads 'yes' and laughed.

"*Timeout*…call *timeout*!" Shadewood's head coach shouted, signaling with his hands raised above his head.

Randy received a stare from the aggravated, beaten man, and returned an emotionless glare before cutting his eyes away as he walked toward his team's bench.

"*Yeah*!" Khalil yelled with his hands up high in the air, as he raced over and grabbed Randy around his waist.

"Stir like *coffee*…Stir like…*coffee*. Stir…like…*motha-fuck'n coffee*!" Khalil chanted, taunting the other team's players as he and Randy passed through them heading off the court.

The other team went to their bench with their heads down as some-one yelled…"That's what I'm talk'n bout…Get these nigga's off our fuck'n court!"

Except for Mr. Shan and Mr. Wyble, almost everyone who knew Randy was in attendance that night…including Zac, Tooch, Omar, the head coach of the college who was sponsoring him for the weekend camp, and even agents Rapth and Smith. Mr. Wyble left the game at halftime to prepare his home for a Christmas party he was having that night, and Mr. Shan remained home to discuss business with his partners.

When the final horn sounded, the crowd rushed onto the floor, and Randy had just scored a career high 41 points.

"Why are they rushing the floor?" Tooch asked, speaking to anyone who would listen. "They make like they just won game seven and shit."

"Actually, the team they just beat won the championship last year..." An eerie White boy said from behind them.

"Oh..." Tooch said with a nod. "Makes sense..."

"They were expected to win it again this year."

Coach Scott, who was in the midst of the celebration, shook his head when he looked over and noticed that Randy did not seem at all happy about their victory. He also caught a quick glimpse of agents Smith and Rapth as they were exiting the gymnasium. Smith accepted something from a woman who was handing out items at the door, and stuffed it into the pocket of his suit jacket as they were leaving. Coach Scott knew who the agents were because Mr. Wyble informed him about Zac's father.

"Yo, do you realize what this could mean?" Khalil asked a sour Randy, as they headed up the ramp to their locker room. "If we keep this up, people are gonna have to start saying that we're the team to beat this year."

"I know..." Randy said in a ho-hum voice.

Khalil opened the door and allowed Randy to go in first, and then let it close behind them as Randy pulled his jersey from out of his long, white, mesh shorts with red and blue trim.

The only knock against Prescott's victory, however, was the opposing team was not at full strength. Their second leading scorer a, 6-foot-8 240-pound senior, who was also currently leading the Public league in rebounds. He sat out due to an injury. They did however have the better of their two top players on the floor.

CHAPTER 36

Minutes later; Rapth and Smith pulled into Mr. Wyble's driveway and looked at the well-lit modern single home, decorated with soft white Christmas lights and red ones scattered about in spots.

"I wonder if we beat the ladies here." Smith asked, from the front passenger seat.

"I don't know. I tried calling Sandra, but her phone just rang…" Rapth answered. "So, I'm guessing they're already here, since she didn't pick up."

"Yeah, they should be." Smith said, as he climbed out of the car.

They headed to the front door, pushed the doorbell, then adjusted their suits and waited patiently before someone opened to the door.

"Hey!" Mr. Wyble said, smiling as he stepped aside and allowed them to enter. "How did it go…Did they win?"

"Yeah, they won."

"That's good."

"Your boy snapped out near the end… He hit three three-pointers in less than a minute!" Rapth said.

"*Three in a row*." Smith confirmed.

"Wow," Mr. Wyble said, looking out onto his front porch before closing the door.

"Flent…glad you could make it." Rapth said, as he walked in and gave his new partner a handshake. "Were the directions I gave you from the Turnpike ok?"

Flent was a very well groomed nice looking Black man in his late 30's, who was about to retire early from the Bureau.

'Yeah, we found it ok. But I have to admit…I cheated a little bit."

"How's that?"

"My wife had a seminar over at the Four Season's, so we just ran straight over from there."

"This here is my lovely wife, Debbie. And this is our beautiful daughter, Inez." Flent said as he grabbed his wife and daughter, bringing them close.

"Hello…" Debbie smiled.

"Hi." Inez said blushing.

"I see why you're retiring early. Who can blame you…you have a beautiful family, man." Smith said, respectfully checking out Inez and her mother.

"These are *our* lovely wives." Rapth said, opening his right arm for his wife as the two women came walking out from the kitchen.

"We 've already met." All three wives said almost at once.

"You boys are late, so you have to pay up like you agreed to do if we arrived first." Smith's wife Tammy said, giggling as she placed a nice wet one on his lips.

And this is my beautiful *future* wife, or should I say '*fiance*', *Kirsten*. Mr. Wyble said, standing next to a beautiful 5-foot-10, 165-pound brunet.

Kirsten was a thick Italian beauty with curly jet-black hair. She smiled and nodded at everyone.

"Say hello to everyone." Mr. Wyble said, as he walked over to Smith and Rapth and placed his hands on their shoulders.

"Hello, everyone!"

Smith and Rapth greeted everyone else at the gathering of about 25 people before following Mr. Wyble into the den.

"Come on so we can get started with this card game sometime before next year." Mr Wyble joked.

"*Boy*, I'd bet you couldn't *wait* to get us back over here…*Could you*? That last game must have really left a bad taste in your mouth." Rapth said, placing his left hand on Mr. Wyble's shoulder.

CHAPTER 37

Coach Scott was back at the school informing the janitor that it was all right for him to go in and shut the water off in the shower room.

"We're all finished in there. You can go in when you're ready." Coach Scott said, thumbing over his shoulder with his left hand.

Randy and the rest of team, who were all laughing and joking with each other, walked down the ramp and turned into a side hallway that led out to the parking lot. Everyone was joking around and carrying on except for Randy. He was taking slow strides toward the exit with his head hung low, clinching the black shoulder strap of his bag hanging over his shoulder.

"Randy, do you still have your plans for tonight?" Coach Scott asked, as he stood under a beautiful red winter evening sky.

"Yes…that's where I'm going right now." Randy quickly replied as he stepped out into the snow, allowing the rest of the team to continue pass him.

"You know…there's still room in the van for one more…if you want to join us for dinner." Coach Scott said, turning his head to the side with a smile.

Randy, still holding on to his strap, paused for a moment, looking down at the ground. He then glanced at Zac's gold SUV, parked across the street with the headlights on, then said, "Nah…it's cool. I'd love to, if I didn't already have plans."

He then pulled his beige skully down over his ears and started away… leaving his coach standing there.

"Hey, Randy" The coach called, after watching him make his way across the gated, snow covered parking lot. The parking lot was covered with snow because it just stopped snowing.

"Yeah, coach?" He answered without turning around.

"You be sure to have a safe and happy holiday, you hear me!"

"Yeah, coach…I hear you!"

"And since I won't be seeing you again before you leave, work hard, for all of us!"

"I'll try!"

He raised his right hand up and kept walking. But no sooner than he reached the entrance of the small parking lot, the visiting team's yellow school bus pulled up right next to him. Some of the players on the bus took the liberty of staring down at him with menacing looks. Randy could tell by their faces that they were trying to let him know that he had not seen the last of them. He just smirked and cut his eyes down to the logo on his hooded team jacket, then shook his head before stepping in front of the stopped bus to continue on his way. With his coach still watching, he crossed the street and got into the back passenger side of the SUV. As the vehicle pulled off, the coach let his players, still clowning, into the van.

"You know, you boys are really lucky that we won tonight, or our dinner plans, I'm sorry to say, would have been cancelled." Coach Scott said, getting everyone to settle down.

"Yeah, right!"

"*Whatever, coach*!"

"Oh, now that's messed up…but, let me ask you this, coach…" Khalil said, from the darkness of the last row. "So, what, you wanted us to leave our plans up in the air because of this game…what if we played hard and still lost…would you still have done it…or that wouldn't have mattered?"

"I'm sorry, but, there is no way that I could've sat through dinner if we would have lost. Psych! I'm just kidding with you boys…You know we would've still gone out even if we played hard and lost…right?"

At first Coach Scott didn't receive a response, but after a couple seconds everyone started laughing.

"Yeah, *whatever*, coach!" Taj shouted from his seat next to Khalil.

"You can go and tell that bull crap to one of those guys on JV. Maybe they'll fall for it." Khalil chuckled, bringing a smile to the coach's face. "I've been playing for you for what…the past year and some games now? I think I should know better."

CHAPTER 38

Tooch was behind the wheel of the truck with Zac in the front passenger seat, and Omar and Randy in the back.

"I've been meaning to ask you..." Zac said as he looked over his left shoulder at Randy. "Are you alright?"

"Yeah, I'm cool...Why you asking?" He answered as he took notice of everyone looking at him.

Tooch looked at him through the rearview mirror and said,

"Cause you damn sure don't look like it."

"Nah, it's nothing...they beat us last year...that's all."

Randy then turned his face and started looking out the side window.

"*Hey*! What the *fuck* you doing?" Zac yelled at Tooch, who had now stopped the SUV in the middle of Broad Street to make an illegal left turn into a gas station.

"What're you *crazy*?"

"*Man, chill*...I got this. Quit cry'n like a *girl*!" Tooch replied as the cars on the opposite side honked at him frantically.

"Nigga, didn't even have the truck a week yet, and already bout to tear the bitch up!"

"Look, I told you... Listen to me when I'm talking to you, lil boy...Shut your mouth!" Tooch yelled before he mashed the gas pedal.

He rolled up onto the pavement and crossed a small barricade, causing the truck to rock hard from side to side.

"You're fast to call everybody else out of their name, and now look at you. You're the one acting like a *Cockhead*!" Zac said, as he looked over at his cousin with a straight face.

Tooch just looked at him and blinked silently as he stopped in front of a gas pump.

CHAPTER 39

At that same exact time, at Mr. Wyble's house, Rapth was at the kitchen counter when he made a mess.

"*Oops*!" He shouted, as he helplessly watched a blender full of Pina Colada spill all over the black counter top.

"*Aw*...What did you do?" Mr. Wyble asked, as he calmly rested back in his chair holding his cards up to his face.

"Looks like you're running low on paper towels." Rapth said, trying his best to stop the spill from drizzling down onto the black and ivory, checkered marble floor.

"*Damn, man*...How much did you spill in there?" Smith asked as he playfully put his right index finger up to his lips and shushed everyone.

"Spare me the bullcrap instigation Smith...Would you please?" Rapth said, looking up at the ceiling as everyone inside the den laughed.

"Is that the last of the paper towels?" Rapth shouted.

"Yeah, I was supposed to stop past the store after the game, but I decided to come straight here. I have to go back out and pick up some more supplies anyway, so don't bother to look in any of the cabinets." Mr. Wyble said as he stood up from his chair and put his playing hand down on the table.

"Fresh out of OJ too, man." Another of his guest added as he waved an empty orange juice carton. "Boy, you can sure tell a bachelor by what he has or doesn't have in his kitchen."

"*Ok*, here I come...Hold on."

"Alright you guys, enough with this boring card game already. You are starting to put us ladies to sleep." Sandra said as she entered the room. "We need to be entertained."

"How about we play Scrabble?" Tammy asked, holding the scrabble game in her hands as she walked in behind Sandra and Kirsten.

"Let me run to the store real quick before we get started. I'll be right back!" Mr. Wyble said.

"*Ah, man*! You can't go and leave us now…we need you. You're our third person." Smith said sounding alarmed.

"The last time we started off against these ladies without you, we never caught back up, and they ended up killing us."

"It didn't have anything to do with you boys being short handed." Sandra said. "And it was your idea to begin with."

"But I can't just leave us in here like this." Mr. Wyble said, after giggling at Sandra's comment. "I'll go and come right back. I promise. It'll only take a couple of minutes."

"Now that's what I'm talking about. Let's get a little revenge game going." Rapth said as he walked back into the den. "The scrabble king is now here to re-claim his throne, baby!"

"If it's that big a deal, *I'll* go!" Inez said, getting everyone's attention as she jumped up from her seat next to the son of another guest.

"No, baby, it's alright…We can handle it." Flent said, signaling for her to settle down and go back into the living room.

"Dad, you heard what he said. It's only a couple of blocks away. You are acting like I don't know the area."

Flent looked at his future partners and at their wives, who were all looking back at him with their eyebrows raised. Then he turned back to his daughter…speechless.

"Relax, I'll be fine, daddy. Plus, I think I need to go get some fresh air anyway." Inez said, exhaling and flailing her eyes to the ceiling.

"Then take someone with you, since you feel that way." Flent said, looking at the young man—who was ready to volunteer.

The young man was a senior in high school and was very close in age to Inez. But she only said that she needed fresh air because he had been in her face the entire evening.

"*Whoa*!" Inez snapped…before the young man could offer his services. "I'll be fine…*please*!"

"I take it she must already have her driver's license?" Smith asked, looking at Ms. Debbie.

"Yes, she does." Ms. Debbie answered, proudly nodding her head.

"What do you need?" Inez asked as she walked over and stood beside Mr. Wyble.

"Are you *sure*?" Mr. Wyble asked, looking at her with his head tilted to the side. "I mean, I'll go…if you're uncertain. It still might be pretty bad out there."

"*No*, I think they've cleared up all of the main streets…and if you're talking about Broad Street…we passed it on our way here." Smith added.

Flent then momentarily closed his eyes, before slowly re-opening them.

Flent was not at all a regular when it came to alcohol consumption, and the few mixed drinks he had that evening were taking some affect.

"I guess this is the part that she gets from her mother…this whole independent thing, you know." Flent said; giggling as his wife looked at him from the corners of her eyes.

CHAPTER 40

While at the gas station, Tooch was standing behind the SUV with the back door raised, fishing through his CDs.

"Where is it?" He mumbled.

"Where is *what*? What're you looking for?" Omar asked looking over the seat.

"I found it."

"What is it?" Omar asked again, as Tooch slid the CD into the 20-disk CD changer.

"My *Big* CD…! Why don't you come in with me?"

"Alright…"

Without hesitation, Omar opened the back door and got out. But before he and Tooch could reach the gas station, Zac leaned over, rolled down the driver's side window and said, "*Tooch*!"

"What, what's up?" Tooch asked as they kept walking.

"Don't be all fuck'n day, man!"

Without saying anything, Tooch went inside the convenience store part of the gas station.

"I know how you are!"

After several minutes, Zac and Randy were still waiting for Tooch and Omar.

"*Now see*, this is the type of bullshit I'm talk'n about!" Zac said, after exhaling deeply in frustration.

"Randy, can you please do me a favor?"

"Sure…" Randy smiled as he placed his right hand on the door handle.

"Can you please go in there and see what's taking that dickhead so long?

But nah, You know what? I have a better idea. Just go get the money from him and put it on pump-one. If their asses aren't outta there by the time I finish, we'll leave both of em."

Randy snickered as he and Zac got out of the truck at the same time.

"This nigga's forever bullshit'n with something, man." Zac mumbled angrily to himself as he removed the gas cap.

As soon as Randy approached the glass door, he spotted Tooch and Omar standing away from the register and talking with an Asian man who looked to be in his mid to late 40's. Randy smiled as he walked in hearing Tooch speak in the man's native language.

"You're very good. How did you learn to speak so fluently…where'd you learn to speak it?"

"You like that, don't you?" Tooch asked, turning and winking at Omar. "I'll teach you that some day."

"Alright…I'll hold you to that too." Omar answered as he nodded his head in compliance.

"Yo, Tooch…give me the money." Randy said, walking up still grinning.

"No, but to answer your question." Tooch continued as he pulled out three crisp 20-dollar bills without looking at Randy. "I have a girlfriend who's in college studying different languages. That's how… I help her with her studies sometimes, you know."

"What is she taking up in college?" The Asian man asked.

"She's studying to be some kind of interpreter or something. I can't remember the exact name of it." Tooch responded, still a little blazed from smoking earlier.

"Ah." The Asian man nodded—impressed.

"Yeah, she's also supposed to be helping me learn to speak German."

Zac stood behind his SUV watching through the window as Randy stood at the register. Randy paid for the gas and something to drink, then threw his right hand up in the air signaling for him to start pumping. Zac stuck the nozzle in the tank and mumbled angrily to himself. He suddenly stopped when he saw a brand new, champagne colored E500 Mercedes Benz pulling gracefully into the gas station parking lot. But the car was not what got Zac's attention. It was a damn fine, light-skinned girl behind the wheel.

Inez pulled up and parked facing the building…to the right of the door.

"*Damn*!" Zac grimaced as he moved to the side of the SUV to continue watching her. Inez had on a short black bubble jacket, a burgundy skully hat, with matching gloves, and a pair of Timberland boots. She also had on her best pair of tight fitting dark blue denim jeans that hugged her curvy buttom perfectly. Just as she went to reach for the door, it popped open and Randy stepped out holding an un-opened bottle of fruit juice in his right hand.

"*Oh*." She said softly, quickly drawing her hand back.

"*Uh*, I'm sorry." Randy apologized.

"No problem." She said, then shook her head stepping pass him.

As she cut her eyes away, she noticed that Randy did not pay her any attention and had gone back to concentrating on opening his drink. Surprised, she cracked a smile then looked over her right shoulder at him… checking him out as she continued into the store. Inez was not only interested in Randy because he was not all over her, but because of his height, build and good looks. Randy, still busy trying to open his drink, barely caught Inez's flirtatious look. But he did a double take as he moved away from the door…and saw her momentarily gaze back into his eyes.

"Damn!" He said, looking at the roundness of her backside as she went into one of the isles.

Randy went up on his juice as he turned away from the door. But he froze and started looking around like he was thinking about something. In his mind, he knew that if he walked away from that gas station, Inez would be 'free game', and that it especially would be over if one of his friends approached her. There was an un-written rule within the crew that no person was to ever step on the toes of another crewmember. 'When it came to rapping to a female' they were to keep their distance and stay clear out of sight. This was established after what happened between Zac and Omar some years back. Randy looked over at the SUV, spotted Zac, and smiled. Zac was hiding behind the truck, trying not to be seen.

Inez grabbed what she came for and headed to the register without being noticed by Tooch or Omar, who were still talking with the Asian-man. She paid for the stuff, grabbed the two white plastic bags off the counter, and turned for the door. Randy, who stood outside and tried not to make it seem like he was waiting for her, opened the door as soon as she approached it.

"Thank you." She said, barely lifting her eyes up from the ground, busy concentrating on where she was placing her feet.

"You *got it*…" He asked in a light voice, checking her out from head to toe up close.

He let go of the door, then waited a few seconds thinking about what he should say next.

"Hey, excuse me...can I help you with that?"

Those were the best words that he could come up with. Inez, holding a bag in each hand, glanced back at him as he lowered his eyes to his feet and smiled as she kept walking.

"No...I got it...I only have to go right here. But thank you anyway."

Inez then pointed her gloved hand at the car and unlocked it with the keyless-entry remote. Randy slowly nodded his head 'yes' as he watched her make her way over to the car.

"I'm sorry..." He said again, carefully strolling over to her.

Inez glanced back at him as she opened the car door then quickly got in, closing it.

"I...hate...to..."

Randy's words broke up after seeing how fast she got into the car, but then he started backtracking to try to save himself from any further embarrassment. But as soon as he turned and started to walk away, Inez rolled the window down and said, "What did you say?"

Once he heard her voice, he stopped and smiled before turning back around. Then he did a slow cool two-step stroll back over toward her. Inez just stared up at him with a studious look clearing her brownish-blond hair from her eyes.

"Uh, I wanted to ask you your name."

"Inez..." She answered smiling pleasantly. "*Why*?"

Her facial expression then became serious looking. A stunned Randy glanced down at the ground then started trying to think of something to say next.

"*Uh...um...*" Randy clearly looked baffled. "*Wait...because...*What do you mean '*why*'?"

He then frowned with a surge of confidence rushing through him and said, "Because I wanna ask you for your phone number before you pull off and I never see you again. Is that a good enough reason?"

Inez looked at the steering wheel with a straight face then back up at him and started smiling. When she blushed, it made Randy want to melt right where he stood.

"*Oh, man.*" He said to himself, after noticing how beautiful she was.

"Yeah...I think so..." She said as she reached down to take out something to write with.

"But what about you? You're asking me all these questions...what's your name?" Inez said as she wrote down her name and number and handed it to him. Randy didn't have a cell phone.

"I'm Randy…" He said, kindly tucking the number into the palm of his right glove.

"Really…and what's your number?" She said with kind of serious look on her face.

Randy paused for a moment, tilted his head to the side, and looked at her silently. Then, he smiled down at her and asked, "*Yeah…alright.* So what now, you're crack'n on me?"

"Yeah, that's it…I'm peep'n your steelo." She laughed lightly.

Randy extended his right hand and took the pen and piece of paper from her…writing his number inside his hand as best he could. As he stood there, Inez took notice of the logos on Randy's jacket. He handed her back the pen and paper before looking back at Tooch and Omar, who were just coming out of the store.

"Hey, I'll give you a call sometime later…ok?"

"Ok…" She said still smiling.

"It was definitely nice meeting you." He said, before turning and walking away.

Inez rolled up the window as she put the car in gear and backed out, staring at the four boys as they all looked at her.

"You lucky *mothafucka*!" Zac said, stepping out from behind the SUV after watching Inez pull out and take off down Broad Street.

"I saw your black ass hiding over there…you ain't slick…" Randy said as Zac smiled and titled his head to the side like he was admitting to being caught.

"You're not slick, nigga"

Randy and Zac then turned to the side clinching their arms tight and shouldered each other laughing. Before Inez pulled out of the gas station she got a good look at all four boys.

"I was like…*damn*, this nigga didn't move…Then I tried to hop back behind the joun, but you saw me."

"I know your ass is dark, but you're not *that* damn dark. I knew that wasn't no damn shadow either."

"*What*…what *happened*…What's up?" Tooch asked, as he and Omar walked over -looking like they were ready to join in on the laughter.

Zac wiped his teary-eyes and suddenly became serious.

"*Yo, man*, can we finally get the *fuck* outta this *gas-station*? We've been out this *bitch* for damn near a half an hour now." Zac said in a stern voice, then turned and walked toward the SUV.

"*Whatever*, man..." Tooch shrugged his shoulders and exhaled -with a nonchalant look on his face as he watched his cousin look him off and go get in the back driver's side seat.

"Yo, you keep doing this shit, man. Every time we go somewhere, you always manage to find something to fuck'n bullshit'n do!" Zac continued as Tooch got into the truck behind the wheel.

"*Yo*...you're horrible at cursing, man. I just wanted you to know that. Shit, like...burns my ears...ya'nom say'n?" Tooch said as he glanced over his right shoulder at Zac.

"If you don't piss me off, you won't have to hear my mouth, now will you?"

"Whatever, man...That private school is fuck'n you up." Tooch said as he quickly turned up the volume to drown out Zac's voice. He then floored the gas pedal causing the wheels to spin as he took off.

"Yo Tooch...Don't forget...tonight I need you to take this ride with me...to go pick up this car, alright?" Omar said, sitting in the front passenger seat leaning toward Tooch's right ear.

"What happened between you and the chick?" Omar asked, turning to Randy. "You get the number?"

"Yeah, I got it." Randy answered with a smile ...unaware that the paper with the phone number on it had slid out of his glove and fallen onto the ground in the gas station parking lot unnoticed.

CHAPTER 41

Inez arrived back at Mr. Wyble's house where she was let in through the front door by Smith.

"Did I miss anything?" She asked smiling.

"*Ah*! Here she is... nice, safe and sound." Smith said, extending his right hand out as if he was presenting her back to the party.

"And *you* were worried..." Rapth said, jumping in laughing.

The living room was filled with the sound of peoples' voices speaking all at once. Mr. Wyble, the agents, and their wives were all huddled around the coffee table where they were playing Scrabble. As Inez walked toward the kitchen, the father of the young man gave his son a nod...to help her with the bags. He quickly jumped up from where he was sitting, went over, and gently took them from her. Inez's mother smiled as she watched the young man's father attempt to help his son land her daughter, then shook her head and silently turned back to the game.

"Hey! Don't anybody move until I get back." Mr. Wyble said, standing up from the couch. "Especially not any of you ladies...I think we have'em this time fellas." He said, pointing at the women playfully, as he clinched his fist.

"Oh, *please*...we're not worried about cheating you jive turkeys. If you win, you win...that's all. We can't win every game, *geese*!' Sandra said, flagging Mr. Wyble as he walked into the kitchen behind Inez and the young man.

Inez walked to the lip of the kitchen, then did an 'about face'...turning back to take off her jacket and gloves. After she hung up her jacket, hat and gloves, she went and sat down next to her mother. Inez did not bother going into the kitchen. She did not want to give the young man any more time to be in her face. She rested her head on her mother's shoulder, exhaled lightly, and closed her eyes. As time passed, the crowd gradually disappeared until the only people left were the agents' families, Mr. Wyble and Kirsten. The young man's family was the last to leave. After Mr. Wyble saw them off, he turned and walked back over to where everyone was sitting.

"*Sheesh*…I'm glad that's finally over." He said, rubbing his face and neck as he sat down on the floor next to Kirsten's left leg as she sat in the living room chair. "Parties are fun while they are going on, but, boy do you feel thee effects once they're done."

There were several seconds of complete silence before Mr. Wyble spoke again.

"*So*…how'd the game go?" He asked, looking back and forth between Rapth and Smith.

"Uh, you have to excuse me for a second guys, I need to use the restroom again." Flent said, as he got up from where he sat next to his wife…holding his belt buckle with his right hand. "I don't know how you drinkers do it, man!"

"Uh…like we said earlier…" Rapth said, as he watched Flent leave the room. "He scored nine straight points late in the 4th quarter, and they all came within a minute. But, he also had a couple of big plays before that, down the stretch, that I feel had already iced it." Rapth spoke with a plain face, trying to let Mr. Wyble know that Randy did all of this while using very little effort.

"Yeah…you could say that…" Smith nodded in agreement "Because *those* plays put the game pretty much out of reach. Then they started having problems with get'n up clean shots. And oh' yeah…before I forget…" Smith said, turning and looking at Rapth as he stood up. "We brought you back something from the game."

Smith went over to the coat rack by the door and pulled out a five-inch tall Prescott Tiger from his jacket.

"They were giving these out after the game…My guess is because they didn't have a Christmas tournament this year." Smith said, as he walked back over and sat it down on the coffee table in front of Mr. Wyble.

"Thanks!" Mr. Wyble said, lifting the acrylic tiger that was resting on top of the letter 'P'.

He then placed the tiger back down on the table, close to where Inez was resting, and she quickly looked at it and turned her head.

"But on a much more serious note…" Mr. Wyble asked, nodding his head in great anticipation. "Do you guys have any new information on his buddy's father?"

"Nah…There is still not much of anything happening with him. He has been keeping his nose clean as far as we know. That's all we can really tell you up to this point." Smith answered. "But we do have a hunch, that like the rest of the bigger guys in the city, he's probably trying to stay as far away from any drug traffic as possible…Or at least until after these next few months."

"And why is that? What's happening over the next few months?" Mr. Wyble asked curiously.

"The Cantone case starts this week, and it's got everyone run'n scared. Once the Italians get a whiff of what they'll be facing and what's gonna have to stand up in court…" Smith said as he started to chuckle. "They will be more than willing to turn states."

"And like we've told you a while back." Rapth said, also smiling. "If we're going to move when there's a break…they're going to want us to bring in anyone they can convince to testify against him. Your kid has an awful lot to loose if he's caught up in the middle of this."

"Yeah…" Smith agreed. "God forbid he's anywhere near that house once we get the call. They will have him brought in for sure."

"*Uuh…Randy*?" Mr. Wyble sighed as he dropped his head back against his chair, and closed his eyes.

Both Rapth and Smith stopped smiling once he mentioned Randy.

"As long as he hangs around with his friends, he's at risk…" Smith said, mimicking as if to say that it was a no-brainer.

"Yeah…that's how it works." Rapth replied, bobbing his head.

At first Inez did not really think much about hearing the name 'Randy' being mentioned. But then she slowly maneuvered her head around the arm of the chair and looked at the small acrylic tiger again, realizing where she had seen it before. It was the same exact color, and was standing in the same exact pose as the tiger on Randy's jacket. Becoming somewhat alarmed, Inez slid her hand down into her pants pocket and slowly pulled out Randy's number.

"Are you alright?" Flent asked Inez, startling her as he came walking out of the darkness of the hallway back into the living room

"Huh, yeah…I'm cool." Inez said smiling, trying to pretend as if she was not troubled.

"*Cool*? You look like you've just seen a ghost." He said as he passed by and sat down next to his wife, leaned against her shoulder, and maneuvered his head getting comfortable. "Let me know when the two of you are ready to go."

"*Ok…*" Inez answered, nodding her head.

"Well, I'm ready now." Ms. Debbie said as she patted him twice on his left thigh.

Seconds later, Sandra and Tammy started to get on their husbands about them losing the game of Scrabble.

"But that's not fair, though. You girls had an X-factor. You can't play with a doctor…that's cheating." Rapth argued after his wife leaned over and whispered something in his ear.

"How is it cheating? You men both are college graduates…" Sandra shot back. "And who is also fluent in several different languages?"

"*Hold up…*" Smith jumped in, as his appearance clearly revealed the amount of alcohol he had consumed. "*Hold up…* knowing or understanding bits and pieces of a few different languages is in no way considered '*fluent*' in different languages. And I've never even heard of half the words she spelled."

"Were they in the dictionary?" Tammy asked smiling humbly.

"*Huh…yeah…*they were…but I've never seen them there until now."

"Then that is not cheating…is it? And I truly can't believe that the three of you could not have caught up, at least halfway," Tammy said.

"Oh, well…I personally blame the liquor." Rapth added as he sat Indian-style on the floor between the coffee table and the couch…and held up a beer in his right hand

"Yeah…it's *definitely* time to go now…they done started blaming the *liquor*. Where's my coat?" Sandra said, laughing with everyone as she got up from the couch.

CHAPTER 42

Over an hour later, Inez was at home taking a bubble bath and reading a book by the light of the red candles she had placed all around the tub.

"Inez!" Flent called, tapping on the door twice before leaning his left ear close to it.

"Yes!" She answered, raising her eyes up from the book.

"Are you alright in there?"

"Yes…I'm fine!"

"You sure?"

"Uh huh…I just needed to get out of those clothes that's all!"

"Alright, baby… goodnight then!"

"Goodnight, Papi!"

Flent stepped away from the bathroom door and went inside his bedroom where his wife was in bed reading.

"Is she alright?" Debbie asked, closing her book as she sat up in bed.

"Yeah, she's fine. She said she just needed to get out of the clothes she had on." Flent told his wife as he unbuckled his belt and stepped into their walk-in closet.

Inez sat in the bathroom staring at Randy's phone number on a piece of paper she was using as a bookmark. Then she closed her book, leaving the small piece of the paper sticking out from the top and placed it on a small shelf next to the tub. She pulled her arms underneath the bubbles, took a deep breath, then laid back and exhaled lightly.

CHAPTER 43

Days later, there was a heavy snowfall up in the mountains where Randy and 99 other male varsity basketball players from around the country were. They were standing in a half circle at the half court mark of a beautiful gymnasium floor, which was connected to an extravagant hotel.

"Guys, I'd like to take this time to thank you all for accepting our invitation and coming up here this weekend. Give yourselves a big round of applause—you are the top 100 players in the country—and you've been specially chosen to be here right now."

All 100 players started clapping. "We've organized this camp this year because we wanted to get all of you on the same court together before you all graduated…and we didn't want to run the risk of interfering with your school work or your team's schedule. So, this is the time we choose, over the Christmas vacation."

The director was a light brown skinned black man that walked with a slight hobbled limp. It looked as if his right ankle was causing him pain, but he showed no signs of discomfort.

"We'd also like to ask that you extend your gratitude and appreciation to our sponsors for affording half of your stay this weekend."

The tournament director then led everyone into clapping as he turned around facing the hundreds of men who were standing and sitting in the arena. Some of the scouts gave nonchalant nods of the head while others waved or watched emotionless.

"Now, however, I'd like to apologize to some of you for the weather conditions that we're facing up here. But, being as though you are in Pennsylvania…and it is winter here…so, what do you expect…?" The director shrugged his shoulders as he received a small laugh from the crowd. "But no, seriously, I hope everyone had a pleasant trip up here…we will do our best to make sure you have a pleasant stay…between your sponsors and our staff we have done our best to try and make sure that this will be an experience none of you will forget hopefully for the rest of your lives. And we hope to accommodate each and every one of you with whatever special needs you may have…because you guys are special…and don't let anybody ever tell you different. Now…*there*. I said it…" The tournament director then turned to his assistants, who all started laughing, with his hands clinched together. "My staff knows I was worrying myself about saying that the whole trip up here—I swear to you…" A small chuckle came from the crowd of 100 boys again.

"So give yourselves another big round of applause," the director said shrugging his shoulders before rubbing his hands together. He had a mischievous look on his face looking at the boys. "This is a chance for some of you guys who've never played in front of some of the bigger schools to show what you can do. If you're lucky, you might land a scholarship," the director said flailing his eyebrows.

A White male assistant in his early thirties chimed in: "Now, I know that most of you, recognized the schools like—Duke, North Carolina, Florida, and so on."

Randy quickly snapped his head around scanning the stands once he heard Florida. Randy wanted to make sure to get a good look at whomever was there representing Florida. Florida was where Randy always dreamt of playing his college basketball. It didn't have to be Florida University, but just as long as it was one of the bigger schools in the state. The Florida scout was an older Black man with a full salt and pepper beard sitting with his legs crossed reading a program. He looked up for a second; slightly raising his right hand, then went back to reading.

"I would also hope that some of you guys, you'll consider attending a division two school if need be…like Shaw University, IUP, Indiana University of Pennsylvania, and so forth. Now, there are also some division *three* schools here, and I know that some of you are probably not thinkin'of going division three, but a lot can happen between now and graduation.."

As the assistant spoke, the director started glaring at a young man turned to another young man joking around. "Did he say something that was funny!?!" the director asked hobbling toward the young man standing on the right of the half circle. The young man didn't hear him at first.

The director then shouted: "I asked if he said something funny?" The director's voice echoed throughout the arena, everyone had now focused their attention on the young man.

"No, he didn't say anything funny." The young man said embarrassed.

"Then what's the laughter about…he must have said something funny… share it with us? We all came up here, to have a few good laughs, *right*?" the director asked, stepping back nodding his head to see if any of the other 99 boys agreed with him.

"C'mon, *share*. We all would like to know what's so funny. Won't nobody get offended, it's only a joke, right?" But the young man didn't say anything and remained silent.

"Tell 'em, Shamond," the player he was joking with said and gave him a light nudge in his right arm. The 6-feet7 kid at first refused to speak, but then he changed his mind saying, "I laughed when he said there were some division three schools up here."

The director placed his right hand behind his right ear to make sure he heard what he was saying. "Ah, I see…" The director looked Shamond off then limped back to the center of the crowd, "Let's just make sure that you're not one of the ones who has to end up going to one of those division three schools, then it wouldn't be all that funny, would it. The director then reached to his chest grabbing his black plastic fox 40 whistle, which hung from a dark red string, and chirped it twice saying, "Alright! Before we get started, let's go grab a basketball and find a corner or some space to warm up. Try gettin' up a few shots!"

As the director spoke a number of his assistants dumped about 30 brand new indoor basketballs out onto the floor from big blue and red duffle bags that went bouncing all over the arena. "Try to at least get yourselves nice and warmed up first, before you start your stretching, that'a way we don't have anyone stretching out cold muscles. That's a quick way to get hurt. Besides, I don't need any of your basketball coaches back home coming after me. I don't need that…" The director turned to his staff then spun back around saying, "Guys if you notice, the city you're from is on the fronts of your jerseys. That's who you will be running with unless you're told otherwise."

Randy, Sean, Chuck, Rob, a 6-feet-9 kid named Kebo who also played for Tech was standing on the court together. Tridane came walking over and stood at the three-point line in an empty corner away from them. Sean did a count and said, "We have one extra."

Randy looked at Sean then glanced back at Tridane walking a nice distance behind them and said, "Yeah, I see somethings never change." Tridane was playing with Philly because it was his home state.

"Al, don't forget we still need to add one more player to Texas, they're short one," another of the assistants said.

"Oh, that's no problem," the director spoke calmly as he stroked his bald chin with his left hand. "We have one extra with Philly so take one from them."

"Yeah, but who?" the assistant asked as they both turned toward the Philly players.

"Alright, Sean," Randy said, putting up his first shot of the camp standing outside the three point line. "Let me have'em. What's the *whose-whose*?"

Rob, Chuck and Sean were also juniors in high school and had kept in contact with Randy over the years. They also still played on the same summer league team.

Rob, by this time, was a 6-feet-2, 180-pound point guard. He was considered by the national media as one of the truest point guards in the country. Chuck was 6-feet-5 with a sturdy 240 pound frame. Sean, on the other hand, went through some serious growth spurts and was now an athletic 6-feet-8, 215 pounds. Sean was also currently receiving offers from almost every big-time and Ivy League school in the country. He was projected to be a future all-American. Randy knew everyone except for the wirey 220 pound 6-feet-9 Kebo.

"Oh yeah, Randy, this right here is my man," Chuck said, leading Kebo over. "His name's Kebo and he's our center. He transferred in this year."

"Well, *damn*, they brought y'all whole ma-fuckin' squad up in this bitch, didn't they?" Randy said, extending his hand out to greet Kebo. Kebo was from Africa.

"Yeah, I was saying the same thing," Sean chuckled, with his right arm around the front of his neck stretching.

"But, what I don't understand," Randy said, now looking confused, "is where is *Duane*. Why didn't he come up…isn't he y'all leading scorer?"

"Yeah, but he had some stuff that came up so he had to go out of town with his family," Sean riffed, now sitting on the floor reaching to his toes with both hands with his legs straight out in front of him.

"Yeah?" Randy smiled and halted his shooting motion placing the basketball against his left hip.

"Yeah…" Chuck nodded. "But why'd I see that nigga standing out in front of a Chinese store out southwest the night before we left?"

"Yeah?" Randy laughed lightly at first but then frowned, scratching the back of his head, realizing that the excuse he used sounded familiar. "Man, that's wild," Randy said, before putting up a shot.

"So, where you from?" Randy asked Kebo as he caught the ball as it came down from the net.

"Africa," Kebo answered in an unnoticeable accent.

Randy laughed and said, "I thought that only happened in movies," getting Kebo to smile and shake his head. Tridane looked at the five boys talking amongst each other then frowned, drifting away to another court.

"But for that question you just asked," Sean said, getting up from the floor and dusting off his backside, "do you want the good news or the bad news first?"

"Just give it to me…order doesn't matter," Randy answered, allowing the ball to bounce pass him into Chuck's hands.

"You'll get the good news first then," Sean said stepping beside Randy. "The good news is, all the juniors have small orange circles on their jerseys—like these." Sean grabbed the front of Randy's black mesh jersey that had "Philly" written on the front, showing him the small orange circle located at the top near his left shoulder.

"Now the bad news is, all the seniors have white circles. So as you can see, there are a lot more of those up here…the law of the land, '*stop* and *pop*'," Randy and Sean said together.

"Don't expect to get too many foul calls if you intend to go to the basket, because it's not happening for us juniors." Randy silently nodded.

Sean began scanning the arena and pointed to a tall dark skinned kid dribbling a basketball in his right hand and talking on a cell phone with his left. "He's considered the best player in the country right now."

Randy leaned his neck to the side checking out the 6-feet-11 inch, 240 pounder wearing a red sleeveless crewneck shirt that was totally different from what everyone else was wearing. He also had on a pair of long, black, baggy mesh shorts that fell well below his knees.

"That's Caron Reed…and you can expect to hear his name called first or second when he becomes eligible for the draft.

"Who's he ballin' with?" Randy asked.

"He's gigging with Cali. Now for the other guys you should know about…" Sean said again, scanning the arena. "Uh, yeah…him, right there." He pointed.

"Who?" Randy asked trying to see who Sean was pointing to.

"Him, right there, standing next to our friend." Sean was referring to a 6-feet-6 brown skinned kid talking to Tridane. "His name's Tyrell Poole and as you can see he's running with New York.

"Ok, ok…" Randy responded in a low tone not at all impressed with the kid's physical stature. Randy didn't think much of him because he was a bit on the knock kneed side, but the kid did have huge muscular calves.

"Randy, you listening to me?" Sean asked.

"Huh? Yeah…finish what you were saying."

"*Because* if we get the chance to face him, and you get stuck guarding him, you might wanna try to stay close to him at all times…or at least where you can get a hand in his face."

"Can he shoot?"

"*Shit, yeah*…he's got what they like to call 'true NBA range' and in my own personal opinion, he's the best shooter in the country, hands down. So please, it'll make all of our lives easier up here this weekend, believe me."

"No problem, man, you make like you don't know who *I* am," Randy smirked.

"I know…but…I know…"

"Yeah, you better…" Randy then turned his attention to a small dunk contest that Tridane was partaking in with a few New Yorkers and players from Washington DC.

"Are they heading over to us?" Sean asked as he watched the director point at them then start in their direction. "They sure are…" Sean said, but no one was listening.

"Huh? What you say?" Randy asked looking back at Sean with his eyebrows frowned. "Nothing…but it looks like they're coming straight for us."

"Who?" Randy asked.

Sean then nodded his head in the director's direction saying, "But the rest of the players, you should pretty much be alright with, just as long as you remember what I said."

There were plenty other players that Sean could have pointed out for Randy, but since the director was heading over to them he didn't have enough time. The director and his assistant walked up and stood right in front of Randy and the other boys. An assistant spotted Tridane waiting for his next turn in the dunk contest and signaled for him to come over.

"Hey, guys…here's what we're gonna do," the director said. "We're gonna take and have you placed with Texas," the director pointed at Randy. "And you other five are gonna run together." The director gave Tridane a small nudge, pushing him closer to Sean, Rob, Chuck, and Kebo. "Texas needs one more, so you're running with them today, alright?" the director said, looking at Randy, who didn't appear at all pleased with the move. Randy and Sean looked at each other and shook their heads before Randy turned and jogged away.

"Guys we're gonna switch you up and see if we can help give the scouts a better feel for who can play with who a little later."

Chuck stood next to Tridane holding a basketball as he listened to the director speak. Suddenly, Tridane snatched it from him, startling Chuck, turned, and went in toward the basket for a layup. Chuck looked down at his hands then back up at Tridane and shook his head saying, "Fuckin' dickhead…"

"Alright, now give me my guys from New York and my guys from California. You boys'll start this thing off!" the director said then hobbled off to the side of the court.

"All games go to 15, win by two, and even though we're counting twos, you can't win with one! Got it?" the assistant yelled as he blew his whistle and handed the director a white clipboard.

"This should be good…" the director said quietly, turning to another of his assistants who was a heavyset Black guy named Bass wearing a pair of brown framed glasses with a small blowout haircut.

The two teams trotted out to center court, where a White female referee in her mid thirties stood, waiting with a basketball. She lobbed the ball up in the air after the boys got set into position and the camp started.

The tap was easily controlled by California's 7-feer-1 center since he was a whole four inches taller than New York's 6-feet-9 center. He tapped the ball to his point guard, who immediately took off up court toward the basket. Cali's 5-feet-8 senior point guard streaked up the court through traffic, then went into the lane where he left his feet drawing several defenders who were all much taller than him. He kicked a pass out to Caron Reed who was standing by himself behind the three point line in the far right corner. Caron caught the pass and rose up, smoothly firing a shot with perfect rotation.

"*Hustle back*!" he yelled, as the ball went spinning through the air and came crashing down through the net. Caron then started smiling as he jogged back on defense, re-adjusting his wristbands.

The two teams traded baskets until they both had scored 13 points each, but that was when Caron Reed proved that he was truly the unstoppable force that he was being so highly touted as. Caron took the ball from his team's point guard on two straight trips down court. Each time he came down, he scored what looked like uncontested baskets. The next game played was Philly vs. Texas. Sean and the rest of the boys ran Randy's Texas team clean off the court, beating them 15-7. But Randy had five of his team's points on a highflying dunk through traffic and two deep NBA range three pointers. Tridane also collected seven points on fast break dunks and a few easy fast break lay-ups that came off of steals that he had taken from Texas' point guard.

The day was to end after each team had faced each other at least once; that came as Randy's team finally put together two consecutive wins.

"Alright, that's it. That's enough for today!" The director said, stepping out onto the floor. "Now give yourselves a big hand for displaying such great hustle and team work out there, especially being only our first day out!" Everyone, including the scouts, applauded the boys' efforts.

"That's what I'm talkin' about!" the director said to those of his assistants who were standing next to him. The director's response showed the boys playing well and no one getting hurt was a heavy weight lifted off of his shoulders. "Now, get yourselves back over to the hotel side so we can assign you to your rooms and let you know who you're room with!"

CHAPTER 44

Later, the boys were on the hotel side getting their rooming arrangements taken care of.

"Sean, who are you rooming with?" Randy asked over the sound of rowdy young men shuffling through the hallway of the beautiful hotel with their big team bags.

"I'm shacking with Rob. What about Chuck?"

"Chuck's with Kebo," Sean said as he slid his keycard into his door, holding his big black bag over his left shoulder. "Who are you with?" Sean asked as he stepped halfway into the darkness of his room.

"I don't know," Randy answered, shaking his head and thinking that he would surely be stuck with the worst possible roommate: Tridane.

"Alright, well, you see my room number; just give me a call when you get settled in. We'll go down to dinner together."

"Alright..." Randy then walked up the partially crowded hallway decorated with plants in gold vases with gold framed pictures hanging on the walls. He made a left turn where he saw two tournament assistants handing out keycards.

"What's your name?" a young White male assistant asked Randy, who was walking like he was almost sulking.

"Randy Murcy," he said in a grim voice.

"Here you go. You're back around the hall in room 3212," the assistant said, pointing Randy back in the direction that he just came from. "You were supposed to have a roommate, but his parents came up and got him his own room. Consider yourself lucky; you're alone tonight."

Deep down inside Randy wanted to shout and leap for joy, but he held it in and acted as if it was nothing saying, "Thank you," and strolled away.

Once Randy got around to his room and got himself situated, he phoned the boys who were about 75 miles away from him at their hotel. "Yo, Tooch, what's up, scrap?" Randy asked after hearing Tooch's voice answer the telephone.

"Uh, my nigga…what's up with you, Mr. so-called big-time basketball star? How'd your first day go, and please don't tell me you let those niggas bust your ass!"

"Nah, man…you know ain't shit gettin' bust over here, ain't happening pot'na."

"I hear dat," Tooch said, smiling big and happy to hear Randy's voice.

"But," Randy started, "I can't speak for them cats they had me runnin' wit, though. I was holding shit down."

"That's what I wanna hear…"

"But, yo, where they at?" Randy asked, referring to Zac and Omar.

"Them two niggas went downstairs to try and bribe the security guards that's gonna be working the doors at the pool party tonight."

"Yeah?"

"Yeah, but now, I told'em, just wait until after the let out. Then we can just go down and scoop up some chicken and bring'em back up to the suite and chill with us, you know."

"Yeah, I hear you."

"But, nooo, these niggas rather go down there now and run the risk of getting' us kicked outta this bitch before shit starts poppin'."

"But, damn, they still card'n?"

"Hell yeah, man! The dude from the radio just came walking through the hallway with a bullhorn, saying that ain't no need to even come down if you don't have proper ID."

"Yeah?" Randy laughed.

"Yeah, then he said they were gonna be broadcasting the names of the people who tried it over the radio when they get back." Randy and Tooch then started laughing together.

"But, yo, tell me more about what happened today."

"Uh, it wasn't really too much happening. They just had me runnin' with some cats from Texas."

"But I thought they said you were runnin' with Philly. What happened with that?"

"Oh, that's how it was supposed to go, but then they switched it up. Since we had one extra player up with us, they decided to have me run with Texas."

"Did you know any of the dudes up here from Philly other than Sean and Rob?"

"Man, they have y'all whole squad up this bitch."

"Word?"

"Yeah, the only two people that weren't from Tech were me and that cockhead, Tridane."

"Yeah?" Tooch asked, letting off a breathy chuckle.

"They must be expecting y'all to do some big things this year," Randy said, smiling as he got up and went to look down onto the highway from his window where the blinds were drawn.

"Yeah, whatever, man. I ain't fallin' for that bullshit," Tooch said, as he sat on the couch with his feet up waving at the air. "Can't nobody convince me that that bunch of pussies are winning anything, that's for damn sure."

"Damn! Why don't you give'em a chance?" Randy laughed again but only this time with his face smirked a little.

"Nah, because I'm not. And the biggest pussy of them all is that damn Duane Jones. He's some real bullshit! *Leading scorer*?" Tooch mumbled. "Yeah…maybe leadin' my *nuts*."

That was one thing Randy knew he could always count on from Tooch: a fair assessment of a team or a pinpoint player report on someone. Even though Randy and Tooch didn't always see eye to eye when it came to Randy's Prescott team's potential, they both knew to always be straight up with each other at the end when dealing with someone else.

"It doesn't matter how many pep rallies they throw. They still gotta show me."

Randy then went and flopped back down on his bed reaching for the TV remote. With the remote in hand, he started flicking through channels.

"So what's up? You ready for us to come and get you?" Tooch asked after a brief pause in their conversation, which caught Randy by surprise.

"What?" he asked frowning.

"You heard me. We're comin' to get you. I didn't stutter, man."

"Ah. Nah, you didn't, but…" Randy stammered.

"Well then, start getting' your stuff ready. We'll be there in about an hour or so."

Just as soon Tooch spoke those words, Zac and Omar came walking in the hotel room door. "Yo, we out!" Tooch said, getting up and heading for the kitchen, leaving the phone lying on the couch.

"Where we going?" Zac asked, looking at Tooch strangely.

"To get Randy."

"Who is that?" Zac asked as he went and picked up the telephone from the couch. "Is this him? Hello?" Zac asked as he held the phone up to his right ear. "What up, baby? How's the tournament?" Zac smiled.

"It's alright. I don't know why everyone keeps calling it a tournament, though. It's more like a damn combine."

"Yeah?" Zac giggled noticing to his best friend's aggravated pitch. "Yo, well, we're leaving to come and get you right now. Tooch is already puttin' his jacket on," Zac said as he handed the telephone to Omar, who was walking up behind him smiling.

"Yo…where my bottle, man?" Omar asked, laughing.

"Shit, nigga, you're the one over there with all the women and alcohol. I should be asking you that." Omar and Randy shared a hardy laugh.

"How long of a ride is it to go get him? You know where it is?" Zac asked Tooch. Tooch was leaning into the refrigerator fishing through bottles of champagne and wine coolers.

"Like no more than an hour and fifteen minutes tops," Tooch said, spotting a bottle of Patron and taking it out.

"Then we should be back around by at least ten, ten thirty then, right?"

"Yeah," Tooch agreed as he started opening the bottle. "What time is it now?"

"Like quarter after seven," Zac said, looking at his watch on his left wrist.

"Alright, we're out!" Tooch said to Omar who was just hanging up the phone with Randy.

"That nigga's crazy," Omar said, as he walked over to the door behind Tooch and Zac.

CHAPTER 45

The tournament director and his assistants were in his room, which had papers everywhere like an office, discussing what still needed to be done for the boys.

"Take all the junior class transcripts and separate them from the seniors'. Then that'a way, we don't have to worry about anybody else's getting mixed up," Al said to an assistant, who was placed in charge of the paperwork.

"Alright, I'll try it that way, but I still don't think it'll make much difference."

The director persisted. "Just try it and see how it works out for you anyway." The assistant walked out of the room carrying two big stacks of papers in his hands.

"So, did they say who they thought the top juniors were?" a young White assistant named Danny asked Al as Al relaxed back in his chair.

"Um, yeah, Blane Lake, three kids up from Philly, Tridane, Sean, Randy Murcy, the Shamond Glynn kid—you know, the practical joker early in the morning during presentations—and a couple of the other kids whose names I can't remember right now." Al spoke in a very sluggish voice as he leaned back in his chair against the wall with his right hand placed behind his neck.

"But I'll tell you what, though, that damn Murcy kid's pretty tough. Don't you think?" Danny asked nodding his head convincingly. "He seemed to be almost at the top of everyone's list that I've seen so far.

"Yeah, he's a lot tougher than I thought he would be, especially from what I first saw stepping off that bus this morning. Once I saw him out on the floor, I was like damn, is this the same kid? I had to check my list to make sure I knew who I was watching."

"Yeah, he's got a really big upside," Danny said, still nodding his head agreeing with Al. "But I wonder what the problem is with him as far as his recruiting is going."

"I don't know, but I'll definitely see if I can find out… I'll ask a few coaches tomorrow," Al said as he sat up in his chair. "I couldn't imagine it being only because of his SATs. Somebody's had to have heard something about this kid."

"Yeah, you never know, though. But I'll try and see what I can find out tonight as well," Danny said as he headed for the door.

"And don't forget to tell those guys that they have a nine thirty breakfast call in the morning—and to get some rest!" Al shouted as Danny went out and closed the door behind himself.

Moments later, Danny was in his room having a conversation with Mr. Wyble about Randy.

"So how'd his first day go? He perform well?" Mr. Wyble asked over the rough textured sounding telephone.

"He did well…I mean, he showed that he could easily compete at the Division1level. But in my opinion, he's gotta be *one* of, if not the *toughest* juniors up here this weekend."

"Were they impressed with his defense?"

"I don't know about that part. I still haven't gotten a chance to speak with all the scouts. But most of the bigger colleges wanted to have a look at his transcripts before tomorrow's session."

"Yeah?" Mr. Wyble asked.

"Yeah, so I'm guessing tomorrow should be a pretty big day for him, with regard to his recruiting."

"Yeah…let's hope so," Mr. Wyble said exhaling.

"But, you know, that brings to mind what I wanted to ask you…" Danny remembered.

"What? What's that?"

"Why does it seem like none of the schools up here have been beatin' down his coach's door for him yet?" Danny asked cautiously. "They all seem to be really surprised…"

"I don't know, and I really wouldn't be able to tell you that at the moment. But I think it may have something to do with some of the problems that he's had in the past."

"*Problems*? like what kind of problems?" Danny inquired.

"You know, the usual dumb high school ball player stuff—being in the wrong place at the wrong time, hanging out with the wrong crowd, doing what you're not supposed to—you know, kid stuff."

"Oh, I see," Danny allowed. "But the funny thing is how fast word got out about him."

"Yeah, it is amazing, isn't it?"

"Yeah, it's almost like colleges have someone working in the schools for them."

"Huh, how bout that? The conspiracy theory; it always works." Mr. Wyble let out a hurtful laugh.

CHAPTER 46

A little more than an hour later, Taya and Tony were exiting Tony's car and heading for a nightclub.

"I sure hope we're not getting here too early," Taya said, folding her arms wincing from the cold as they started walking.

"Girl, ain't nobody getting' here too early. I already told you, this place is usually packed on holiday weekends."

"Man, I don't believe ya'll tryin' to make a nigga pay an extra twenty dollars just over a damn flyer!" a short Black man said to a pair of bouncers who were standing in front of him. He was standing just inside the club's doors.

"Hey, man…it's the rules," one of the bouncers said, shrugging his shoulders emotionlessly.

"Step right this way," the second of the two bouncers said, letting Taya and Tony in as he stepped to the side of the rope holding it for them.

"What?" the man bellowed after seeing Tony, who was dressed in complete drag, get in totally free because it was ladies' night at the club. "You gotta be kiddin' me…and he doesn't have to pay, right?" the man asked, resting his head back in between his shoulders with his lips turned up. "This is some bullshit!" He then began reaching down into his pants pocket for his money.

CHAPTER 47

Meanwhile two FBI agents were following Mr. Shan as he pulled into the parking lot of a soul food restaurant. The two agents, one Black, one White, pulled to the side of the road. Mr. Shan was driving a late model black Cadillac DTS.

"Hey, are you there?" a voice called, clacking through the speaker on Rapth's cell phone.

"Yeah, we're here. What's up?" Rapth said as he, Smith and Flent were now stationed inside a gray van parked down the street from Mr. Shan's house.

"We should be there to hand him off in, uh, say, fifteen minutes?"

"No problem," Rapth answered then sat his cell phone back down on the table in front of him. "So, what were you saying?" Rapth asked turning his attention back to Flent. Flent was in the middle of telling them a story about Mr. Shan.

"But anyway, like I said, he wasn't that deep in the game when his son's mother was killed…"

"This is Zac's mother you're talking about?" Smith asked looking attentive.

"Yeah," Flent nodded, slowly closing his eyes. "Word is, they were having problems with him messing around after they graduated high school and at the time she had just found out that she was pregnant with his son Zachary. They made some sort of a so-called agreement, that if he left the other women alone, and stopped dealing, she wouldn't get rid of the baby."

"So *she* never got the abortion and *he* never stopped cheating or selling drugs, right?" Smith asked sarcastically.

Flent nodded as he continued, "But one night, around six or seven months after she had the baby, they pulled to a traffic light on the Boulevard. A Buick pulled up next to'em on the drivers' side and a women yelled out, 'Uh huh! I knew you weren't *shit*, you *cheatin' motha-fucka*!'" Smith and Rapth could see all of what Flent was saying vividly.

"But before Shan could turn to look to see who it was, Carmen, doing what any female in her position would do, pushed him outta the way to look for herself." Flent paused and brought complete silence to the van. "When she looked over, there was a guy hanging out the passenger side window of the car with a sawed off 12-gage shotgun."

Rapth sighed and Flent continued, "He didn't even bother to readjust his sights and just pulled the trigger." Flent closed his eyes and shook his head with deep sympathy for her. Smith and Rapth were both cringing.

"Yeah, it was definitely not a pretty sight out there that night."

"Did they ever say if they caught the person who did this?" Smith asked.

"Nah," Flent shook his head again slowly. "At the time, I was just a regular plain blue cop. I never had a chance to go and actually see what was going on with the case. You guys know how it works: once homicide gets their hands on it, you can forget about it." Flent was one of the first police officers to arrive at the scene that night. "But that night," Flent recalled, "Shan cried like a baby."

"Damn…then again, could you blame him?" Smith said sarcastically after first feeling sorry for Mr. Shan. "Hell, he's lucky that none of her relatives came looking to do the same to his ass."

As Flent and Smith traded words, Rapth's cell phone rang again.

"Rapth, you boys there?" the voice of the Black FBI agent asked.

"Hold up," Rapth said, picking up his cell phone from the table. "Yeah, go ahead."

"He's around the corner from you guys right now. You should see him any minute now."

"Alright, we got 'em," Rapth said, then turned and started watching the small camera monitor that was also sitting on the table in front of him.

Moments later, Mr. Shan came driving down his block and parked in front of his house. He got out of the car looking around his dark and empty block before heading toward his house.

CHAPTER 48

Back up the mountains, Randy's room phone rang and he came walking out from the bathroom fully dressed and answered it. Randy was dressed in a thick black hooded sweat suit with the camp's patches on it. The patches were placed on the front right side of the chest and on the front left side pants pocket.

"Hello? Yeah, alright. I'll be right down," Randy said, then quickly went over to turn off his lamp before heading out of the room. Randy also had on a fresh pair of Timberland boots that Zac had bought for him the day they went shopping. Down stairs in the plush four-star hotel lobby, there were basketball players from all over the country lounging around and getting better acquainted. They were dressed in sweats, t-shirts and shorts; all displaying the camp's patch logos on them. The players were on the rugged floors, sofas and standing up against the walls; it was pretty safe to say that they were where ever they were comfortable. Some of the players were in the poolroom taking a dip in the pool. The poolroom was made of walls of glass trimmed with gold. The glass walls provided an excellent view of the expressway that sat 35 feet beneath it and 120 feet away. Zac, Omar and Tooch stepped inside the lobby through the automatic doors and received an all but welcomed man's stare from the players. Tooch, who was the last to step inside, looked around at the players who were now staring at them and hissed, looking back over his shoulders at Zac and Omar.

Tooch didn't hesitate: "Looks like a romper room for teenagers in this bitch."

"Yeah, tell me about it," Zac mumbled.

Moments later, the elevator doors opened and Randy stepped off looking around.

"Where's *he* going?" One of the players who was laying on the floor next to a couch asked another player. Randy looked around the lobby making sure there weren't any tournament assistants around, and then bolted across the lobby toward the automatic doors walking quickly. Zac, Tooch and Omar all smiled as he approached then stepped aside to let him go out first.

An hour and some minutes later, the boys arrived back at their hotel where they walked through the lobby and turned a corner finding themselves face to face with two big Black security guards who were dressed in all black. The security guards were both standing outside two big white doors with their gigantic arms folded. As the boys approached the one on the left nodded his head at Zac then stepped aside opening the doors for them. As soon as the doors opened the sound of water splashing and loud music blaring poured out into the hallway on them.

"*Oh*, my *goodness*!" Randy said in awe, looking at the large crowd having a ball in an almost Olympic sized, fancy and elaborate swimming pool.

"Welcome to the party, man..." Omar said, wrapping his left arm around Randy's neck. "I knew we were gonna find some way to get you here." Omar smiled as he watched Randy looking around wide eyed at the women. Randy then looked up to the ceiling and became even more impressed after seeing that it was made of glass, revealing the brisk night time sky.

"Yo, how much did you have to give 'em?" Tooch asked Zac as they stood a few steps behind Randy and Omar. "Nothing...it was free. They let us in with the tickets. They just said 'as long as they don't see us with any alcohol." "*Maaaan*...I'm goin' back up to my damn room, where the alcohol is," Tooch said, immediately turning back for the doors.

"Hold up, yo...damn, man. At least let's go over and tell the chicks what suite we're in," Zac pleaded. Randy and Omar both turned around to see what was going on with Tooch and Zac.

"Man, these nigga's trippin'!" Tooch grunted, seemingly aggravated with his eyebrows raised. "I ain't standin' around down this ma-fucka sober, like I'm in some fuck'n 'youth help group'. Shit."

"Alright..." Zac said raising his arms up some then looking at Omar. "Well, O', go tell them right quick, please. Then we're out, *ok*?" Zac said to Omar, then turned and looked at his zero tolerance cousin.

Omar left the three boys standing almost near the doors and went over to probably two of the badest chicks in the room. The two ladies were relaxing poolside in their bikinis on long beach chairs. One of them, wearing a royal blue, string bikini, spotted Omar strolling over and sat up giving him her left ear. She nodded her head 'yes' slowly as Omar whispered into her ear then turned and looked at Zac, Randy and Tooch, through her mirror tinted sunglasses. As soon as Omar walked away, the girl said something to her girl friend then leaned back relaxing again.

Later that night, upstairs in the boys' suite, the boys had their own party going with about 10 girls and four other guys. They had plenty of alcohol and food to eat. Everyone at the party was either standing or sitting around getting drunk, or they were playing cards or lounging in the Jacuzzi. Zac and Tooch,were both standing over by the bar while Randy and Omar were sitting over on the couch in front of the balcony's sliding doors next to each other. Omar, who was already 'twisted,' as was Randy, sat slouched down with his neck leaning forward and clinching a half full bottle of Corona with both hands between his legs.

"You see, I blame most of our problems as the youth on some of the rap music," Omar slurred.

"What? Man, I think yo ass is *definitely* drunk now," Randy said, chuckling as he looked down at Omar sitting next to him on his left.

"No, no, hear me out, hear me on this one…I'm serious," Omar begged, raising his bottle up some from his lap. "Because, you have to remember a lot of the lyrics…who are they talking about? Who are the ones really not making that much money and feel they have the most need for it? It's us—young people—the younger generation. So when they say, 'I'm ballin', and you ain't; I'm taken trips all around the world, and you ain't. Who da fuck you think is gone be the most effected by that shit? Because it damn sure ain't gone be the older ones. A lot of them, they already realize that they probably ain't gone ever be rich, unless they hit the lottery or some lucky shit like that. Plus, besides, a lot of the older people do be taken trips and stuff.

"I think I feel you," Randy said, nodding his head in a deep stare while glaring across the room feeling the effects of the alcohol.

Omar continued, "But say, when some kid that works for McDonald's takes his or her lil' paycheck they get every two weeks, and they go get one of these rapper's CDs talkin' like this. You know, to listen to on their way home or to work. How you think they're gonna feel after listening to those lyrics? Then people gone try say they wonder why young people don't take pride in anything any more."

"But, maybe those lyrics might make people wanna do better." Randy shot back with his speech slurred almost as badly as Omar's.

"But not everybody *can* do better, is what I'm sayin'. Some peoples' situations don't call for them to have room for immediate improvement. But so what then? Fuck 'em, I guess then, right? That's how we're gonna to look at it, huh?"

Randy just shrugged his shoulders and shook his head slowly before going back up on his Corona that he was holding in his right hand. Over by the bar, Tooch, holding a bottle of Belve in his left hand, had just finished whispering into the same girl's ear that Omar had whispered to downstairs in the royal blue bikini. Tooch pointed her over to Randy then smiled deviously as he watched her walk away. The girl looked at Randy, who was now only wearing his sweat pants and a black tournament t-shirt, then ran her tongue across her bottom lip sizing him up. Given the current setting of where the boys were and what Randy now had on, Randy was like a celebrity in her eyes. Tooch had also spruced Randy up so well that the girl thought that he was about to go straight to the pros from high school. The girl made sure she made strong eye contact with Randy as she approached him, then she nodded her head and ducked into one of the two rooms to her left. Randy froze, slowly lowering his bottle from his lips, then started looking around to make sure that it was him she was looking at and not the alcohol causing him to hallucinate. Randy looked down next to him at Omar, who was still yapping away, then hurried and got up saying, "Hey, O', hold that thought, baby. I'll be right back..." Omar watched Randy go into the room behind the female then disappear into the darkness of the room with the door closing behind him.

"Ain't this 'bout a bitch," Omar said, after watching the door close. "I saw her first..."

CHAPTER 49

In Philly at the nightclub, Taya and Tony were now sitting at a tall, round, glass table having drinks.

"What time do you have?" Taya asked Tony as he swayed from side to side listening to the music while sipping from his light lime green straw.

"Almost eleven-thirty, why? You ready to leave already?" Tony answered politely, then looked at Taya with a sarcastic smirk on his face.

"No, not yet."

"Bitch, please, we just got here…you're not pulling that early bird shit on me tonight."

Taya didn't say a word back, but she slouched her shoulders and placed both of her elbows up on the table in front of her.

"*See*, that's what your problem is. You need to bring your ass out more, Tay, and maybe you just might find somebody worth while," Tony said, dancing on the stool as the songs changed.

"Yeah, but I hate when you say 'we need to go out' and then you bring me straight to a club. Ain't nothing in here but a bunch of men lookin' to catch something…most of'em have wives or girl friends that they're not going to tell you about."

"Now, you need to stop, you sound like one of those old hags that sit at home watching too many damn TV shows."

"Ain't no 'I need to stop.' You know what I'm saying is true. After all the damn horror stories we've done heard about women meeting men in clubs," Tony was speechless at first but then he hid his face behind his drink.

"Yeah, well, some of us only plan to fuck 'em and leave 'em alone anyway!"

"That's because your ass is a little ho, that's all that is…ain't nothing else to it."

"I'm glad to hear you're expressing your true feelings, that means you care so much about me…and besides this is a lounge spot," Tony giggled.

Tony, dressed in a tight fitting aqua green color two piece ladies' dress suit, reached over and grabbed a waitress by her left arm as she passed by their table. "Uh, I'm sorry, honey, but can you please do me, I mean, us, a favor if you're not too busy."

"Sure, what can I do for you?" the attractive young White waitress in her late 20's asked, placing both her hands on her knees as she leaned forward in front of them.

"Can you bring us two more double shot long island ice teas, please? And get rid of this wench's Kool-Aid for me. Thank you." Tony downed his drink after moving his straw then grabbed Taya's barely touched drink and handed them both to the waitress. The waitress took notice to Taya's frustration then let out a small chuckle.

"Two double shot, long islands, no problem. I'll be right back." As soon as the waitress walked away, four well groomed and well dressed men passed by. None of the men, however, were gay, but the last one extended his left hand out and lightly pinched Tony's cheek. He must have been wasted and didn't notice. Tony immediately sat straight up with his back arched like a young school girl ready to scream. Tony smiled deviously at Taya then looked back over his left shoulder at the man.

"Yeah, but there's one thing that I am definitely certain about…"

"And what's that?" Taya asked.

"There's always good reason to have a nice dog around the house at night…*ew*…" Tony lustfully sucked air in through his clinched teeth. The four men made their way down a small flight of stairs and across the dance floor. Diego, was also at the nightclub, standing across the dance floor, noticed Taya and Tony sitting to their table. Diego and his much taller and lighter cousin Blanko—who earned his name because of being the lightest person in their family—were sitting and standing over near the bar.

"Uh, yo, look at who it is!" Diego yelped pointing at Taya. Diego only spotted them because he was watching to see where the men were going; he had plenty of enemies and never knew when someone would be coming to do something to him. Blanko turned and squinted his eyes, to see who Diego was pointing at.

"Who?"

"The girl right there, sitting with the chick in the light green outfit."

"Ah, I see her. What about her? Who is she?"

"She's the chick from the hood. I think I'm gonna go over and talk to her."

"Yeah, that's good…you go over and do that…" Blanko said, then turned back to his conversation with a beautiful mami who was sitting next to him on a stool to his right.

"So, anyway, I tell the guy, 'you either order me the truck the way it was when I first saw it, or we're gonna have a serious problem in your place of business.' You know, I can't stand that." The women just looked at Blanko, smiling from ear to ear as she listened to his thuggish story.

After Diego made his way across the dance floor and got close enough to see Tony and Taya's faces, the first thing he noticed was that Tony was not a woman. Diego, however, didn't make it obvious.

"Hey, excuse me," he said, never taking his eyes away from Taya. "I apologize for running up on you like this, but do I know you from somewhere?" he asked calmly, pointing at Taya.

"No…" Taya quickly shot back, causing an almost instant dead silence.

"Oh, well, anyway, I'm Diego and I thought I recognized you from Frankford," Diego said, as he slid aside allowing the waitress to set their drinks down on their table. Taya and Tony looked at each other with surprised looks. They at first thought Diego was just another crumb using cheesy pickup lines. Tony flailed his eyes with his face turned so Diego couldn't see him as if to say 'What the heck?'

"Huh? Yeah, I thought you looked a little familiar too. So, what's your name again? What else brings you from all the way across the club?" Taya asked now turning her attention to Diego.

"Nothing, I saw you over here and thought it wouldn't be a bad idea to come holla at you. Nothing else to it, mami, and since every time I see you, you look like somebody just stole your puppy. I felt I could try and get you while you're not in a bad mood."

Tony mumbled to himself 'stole your puppy' in disbelief, then said, "Yeah, that's her," flailing his eyebrows again.

Diego looked at Tony, giving him a quick smirk, then cut his eyes back to Taya. As Diego started to speak again, the well dressed man that pinched Tony's cheek, returned requesting a dance. He didn't say anything and extended his right hand out guiding Tony away by his left hand. Diego winced as the man helped Tony up from his seat, then causally went back to conversing with Taya, just before she could turn around and see his reaction.

"Also, is it alright with you if we exchange numbers so we can hook up… if it's ok with you." Diego asked, still watching the guy lead Tony away.

"Well, here, why don't we do this…I'll take your number," Taya said, as she began digging through her small black purse sitting in her lap. "And I'll give you a call."

Diego reared his head back again caught off guard by Taya's attitude. Diego ripped a cunning smile then stared across the club at his cousin Blanko, who was now looking over at him and raised his glass in the air. Blanko then spun back around and went back to talking to the lady sitting next to him.

"So, how long has your man been down?" Blanko asked.

CHAPTER 50

Back up in the mountains at Randy's hotel, the tournament assistants were finishing up their room checks and making sure all of the players were in their rooms by eleven.

"Murcy's not in his room..." the heavyset assistant named Bass told Danny, as he walked up and stood next to him in the middle of the now empty and quiet hallway.

"Yeah? And why not? I mean, did you check the right room?" Danny asked before he started flipping through some of the pages with players' names and room numbers.

"Yeah...I'm sure. I even asked a few of the boys who walked pass me in the hallway if they had seen him."

"And what'd they say?"

"They all said 'no, they hadn't seen 'em."

"Well, does Al know? But hey, wait a sec, you know what..."

"What, what's up, dawg?" Danny's eyes popped open like he had just been struck by lightening.

"You should go up and check with that other kid from Philly. You know, the one who has the single room, remember?"

"Yeah, I remember. But if it's the same kid we're both thinking about, I asked him already, while he was out in the hallway. He hasn't seen him either."

Bass walked over to the elevator, door already open, and got on saying, "But I'll go up and check with him again anyway."

Bass took the elevator up eight stories. He got off and knocked on Tridane's white with brass trim door. Tridane's door didn't look anything like any of the other doors that were on the lower levels of the hotel. In fact, his door looked more like it belonged on an expensive home somewhere. Bass knocked on the door twice then spotted the doorbell beneath the peephole and started pressing it.

"Oh, boy…" he said exhaling as he waited patiently with his right hand resting on the right side of the doorframe. Moments later, Tridane came to the door, flinging it open and looking like he was being both annoyed and disturbed. Tridane stood there wearing a thick white hooded hotel bathrobe with his toothbrush hanging halfway out of his mouth. He had light blue toothpaste covering his bottom lip as he stared straight at Bass.

"Hey…hey…have you seen Randy Murcy? Is he in here with you?" Bass asked stuttering at first. Bass looked over Tridane's left shoulder at Tridane's fine ass light skin girlfriend. She was just standing up from the Jacuzzi and tying her thick hotel bathrobe belt around her curvy waist. She walked toward the back of the hotel room after looking at Bass and went into the bedroom. Tridane looked over his shoulder at his girl then turned back and looked at Bass, eyes half squinted.

"Well, if you see him, please tell him that we're…" Bass was cut short by the fancy white oak being slammed shut in his face. "Ew…little, skinny, black snake lookin' motha-fucka." Bass groveled at the closed door then started away. "Need to teach that damn boy some respect, instead of pampering his black skinny ass." Bass stepped back onto the elevator, which was waiting with the door open, and pressed the button closing its doors.

CHAPTER 51

Over at the boys' hotel, Tooch walked out onto the balcony and started staring down at the clean-up crew through the glass ceiling of the poolroom. Tooch was holding a lit Swiss & Sweat cigar in his left hand and a bottle of Moet in his right. Omar and Zac came walking out next and stood beside and behind him; also staring down at the clean up crew. Omar stood to Tooch's left while Zac stood almost behind him also on his left. Moments later, Randy stepped out with his eyes squint joining the boys on the balcony. They were all taking in some fresh air. They stood there staring off into the distance underneath the clear and cold full moon sky. Tooch waited a few moments, then glanced over at Omar and winked cracking a quick smile. "So…how was it?" Tooch asked going up on his bottle to cover his smile.

Randy leaned forward on the black railing with his arms folded down in front of him then looked up to his left at Tooch and said, "Yeah…you seen how she looked…" Randy nodded. "What'd you expect me to say?"

"Nothing…" Tooch replied, double swigging the bottle. "But, are you alright though?" Tooch asked next.

Randy stood back up from the railing, looking at Zac and Omar before looking back at Tooch and said, "Nigga, why you asking me so many damn questions?"

"No reason…" Tooch smoothly answered, still with a distant and glazed stare in his eyes. Tooch glanced back over his left shoulder at Zac and smiled, but Randy didn't see him. He took a pull from his cigar and asked with a chest full of smoke, "But, did you get the number?" Randy stood there for a few seconds looking at Zac and Omar smiling at him then shook his head. Zac and Omar both had looks on their faces like they too were waiting on his response.

"Yeah, I did..." Randy answered humbly after a few more seconds went by. Tooch held his breath for a moment then bust out laughing and went charging back into the room with smoke escaping from his mouth and nose. Zac and Omar followed right behind him. The three boys left Randy standing out on the balcony by himself looking confused.

"What's so funny?" Randy asked, as he approached them now leaning up against a wall and resting against each other laughing. "I don't get it... what's the joke?" he repeated.

"Ah, ah, yo, the boy is wild!" Tooch cooed, then started coughing. Heavy amounts of weed and cigar smoke that day had now made his lungs sensitive.

Over by the bar, the girl that Randy had just been with was sitting down next her girlfriend.

The two girls fixed their eyes on Randy, Zac, Tooch, and Omar. The girl in the royal blue bikini had been giving her girlfriend a few words of encouragement that would possibly land her in a bedroom with Zac.

"Hey, yo, Tooch!" one of the guys, who was sitting on the couch playing cards on the coffee table said waving Tooch over. Tooch looked up with his eyes bloodshot red from laughing and caughing.

"Hey, but, yo...school your boy on the do's and don'ts with these chicks..." Tooch said, looking at Omar as he and Zac both walked away laughing. Omar stepped in front of the still confused Randy and said, "Look, Ran, the reason we're laughing is because you don't take none of these chicks you've boned number." Omar stood beside Randy placing his left arm around his shoulders and pointing over to the girl saying, "It's like, you're just asking for 'em to give you something, you see." Meanwhile, another guy had her full and undivided attention and she was looking up at him with a submissive look like she was buying whatever he was selling.

"But, anyway, let's go over and see what Zac an 'em are getting' into," Omar said as he and Randy went over and joined Tooch and Zac over on the couch.

Time passed and Zac stood up from the floor, slamming his card hand down on the coffee table in front of himself in celebratory fashion shouting, "Yes!" He raised his hands up in the air. "Now get that ass up, and get in the room," Zac flexed, then pointed to the bedroom located directly beside the room where Randy was earlier.

"That ass is mine," Zac chuckled playfully. "Try'na take my money... what's wrong with you?" The girl that Zac was now talking to was the girlfriend of the chick Randy had. She stood up from sitting Indian-style on the carpeted floor gently placing her playing hand down on the coffee table, next to Zac's. She next handed her girlfriend in the royal blue bikini the wad of money that she had already won off Zac.

"Damn, I would've just paid for the ass, as good as she looks. Fuck the card game," said the same guy who called Tooch and Zac over. As the girl stepped pass Tooch and the guy, she took her two index fingers and pulled the seat of her string bikini down out of her backside, letting it snap back, causing her round butt to shake.

"*Damn…*" the card game being played consisted of betting money for sex. Whatever a female felt her sex was worth was what they wagered for; only if the guy agreed. If the guy won, the girl would have the choice of either paying him the amount of money that she lost, or giving up what she originally wagered and lost. In this girl's case, it was a no brainier. She had already won nearly $1,700 from Zac and had clearly no intention of paying him back. Zac probably wouldn't have wanted the money back anyway. Everyone in the party laughed as they watched the two of them go into the bedroom. Then they all turned and went back to what they were doing, as if everything was normal.

Time passed and the boys' suite was vacated by all of its party guests. It was left littered with champagne and beer bottles, plastic cups, paper plates and all kinds of other debris left all over the floors and tables. Tooch, laying on the opposite end of the couch from Omar, who was lying on the floor, rolled to his right and his left arm fell to the floor. His hand hit the floor with somewhat of a heavy thud but didn't wake him. Seconds later, his watch's face lit up sky blue. Tooch tried to raise his arm and stop his watch from beeping, but he just let it fall back to the floor and continue on chirping. As the beeping continued, Tooch covered his head with a pillow, pulling it tight to his right ear with his right hand. Tooch facing the back of the couch had his left ear pressed down into the cushion. Unfortunately, the longer Tooch's watch beeped, the louder it became. Tooch took a deep muffled breath underneath the pillow, exhaled then rolled over onto his back. He stared up at the ceiling for a few moments before checking his watch with his eyes squinted from his vision being blurred. Tooch looked at his watch once then checked it again as his eyes popped wide open. His watch now read 5:23 am. He looked around the living room and noticed Randy and Omar still both asleep. He nudged Omar. "O', O'…" he grumbled, pressing Omar in the right side of the head with his right foot.

"Huh?" Omar groaned, rolling to his left side, folding his hands and tucking them down in between his thighs trying keep warm.

"Wake up, we gotta get Randy back!" Tooch said still pressing his foot against the back of Omar's head. Omar laid there silently and motionless for a few more seconds then reached over snatching his cell phone from the floor next to him.

"Oh, shit!" He said checking the time.

"Go wake up, Zac," Tooch said waking Randy who was still asleep on the love chair.

Omar did somewhat of a run-walk to Zac's room.. He knocked on the door once then opened it. Zac and the girl were in bed naked and partially covered.

"Zac, yo, get up. We have to get Randy back."

Zac opened his right eye looking up at Omar.

"What?"

"We gotta roll. We have to get Randy back before he gets in trouble."

Both of Zac's eyes popped open as he gained conscious.

"Yo, I got a headache like shit," Zac said minutes later as he stood in the bedroom door holding his forehead with his right hand.

"Quit bitchin' and come on!" Tooch said as he, Randy and Omar walked pass with their coats already on. "You *need* to learn how to control your liquor."

But Zac didn't say anything and looked at him with a straight face raising his eyes up from the floor.

A little over an hour later, Al sat in his room at his desk, sipping coffee from a white hotel coffee mug and skimming through some paper work. He saw the headlights of a vehicle pulling into the hotel run across his window blinds. The lights hit Al in the face as he raised the white coffee mug to his mouth. He got up and slowly made his way over to the window to see who was arriving at this time in the morning. Al was wearing a thick white hooded hotel bathrobe like the one that Tridane and his girlfriend had on earlier. He peeked through the blinds sipping his coffee, he noticed a middle age White gentleman, who was dressed in a gray suit, getting out of a taxi. The man, carrying a black briefcase in his right hand and his beige trench coat draping over it, closed the back passenger side door, then walked into the hotel through the automatic doors. Al let go of the blinds once he saw the man walk into the building then turned and went back over to his desk. He sat his coffee mug down beside the lamp before switching it off. The lamp that Al had just turned off only lit up a small section of his darkened room. He got into bed after taking off his robe, and just as he settled in underneath the covers exhaling and closing his eyes, Zac's gold SUV pulled up out front with the headlights off. The front of the hotel was completely covered with snow except the driveway and the skies above revealed the start of daybreak. Tooch pulled up right in front of the hotel and Randy jumped out, sprinting into the building. The automatic hotel doors opened for a few seconds and Randy's head popped in looking around cautiously. The only person in the lobby was a female clerk, sitting behind the tall hunter green marble front desk reading a magazine. She noticed Randy but didn't make it obvious as she just kept her head down, reading. Randy quickly sprinted across the lobby and into an already open elevator, pressing the bottom button to close the door. The girl raised her eyes from the magazine then frowned, as she looked to her left at the clock on the wall.

Randy went up eight floors to his room, but as soon as he went to step off of the elevator, he spotted Bass who was just turning the corner down the hall on his right and stepped back inside the elevator. Bass had his head down, though, and didn't see Randy, so Randy quickly stepped back into the elevator and pressed the button, going back down two floors to remain undetected. Bass looked at the elevator suspiciously as he walked pass but didn't think much of it and just kept walking. The elevator doors opened for Randy again and this time he slowly peeked his head out, looking both ways up and down the hallway. Randy exploded from the elevator, heading to his right toward a white door that led to the stairwell, and in the opposite direction of Bass upstairs. Randy pushed through the door and found himself face to face with the same older White gentleman who just exited the taxi. The man and Randy both froze for a split second as they stood there looking at each other. Randy then turned to his right and darted up the stairs almost stumbling. The man stood halfway up the flight of stairs, frozen in his tracks, as he stared at Randy, who flew up the rest of the stairs before exiting the stairwell. The man finished climbing the rest of the stairs and pulled open the door to leave the stairwell. He found himself yet again coming face to face with another person. "Huh…" He jumped after noticing Bass.

"Hey, what's going on?" Bass asked, frowning as he did a quick double take, continuing on his way. The man started walking again and looked up at the ceiling exhaling, looking like he now understood why the kid in the staircase was just running.

CHAPTER 52

Weeks later, just after the holiday vacation, Randy sat inside Coach Scott's office getting yelled at by Mr. Wyble.

"I can't believe you'd go all the way up there and do something like this!" Mr. Wyble yelled at Randy with his eyes looking like they were about ready to pop out of his head. "This is your life that you're playing with here, you know that!" Mr. Wyble turned and looked out the window, then his face lit up like he had just had a bright idea. "But you know what, you know what, let me calm down because this isn't my problem anymore." He started smiling, pointing to the ground with both hands.

"What do you mean, it's not your problem anymore?" Coach Scott asked, sitting behind his desk with his arms folded.

"I'm through. I'm washing my hands of this mess..."

"You can't just *wash* your hands of this. This is something we *both* agreed we'd take on *together*. It wasn't just *my* idea. This is what you signed on for, remember?"

"Yeah, but now that I think about it, what in the world was I thinking?" Mr. Wyble had a lost look on his face. "I...I, I don't know what I was thinking."

"So now all of a sudden you're pulling out, right?"

"Hey, look, listen, I'm going home. You can call me or reach me there. Give me a call later; we'll talk about this some more." Mr. Wyble, without saying anything else, left the office, slamming the door shut behind himself.

Khalil, who was standing outside the door, ear-hustling heard everything, but he quickly turned and acted like he was drinking from a water fountain on the wall to the left of the door. Mr. Wyble glanced at Khalil as he came out, then did a double take before hurrying off. Khalil peeked up from the water fountain, and stood up as he watched Mr. Wyble go out the doors that lead outside into the parking lot.

Back inside the office, Coach Scott had nothing else to say to Randy as he looked around his office rubbing his face. "Well, I guess now you can go." Randy slowly lifted up from his chair, grabbing his bag and casually strolled to the door.

"What's up? What happened?" an inquisitive Khalil asked.

"Nothing..." Randy mumbled.

"You sure?"

"Yeah, come on, let's go." Randy walked away from Khalil, leaving him standing there in front of the fountain with a confused look on his face. Randy, Taj, Khalil, Pooh and three other players from the team came out the building and started walking down the street together, and as usual, everyone was joking around except for Randy.

"Hey, you sure you're cool, man?" Khalil asked Randy again. The other five guys turned to look at their star teammate.

"Yeah, I'm good, but, hey, look, I'm gonna catch up with y'all fellas later. I need to get some air, or take a walk or something."

"You need me to come with you?"

"Nah, it's good. I'll hit you up later." Randy gave Khalil and the rest of the boys handshakes and hugs before turning and walking in the opposite direction down Broad street headed north toward City Hall. Khalil looked back over his left shoulder at Randy as he walked away with his head down.

While Randy walked, he thought about some of the things that Mr. Wyble was getting on him about back in the office. Mr. Wyble said he was 18 years old in the eleventh grade and still didn't have a job or his driver's license, and it didn't make sense because he wasn't all that serious about his school work. And, that if he was, he would have at least taken the SATs by now. He said that these were the types of things that should let people know what kind of person they were potentially going to be in the future whether they understood it or not.

After taking all of what was said to him into consideration, Randy made a pact with himself that he would turn over a new leaf and try refocusing his attention on the important things in his life. That would mean, for the time being, not spending as much time with the fellas—at least until after his situation improved. One of the biggest reasons that Randy didn't think hanging out with the fellas was such a big problem was because they hardly ever left the house, so, every time Mr. Wyble would preach to Randy saying "you need to stop running the streets with your friends and stay in the house," Randy would think that if he was wrong about that part, he must be wrong about everything else that he had to say about the situation as well. This is also a major problem with dealing with the youth today, because if you say just one simple thing wrong or out of place, their ears will shut off faster than you can blink and they will become numb to everything else you have to say. It's sort of like turning in an essay to a professional and wanting them to take your writing seriously, but then as soon as they find something misspelled or worded improperly, they won't want to read anymore or take your work serious. For the next month and a half, Randy jumped out of bed as soon as his alarm clock went off and got washed, dressed and ready for school in good time, instead of his usual pattern of laying around until he would miss the last bus that got him to school on time. All of his reports and homework were also turned in on time or completed as soon as he came home from practice. Randy even worked on some of the areas that he was weak in, like Algebra, English, and so on. He read every chapter of every book he was assigned and aced each and every test he was given over this period of time. His teachers took notice to his changes and began dealing with him in a much more respectful manner.

This also came while Randy was still posting big numbers on the ball court. In fact, since his trip up to the mountains, his game had elevated a level or two higher. Randy studied as hard as he could to prepare for the SATs and his driver's license test and took both of them on the same day.

Mr. Wyble was still keeping tabs on him, but from a distance. He would buy newspapers to check up on his stats and would read to see what was going on in his life. But he would always call Coach Scott if he had any real questions. In one newspaper it read: "Murcy surpasses 1,000 point milestone." Randy had scored his one thousandth point in a quarter finals playoff game, while also leading his team to victory.

CHAPTER 53

Inez's best friend, a pretty dark skinned Black girl named Kendra, was sitting with her knees on the floor while leaning on Inez's bed. A newspaper was sprawled out in front of her as she was trying to convince Inez to give Randy a call.

"Look, it says right here, 'when asked if he had a girlfriend, Randy giggled and shook his head, almost like he was embarrassed.'" Kendra went on reading the article to Inez: "It's not that I'm not into females right now, but it's just that most of my time goes into practicing and my school work. Pretty much, the way I see it, if it happens, it happens...' Now see, *girl*, I'm telling you that you're *crazy*. Talkin' 'bout, 'what if he has a girlfriend now.'"

"But it could've changed by now," Inez said, sitting up against her headboard with her feet pulled close, clutching a pillow tight to her chest.

"What is this..." Kendra started ruffling through the newspaper to see what date it was printed on. "This paper's from the day before yesterday, girl. What're you talkin' about?"

Inez looked at her other girlfriend Billy, who was sitting at the foot of her bed staring back at her over her left shoulder. Inez's other friend was a beautiful Black and Vietnamese girl named Billy. She was also in the eleventh grade with Inez and Kendra. Inez and Kendra were both around the same height while Billy stood 5-feet-5.

"And I know one thing, if my man played ball, and he tried to act like he was going to leave my name out, when somebody asked about us, I'd be like, 'oh, you don't wanna answer questions about us?' Then I'd be like, '*bam-bam-bam*!'" Kendra started flailing on the bed like she was fighting, which caused the newspaper to ruffle and Inez and Billy to laugh.

Inez's mother heard the commotion as she passed by the room and stuck her head in asking, "Are you ok?" Kendra heard her voice then tried to play it cool by fixing her shirt and scratching the back of her neck answering, "Yes…I'm alright." Kendra gritted her teeth, embarrassed, and raised her eyebrows as Ms. Debbie pulled her head back out of the room.

"What's so funny?" Flent asked his wife as she came down stairs grinning.

"They're upstairs trying to convince our daughter to call some boy." Flent looked around with his reading glasses resting on the bridge of his nose. He shrugged as if it was nothing before going back to his reading.

Back upstairs, Inez was still pleading her case to her overly persistent girlfriend. "You don't know what kind of guy he is. He could be one of those guys who has lots of girls because they all know he's going to college and maybe the pros…or NBA.. And I'm not about to get in a fight with some girl over her man—especially not over a *man*."

"You're exaggerating now, Inez."

"No, I'm not. I'm serious," Inez said, shaking her head convincingly with her eyebrows raised. "We both know how those girls are over at that school; they claim stuff that's not even theirs…" Billy nodded her head in agreement.

"But you don't know if he is in a relationship…and besides, you ever think they might do that because you have something they want?" Kendra asked.

Inez's whole demeanor changed as she said, "Yeah, I know. But I just hate meeting people and going through that whole getting to know each other thing."

"All she's telling you to do is give him a call," Billy added.

"Thank you…" Kendra said, snapping her head and looking at Billy sharply. "No one's asking you to marry the darn boy."

Inez thought to herself for a few seconds then lifted up her head saying, "But what about Josh?"

"*Ahhh*!" Kendra yelled, flopping her upper body back down on the bed again and crinkling up the newspaper. "You are kiddin' me, right?" Kendra asked, showing her gorgeous smile being sarcastic. "You have to be…because he's a *guppy* compared to Randy. Inez, he still wears his sweaters wrapped around his shoulders. You can call me ghetto, but this is *not* the *Fresh Prince of Bel-Air*."

"I know, but he's cute and he's smart…" Inez said, looking deep into Kendra's eyes. "Do you know how many offers he already has from some of the top Ivy League schools?" Inez was praying that Kendra would somehow understand where she was coming from.

"I understand that, I do…but, I'm sure Randy does also. Maybe not *Ivy League*, but Duke counts, doesn't it?" Kendra asked nodding her head slowly. "All I'm saying is give him a call. You never know. Just give him a call and see what happens. That's all." Kendra then opened her hands up like she was now washing her hands of the subject. Inez turned and looked at Billy, who just shrugged and nodded as if to say, "It isn't asking too much."

CHAPTER 54

Later that night, Inez finished straightening up the kitchen and went upstairs to her bedroom. She laid across her bed, thinking to herself. She reached over to her right and grabbed her cordless phone and Randy's phone number, which was still written on the same small torn piece of paper. She started dialing. The phone rang four times before Randy's voice picked up saying, "Hello?"

"Hi, can I speak to Randy, please?" Inez asked using her softest voice.

"This is him…who's calling?" Randy's voice sounded like he might have recognized Inez's voice.

"It's Inez…" Randy's head popped back because it was who he thought it was.

"Hey, how are you?" Randy asked, now sounding a bit refreshed.

"I'm fine, and you?"

"Ah, I'm good. I'm glad you finally called me."

"Oh, really?" Inez teased.

"Yeah…really."

"But didn't I give you my phone number also? Why didn't you call *me*?" Inez questioned.

"Because I somehow lost your number the same night you gave it to me—like an idiot," Randy admitted.

"Ah…" Inez said slowly, nodding her head once.

"So, what's new?" they both asked at the same time and started laughing together.

"Uh, I'm sorry, you can go first, it's ok," Inez said.

"It's alright. But I'll go first since I lost *your* number," Randy insisted still laughing a little. "Uh, nothing really. I've been spending most of my time tryin' to keep up with books and practicing. That's all…what about you?"

"I've been doing pretty much the same. Nothing different…except, I've been spending a lot more time over in Jersey recently, since both my parents have been working long hours lately."

"Yeah? What's in Jersey?" Randy asked.

"My girlfriend Kendra lives over there, so that's where I go during the weekends."

"Ah, that's good. Well at least you're having fun, right?"

"Well, not really…" Inez said, frowning a little.

"And why is that?"

"She kind of has this big thing where she's into guys real heavy—or should I say *men*."

"Oh, I see." Randy said.

"But, so did you take your SATs yet?" Inez asked switching up the subject.

"Yeah, I took 'em about three weeks ago. *Why*?" Randy quickly answered.

"No reason, just a question."

"Have you taken yours yet?" Randy questioned.

"Yes, I took mine last year, so I could get it out of the way early."

"So you took 'em in…what grade are you in?" Randy asked, squinting.

"Eleventh…"

"So you took 'em in *tenth*? *Damn*."

"Yeah, my parents don't play around with that stuff. They were expecting me to take 'em and be done with them before I was a senior," Inez said.

"Ah, I see," Randy answered, nodding his head back impressed. "So what did you get?"

"1220."

"Damn, that's what's up…"

Downstairs in Inez's house, Flent came in through the side door which led from the garage into the dinning room, wearing a brown sports coat, a white shirt, a pair of blue denim jeans and a rust colored pair of loafers. He walked into the dinning room, plopped a manila envelope down on the table, and went to the closet to hang up his jacket before he turned and walked into the kitchen. Inside the envelope, were a series of black and white photos from Mr. Shan's indictment.

"Hold on for a second," Inez said, raising her head to listen. "Hold up." Inez sat the phone down on her bed and slowly got up, tiptoeing over to her bedroom door. She stuck her head out into the hall and peeked toward the bottom of the stairs, but she couldn't hear anything because her father had momentarily stopped moving. Inez crept over to the top of the stairs and leaned forward, holding on to the banister.

"Phew…" her father said exhaling again.

"Daddy, that you?" she asked, relieved.

"Yes, it's me. What're you doing?"

"Nothing…you just scared me because I didn't hear you come in…"

"Oh, I'm sorry. I came in through the garage."

"It's ok. I'll be down in a minute, alright?"

"Ok…"

Inez turned and went back into her bedroom. "Hello?" she said, picking the phone back up.

"Is everything alright?" Randy asked.

"Yeah, it's fine. My father just came in from work," Inez answered.

"Sounds like he scared you."

"I was. I usually hear him when he comes in…my room faces the front of our house, so I hear practically everything."

"Ah, he's getting in kind of late, isn't he?" Randy questioned.

"Yeah, this has been his schedule lately…"

"What does he do?" Randy asked, but Inez didn't hear him because her father called her at the same time.

"Hey, well, listen…I'm gonna have to give you a call back later?"

"Uh…" Randy sighed playfully.

"Yeah, I know. I'm sorry. My dad's complaining that we haven't been spending enough time together, since he's been working late and I've been staying over in Jersey. Plus, this weekend I'm supposed to be staying with my girlfriend again."

"Nah, I'm just kidding. I understand." Randy sounded like she didn't have to apologize.

"I would say I was going to give you a call tomorrow, before I left, but I'm not coming home after school."

"Oh, well, whatever…it's cool. Just give me a call whenever you get a chance, alright?"

"I will," Inez smiled. "Do you have a pen near you?"

"Yeah…why?" Randy was already holding a pen in his right hand because he was doing schoolwork when she called.

"Because I want to give you my number, *again*," Inez teased.

Randy's face lit up as he wrote the number down. They both said their goodbyes and hung up. Randy held the phone out in front of him in his left hand, staring at it as he bit down on his bottom lip in lust and clenching his right fist in celebration. Randy was surely happy to hear from her after realizing he lost her number, and truth be told, he thought he would never hear from her or see her ever again.

CHAPTER 55

On Friday, Prescott was at a major university playing in the semifinals in front of 8,000 fans. They were less than two minutes away from punching their ticket to play for the Public League championship. They led the opposing team 92-72. Randy received a pass from Pooh then turned and looked at Coach Scott to see what he wanted him to do.

"Give it to Khalil!" Coach Scott ordered. "*Run the clock*!"

Randy started smiling as he dribbled to the top of the key, calling out, "*Lil*!" Randy was smiling because he knew that there was nothing that Khalil loved to do more than show off his ball handling skills for a guy his size.

"Lil!" Randy called, waving him over. Khalil spun off a defender down low, then came charging up to the top of the three-point line taking the ball.

"Spread out!" Randy yelled, motioning everyone from the middle of the floor as he went and stood in a corner next to Taj. The opposing team's point guard stood at the top of the key in front of Khalil, looking up court at his coach to see what he wanted him to do. Their coach looked at the game clock seeing that there was only 1:30 left and shouted, "Go man!" The coach looked at his assistant with his arms folded saying, "There's no need in fouling, just get this shit over with."

Randy leaned forward, placing both of his hands on his knees, and started smiling as he watched Khalil yo-yoing with the defender.

"You think you should help him?" Khalil asked one of the defender's teammates.

"That nigga's crazy," Randy said, smiling up at Taj. Randy looked back over his left shoulder at his fellow classmates going wild in the stands behind him. "Damn…they're actin' a fool," he said, frowning with a smile, tooting his nose up for Taj to look back. Randy watched the madness in the crowd for a few seconds then covered his face with the bottom part of his jersey.

A crazed White male student yelled as he pointed at Randy shouting, "*You, maan…you*!" Time wound down and Khalil threw a shot up without any intent on making it, then ran over and grabbed Randy screaming, "*Yes*!"

When the horn sounded, the bleachers cleared and everyone ran out onto the court to celebrate with the team. "Hey, go shake hands!" Coach Scott shouted as his team started to walk over toward the bench.

"Randy, man, my goodness, man!" Khalil said almost crying tears of joy after they shook the opposing team's hands. "I don't believe we're going to the *championship*!" This indescribable happiness that was now overwhelming Khalil was because no one, including the students at Prescott, expected the team to earn a trip to the championship—everyone that is except for Randy. The year went exactly as Randy had planned and expect for the two close losses they had suffered midway through the season, everything worked out fine.

"You were right, man. You were so right!" Khalil said holding his white #2 jersey up in his face so that no one could see him, in case he would have started crying.

Randy looked around at the crowd jumping up and down and celebrating with some of his teammates and said, "Lil, don't lose your focus, man. We still have one more to go. You dig?"

Randy, Khalil, Taj, and Pooh then all stood there staring at the crowd, emotionless. Coach Scott noticed what was happening over on the other side of the court with his star players and waved for the reporter, who was on his way over to them, to back off.

"I'll call 'em later…" the reporter, who had interviewed Randy before, said under his breath. Coach Scott gave him the thumbs up signal before watching him turn and walk away.

Randy had finished his junior season averaging a little better than 30 points a game at 30.3 and still had not yet gotten pass "clearinghouse" or signed a letter of intent with a big-time Division one school. Clearinghouse meant that he would be able to come in and play right away for a division one college as a freshmen.

CHAPTER 56

Meanwhile, as night fell, Zac and Omar were sitting and waiting outside in the SUV for Tooch to come out of a store. Moments later Tooch opened the back passenger side door of the SUV and hopped in, saying, "Yo, what's up with Randy? Anybody hear from him?"

Zac put the truck in gear and pulled off as Omar answered, "Nah, I haven't spoken to him in a couple days." Omar was now lounging back in the front passenger seat. "He's still on that busy shit with his books and all, you know."

"Well, we're gonna swing by and get 'em before we bounce. I know he'd wanna come with us," Tooch said, shaking up a sealed bottle of juice.

About a half an hour later, Randy arrived in front of his house. He climbed out of Khalil's mother's rowdy minivan listening to his teammates picking with him. "*You* man, *you*!" someone's voice said getting everyone to laugh even harder.

"Y'all boys are crazy," Randy said, as he stepped up onto the curb. "Alright, y'all drive careful. Be safe," Randy told Khalil's mother, who was behind the wheel, then turned to unlock his front door. He turned back around waving before he went inside saying, "Alright…thank you!"

As soon as Randy went inside his house, his whole demeanor changed. He closed the door and sat his bag down on the floor beside his left leg. He started looking at some unopened mail that was sitting on the cluttered and red juice stained glass coffee table. There were three letters sitting next to two half-filled glasses of red Kool-Aid and two of them had Randy's name on them. He reached down, picking up the letters, holding them in front of his face, dropping the junk mail letter to the floor. He held the one envelope that he had been waiting for, with his SAT scores inside, but he had a look like he didn't know what to do with it. He stood there, thinking to himself for a moment, trying to build up the courage to open it. That courage took a while, however, as he stood there motionless.

Minutes later, Randy carefully lifted the right side of the envelope flap up; a few seconds later, he did the same to the other side, and before long the entire envelope's flap was completely raised. Randy removed the folded white piece of paper from inside the envelope, letting the envelope itself fall to the floor. He said a quick prayer to himself with his eyes closed. "Lord, please, I ask of you, please, let me have scored well enough." Randy took a deep breath before re-opening his eyes to read the letter, but once he read what the letter said, he allowed it to also fall freely from his hands. 510 is what he scored. Randy clinched his eyes shut tight, placed his right hand over his eyes, and his left hand on his hip thinking to himself about everything Mr. Wyble said. He now felt that Mr. Wyble could not have been any more wrong about his situation. Randy was feeling like his friends had nothing to do with him not getting accepted into a big time college; it was solely on him and no matter what he did or where he went with them, as long as he made sure he did his best to prepare himself , that was all that mattered.

But just before Randy could start feeling sorry for himself, the sound of heavy base coming from a vehicle in front of his house got his attention. There were then three knocks at his front door and the sound of an all too familiar voice giggling. Randy walked over to the front door and opened it with a grim look on his face and there stood Omar wearing a huge smile.

"Yo, what's up, scrap'a. You comin' out or are you still stuck in study-hall prison?" Randy shook Omar's hand then looked at Tooch, who was standing up against the back door of the SUV, then at Zac who was sitting behind the wheel and answered, "Yeah, but let me do something first." Randy stepped back inside. Omar smiled as he went and climbed back into the front seat of the truck. Randy, who never took off his team jacket, went back inside to trash his horrid SAT scores so that no one else would see them. He came out and closed the door behind himself, but as soon as he stepped down from his top step two crackheads, one male and one female, approached him.

"Hey…is Tootsie around?" the middle aged Black male, reeking of musk asked. Randy listened to him then looked at the boys who were watching from the SUV. He looked back at the two crackheads answering, "*Fuck no*! If you don't get the *fuck* away from me, *man*, I'll beat the *shit* out *both you*!"

Randy's shouting helped him get rid of some of his frustrations. The boys stared down at the crackheads, like they were waiting for them to give them a reason to get out of the truck. But the crackheads both apologized and took off, walking briskly down Tackawanna Street. Randy climbed into the back driver side seat of the SUV.

"Where we going?" Randy asked a short while after he noticed Zac had pulled onto the expressway.

"The game…" Zac answered.

"What game?" Randy asked, puzzled.

"Sean and 'em are playing New Jersey tonight; it's a playoff game," Tooch said.

"Oh," was all that Randy had to say before he turned and started staring out the window.

"But, yo, we heard y'all won earlier," Omar added.

"Yeah…" Randy nodded like it was no big deal.

CHAPTER 57

A short while later, the boys arrived at Tech. They got out of the SUV and started walking up toward the big beautiful gymnasium together. "Damn, it seems like every time I come here, this place gets bigger," Randy said, walking a few steps behind the boys.

"That's because they're always adding some shit on," Omar said. "Seems like every time we go home for the summer and come back they added a new department or lab."

"No bullshit," Zac complied.

Minutes later, the boys were walking down the white marble hallway, which was lined with gold and wooden framed trophy cases, and headed toward the arena. The trophy cases were filled with championship trophies that the school's many sports teams had won over the years.

"They remodeled most of the inside too," Omar continued, looking around the spotless hallway.

"Yeah, but I can see they didn't redo the trophy cases…" Randy said, laughing as he looked down at the last championship trophy that the boys' varsity basketball team had won. It was more than five years ago.

"Uh, yeah, I know," Omar cooed. "It's been a while; they haven't won shit since we've been here."

"Damn…" Randy shook his head. Omar pulled two large burgundy doors open and led the boys into the arena.

"But I can see y'all still know how to pack a house, though. Damn!" Randy cringed as he looked around at the ruckus crowd of nearly 15-thousand roaring fans. The Tech school band was playing and had the whole place rocking with perfectly toned music. Randy noticed the size of the band and smiled after realizing that it was almost twice the size of his school's varsity football team.

"Come on, let's go find somewhere to sit," Zac said, having to yell over the loud music.

"Hey…isn't that Randy Murcy?" a kid asked one of his friends as the boys made their way pass them.

"I'm not sure," his friend answered. "Hold up, wait…let me see. Yeah, that's him," the kid said after spotting the Prescott 'Tiger' on the back of Randy's jacket. "See the Tiger?" A few other students also noticed Randy and started whispering and pointing as the boys walked pass.

"*Uh, shit…*" Omar said.

"What? What's up?" Tooch asked turning and looking back at Omar as they continued walking.

"I think we've got us a celebrity sighting on our hands," Omar giggled leaning forward toward Tooch and Zac, who were walking in front of him.

"Why is that?" Zac asked before turning and looking back at Randy. Randy didn't notice the attention he was getting either because he was too busy watching where he was stepping and looking at what was going on down on the basketball court. Tooch turned around next and took notice to what was happening then said, "Oh, goodness," in a joking voice.

"Here, we can take it down right here, yo," Zac said, stopping in front of four empty seats in a row.

"What? What's up? What're y'all talkin' about?" Randy asked as he came walking up to the seats.

"Nothing. But look…" Omar said and then nudged Randy for him to turn to see the kids whispering and pointing at him. Randy looked at the students with a blank expression on his face, then he turned and looked at Tooch, who was fighting back a smile, and said, "Yeah, you see it. They know. They know who the fuck I am."

Tooch shook his head and covered his eyes with his left hand as he and Randy both shared a laugh saying, "*You cheesy, man.*"

Down on the court Tech was in the midst of a seesaw battle with New Jersey. They lead by the score of 74-71 only a minute into the forth quarter. Tech's lead expanded to 77-71 after Duane Jones knocked down a three pointer. The crowd stood up, then got even louder once Duane threw his hands up in the air like he was trying to pump them up.

"He's such a *bitch*," Tooch said, with his face frowned, flagging down at him. Randy looked at Duane then at Tooch and started smiling. Again, Randy knew that there was one thing that he could always count on from Tooch and that was an excellent assessment on ball players. Yet, Randy still stood there, along with the rest of the crowd, and applauded Duane's play.

"Randy, Randy, yo," a voice called. Someone then placed their hand on Randy's right shoulder. Randy quickly spun around and there stood Khalil, Taj and Pooh, all wearing their Prescott team jackets also.

"*Aaaah...*" Randy smiled. "Yo...what're y'all boys doing here?"

"We came down to check out his cousin, remember?" Khalil said, shaking Randy's hand and thumbing back at Taj. Randy had prior knowledge of Taj and Tridane being related by marriage so he wasn't surprised.

"Big Prescott all up in ya' motha fuckin' kitchen! Now what, nigga?" Randy said turning back to Tooch. "You got the real *big boys* in this bitch now."

"Man, *whatever...*" Tooch said after looking at Randy and his three teammates.

Over on the other side of the court and up in the stands Inez spotted Randy. She started smiling as she blinked her eyes; trying to make sure that it was really him.

"*Kendra, Kendra*!" she said, pulling on Kendra's left arm to get her attention. But Kendra was busy running her mouth with Billy and some other students who were sitting near her and didn't notice Inez at first.

"What's up?" Kendra asked frowning as she turned around.

"*He's here*...I mean, I'm not sure, but I think he is," Inez stuttered.

"Who? Who's here?"

"It looks like him—*Randy*."

"*Eww, eww...for real*? Where is he?" Kendra asked as she got excited and started looking around.

"Over there," Inez pointed.

"Where, I still don't see 'em."

"Right there! The one over in the blue jacket with the red sleeves. He's got a red bucket hat on."

"I still don't..." Inez only recognized Randy because he momentarily lifted up his hat from covering his face.

"He's right there! Standing with the other three guys...they all have on the same jacket. Now he's talking to the guy from your Spanish class." Inez wrapped her right arm around Kendra's neck and pointed with her left hand. Inez was referring to Tooch as the guy from Kendra's Spanish class.

"Ahh, I see 'em." Randy was now standing directly in front of Tooch and was still very much boasting about his Prescott squad, while looking quite rugged.

"That doesn't mean *shit*...I told you already. I'm standing here right now, and I'm telling you again, so when it happens, don't come to me later and say that I was right, cause I'm not gonna wanna hear it," Tooch said, waving his hands out in front of him. Tooch was not an 'I told you so' kind of guy, even though he very much disliked when people would not listen to him or take his advice.

"Fuck outta here, *man*…it *does* mean something?" Randy said swelling up. "*Shit*…it's the same *damn* team we blew the fuck out in the beginning of the season. Now we have to play 'em in the championship. *Bitch, you crazy*." Randy had his right index finger poking Tooch in the chest. "Like their man's gonna make a difference. He doesn't even score."

"You see 'em?" Inez asked.

"Yeah, I see him now. But come on, let's go over there, so you can say hi," Kendra said grabbing Inez's right arm as she started to get up.

"No! Girl, you crazy?"

"What? Why not?" Kendra asked looking at Inez strangely. "You said that the two of you hit it off well last night, didn't you?"

"Yeah, but so, what does that mean? I can't just go run up on him now while he's talking to people after one conversation."

"Girl, you're losing it. Have you seen yourself lately? Men love that shit. What man wouldn't like a fine, young, lil' honey dip such as yourself, to come run up on him while he's talking with his friends—especially his niggas. Girl, men love that…"

"But I still don't think it would be a good idea," Inez said as she glared over at Randy, clearly looking like she was thinking to herself what she should do.

"Just come on," Kendra said, pulling on Inez's right arm as she started to stand up again.

Inez looked back over at Randy as Kendra held her by her arm then said, "Give me a second."

"Hey, Randy! Randy!" another voice called out.

"Yo, Ran! Randy," Omar said, getting Randy's attention away from Tooch who was now speaking his peace.

"Yeah?"

"That White dude down there is calling you, yo," Omar said, pointing to their right and down at a middle aged White man who was standing by the far right basket waving. It was the reporter from Randy's game earlier; the same guy that had done Randy's interview before the Christmas break.

Randy looked over and noticed who it was, then said, "Uh, it's the reporter from the newspaper…I'll be right back." Randy excused himself before making his way down the stands.

Moments later, He arrived at the bottom of the stands where he walked over and shook the man's hand.

"Hey, what's up, Randy. I didn't know you were gonna be here. I was planning to try and catch you at home."

"Yeah?"

"Yeah, I couldn't get to you earlier. I had to hurry and get down to the office, then get over here and have everything set up before the game." The reporter pointed to his photographer who was standing underneath the basket behind a tripod taking pictures.

"Oh, I hear you..." Randy said.

"But hey, listen, if you want, we can do your interview right now," the reporter offered.

Randy's head popped back after he heard what the reporter just said. He looked around, wide eyed, and said, "*Now*?"

"*Sure*. I don't see why not, but it's up to you. Where ever you feel comfortable."

"Ah, well, ok. I guess..." Randy said reluctantly.

Inez and Kendra both watched as Randy made his way down to the reporter. They saw him stand there and started talking then looked at each other with their eyebrows raised.

"Alright, this is perfect," Kendra said, nodding her head. "He's over there now, and away from his friends, so we can go over and you can say 'hi' to him."

"But he's talking to that man now..." Inez pointed. "I still don't think it is a good idea..."

"*Uh*, girl, *hush* and come on. You're a disgrace to me, Billy and every other good looking woman in the world," Kendra said as she pulled Inez by her arm again and lead her out of their seats with Billy following them.

"Oh look, there's Josh," Inez said referring to a tall light skin kid who was standing up against a wall and talking with some of his friends. The boy had on a hunter green v-neck sweater with the white collar of a button up shirt sticking up from the neck, a pair of light blue denim jeans and a beige pair of brown loafers with no socks. He had the bottoms of his pant legs rolled up and you could clearly see his ankles.

"Girl, later for that dork," Kendra said, yanking Inez again. "We're tryin' to go get you a 'pretty thug.'"

"*Alright*, *alright*, Kendra. But *wait*," Inez said, yanking her arm away from Kendra causing her to stop. "I can't just walk over there and look stupid. I'm gonna have to have something to say."

The three girls ducked back behind the stands where Randy couldn't see them, but Josh, who noticed what was going on frowned. Even though Josh continued with his conversation, he could still clearly tell that there was some sort of encouraging going on by the look on Kendra's face. She was talking to Inez animatedly and kept peeking around the stands at Randy.

"We can just go over there and say that we're looking for someone."

"You are a horrible liar," Inez said defiantly.

"No, I'm serious. Just be like, we can walk over there and you can say, 'Is that her? Oh, that ain't her, but oh hey, what's up Randy?'"

"Oh my *goodness*. You're a horrible actor too," Inez said helplessly placing her right hand on her forehead as she closed her eyes.

"Hey, well, look. Couldn't we just say that we were going over to use the ladiesroom?" Billy asked as she pointed to the restrooms that were just pass Randy and the reporter.

"Yeah, there you go, that's it, now come on," Kendra said, pulling Inez's arm as she started walking.

Inez quickly snatched her arm back and gave Kendra a sharp look saying, "Look, now, if we're goin' over there, you can't pull on me. I'm nervous enough as it is..."

"Alright, I won't pull on you, but just come on."

"And you can't act up, either," Inez said making a face like she was demanding this of Kendra, but her voice sounded more like she was pleading for her not too.

"Alright, I won't. Now would you come on!"

The girls started walking over and after only a few steps, Inez had to slap Kendra's hand down from pulling on her again. Randy stood in front of the reporter with his arms folded, watching him write down everything he said in a small yellow notebook. He looked over the reporter's right shoulder and noticed the girls coming straight toward him. At first Randy didn't recognize Inez, but then she smiled and waved at him and her face immediately popped back into his head. Randy truly wasn't in a million years expecting to see her pretty face at the game, nor was he expecting to see her wearing a Tech school uniform. Once the ladies got close enough to hear what Randy was saying, Randy immediately started using his best NBA interview impersonation voice.

"Yeah, well, you know...we just wanted to come out and rebound well, and uh, fill the passing lanes, just get out and run together, as a team, you know? Like coach wanted us to do all week, you know, bring everything together..."

The reporter frowned as he listened to Randy's voice change, trying to figure out why he now sounded so much like Michael Jordan. He looked over his shoulder and saw the girls walking by smiling and he just shook his head. The reporter tried not to make it seem obvious that he knew what Randy was doing so he just continued asking him questions normally.

"So, what do you think your coach's take was on your team's effort out there today, especially coming into the championship week? Do you think he may still be a little worried or concerned about you boys being ready?"

"I think he shouldn't be worried, but, knowing coach, he'll still find something to worry about. But that's just coach," Randy said, waving to Inez with a gracious smile as she walked pass. Kendra made sure she got a really good look at Randy as they passed by, and when Randy looked at her, she was cheezing from ear to ear. Billy, though, just gave him a submissive stare and didn't smile or do anything except blink.

"And what's the feeling like for you guys, since no one was expecting you boys to do so well this season? Since you've already beaten the team you're getting ready to face in the beginning of the season by a large margin," the reporter continued.

"It feels great knowing that no one believed in us at the beginning of this season. But, it's the same as usual; no downtime during the season, you know, we know what we're gonna be there to do and we know what they're gonna be there to do. Plus, they're still the defending Champs until we beat them."

The girls caught some of what Randy was saying and were very impressed. With the huge roaring crowd and the band playing in the background, the ambiance only made Inez want to talk to Randy even more. Now she could clearly tell that, like Josh, Randy was *about* something.

"I think he looks cuter now than I remember," Inez said, frowning.

"Now, see, look at you," Kendra said, smiling.

Randy finished up with his interview then shook the reporter's hand before turning and starting toward Inez, who was now standing outside the ladies room.

"Oh, we're goin' inside," Kendra said, after seeing Randy on his way over.

"What's up, lady?" Randy said to Inez, who was just realizing that he was bowlegged. "I didn't expect to see you here."

"Yeah, me either," Inez said, looking up from his legs. Randy smiled then pulled lightly at the left shoulder of Inez's black uniform sweater.

"Who's Randy over there talking to?" Omar asked, turning and looking at Tooch. The six boys all turned and looked over at Randy at the same time.

"I don't know," Tooch answered.

"Oh, I think I know who that is," Zac said, with his eyes popping wide open.

"Who is it?" Tooch asked.

"That's the female he met at the gas station, remember?" Zac looked at Tooch and nodded his head like he was trying to get Tooch to remember.

"Oh, yeah, I remember her now," Tooch said, nodding back. "She goes to Tech!" Tooch said, frowning.

"Yo, guess who else that is?" Zac asked Tooch again but this time his eyes got even bigger.

"Who?" Tooch now had a lost look on his face.

"She's the one you always call stingy when you see her in the hallway!"

"I, do?" Tooch said tilting his head to the side with a bit of a smile on his face.

"Yeah…"

"Oh, shit!" Tooch said becoming happy. "That's *her*? That's who that is?" Tooch looked back at Randy and laughed.

"Yeah, you remember now?" Zac asked.

"Yeah, but, ok big *Randy*. I see you pa," Tooch looked back at Zac and Omar and said, "That's my man! *Haa*! I knew one of us could get her!"

CHAPTER 58

Down on the court, Tridane stripped Duane Jones clean of the ball and flew up the court for an easy and uncontested two-handed backwards dunk, cutting Tech's lead to three with 4:05 left in the game. Randy watched the whole play and just shook his head silently.

"I see you're still speaking to reporters—even while you're in *my* school," Inez smirked playfully.

"Yeah, you know how it is. But, yeah, you know this is the school my mans and 'em go to."

"Really? I didn't know," Inez purposely gave Randy a clueless look like she was lost.

"Yeah, but anyway, this is a more than pleasant surprise to see you here like this," Randy said. Inez nodded her head in agreement as she momentarily looked away from Randy, running her tongue across her top teeth. Even though Inez was unaware of if, this was truly one of Randy's turn-ons when it came to females. Randy almost fainted after he saw what Inez just did with her mouth. Inez noticed the look on his face as he was now staring at her lips and asked, "What's wrong? Do I have something on my face?"

"Huh? Oh, uh, no…I was just checking out the color of your lip gloss, your make up looks nice on you," Randy said, snapping out of his temporary trance and frowning, as he looked away from her while thinking about the dumbass response he just gave.

"*Sheesh*…hey, well look, I'm goin' back up to my seat before ole' Otis over there starts tryin' to make his way over here," Randy said after taking notice to an older security guard who was clearing people off the floor level. "He looks like he might wanna start takin' people down to the ground."

"Y'all gonna have to clear out from over here and go back to y'all seats," the older Black security guard said, getting Inez's attention while she was unknowingly staring at Randy. Inez looked at the security guard and smiled at Randy's comments. She looked back at Randy, who leaned up from resting against the wall, listening to him say, "But try to be around after the game. I wanna talk to you a little more. Alright?"

"Alright…" Inez watched as Randy walked over and stood in a line behind some people going back up to their seats before turning to her right and looking in the crack of the door at Kendra and Billy. The girls were hiding behind it.

"*Eww*…you *owe* me," Kendra said as she and Billy stepped out smiling. "Say that you don't! Say you don't!"

Inez looked at Kendra and shook her head saying, "Yeah, ok, I owe you…"

"Yup, and that's all I wanna hear," Kendra said.

"Ok ladies, y'all gonna have to move it. It's time to get back to y'all seats. We need to clear this out before the end of the game, y'all hear me?" the security guard asked as he stared directly into Kendra's eyes through his thick bifocal glasses. The game, however, was in its last few minutes of regulation as the game clock now showed 2:37 remaining. Tech was still ahead 87-85.

"What'd I miss?" Randy asked as he stood back next to the fellas.

"Nothing much, except for your homies getting' ready to blow the game," Omar said.

"That was the female from the gas station, wasn't it?" Zac asked smiling.

"Yeah…" Randy answered blushing a little.

"How come you didn't tell us she went here?" Zac asked.

"I didn't even know," Randy said.

"Ah, man!" Omar shouted in despair. Down on the court, Duane Jones attempted a bad pass that was nearly picked off by Tridane; luckily the pass was deflected out of bounds. The two teams both scored a few more baskets and found themselves knotted at 91-91 with 1:03 left to play. Tech was clearly the much bigger and what looked like the better team, but New Jersey was able to stick with them. Tridane, who received some help from a wirey 6-feet-7, 200 pound kid named Stacey Curtis, who pitched in 25 points, was in the midst of posting a career high 56 points and was still looking to drop in more for New Jersey. Tridane, like Randy, was a scoring machine and had very bad intentions when he was out on the court. Tridane's facial expressions made him always seemed to resemble that of an angry snake. Sean came down court and missed a wide-open jumper from the left side in rhythm. The ball skimmed off the side of the rim and landed in Stacey Curtis' hands. Stacey quickly turned and passed the ball to Tridane, who caught it then weaved his way up court through traffic using his yo-yo of a dribble straight to the basket. But Chuck, Tech's enforcer, immediately chopped him down out of the air as soon as he left his feet causing Tridane's father and the New Jersey fans to stand up shouting in dismay.

"Where's the damn foul? He should be ejected for that!" New Jersey's coach stood up from his team's bench and got into the face of one of the referees who was passing by their bench. The crowd also started chanting the infamous chant "Asshole."

"It's two foul shots coming up! Two shots!" the ref that called the foul said as he ran over to the scores table, trying his best not to look over at New Jersey's head coach, who was presently being restrained by two of his assistants. Chuck showed no remorse for Tridane who was grimacing as he was helped up from the floor by some of his teammates. Tridane made his way the top of the key, walking with a slight limp, where his team had huddled. After the huddle, Tridane went to the foul line and sank both foul shots, giving his team a two-point advantage. Rob brought the ball up court, jogging lightly then shouted, "set it up," as he raised his right hand in the air and looked up at the game clock.

"Four spread!" he yelled and caused his team to separate to go start setting picks for one another.

"What was that?" Khalil asked Randy after watching Duane Jones run the wrong way around a pick.

"I don't know," Randy said squinting his eyes and shaking his head as he then turned and looked at Tooch.

Sean received a pass from Rob and drove baseline, throwing down a very athletic looking left handed dunk pass two people.

"Ok, *Sean*!" Randy cheered after seeing how Sean had to twist his body in order to make the play work.

"*Ooh…ah*!" the crowd roared. The score was now 96-96 with only 36 seconds left to play.

"D-up, d-up!" Sean cried out as he came down from the rim and sprinted back on defense. New jersey's point guard received the inbounds pass from Tridane then tapped it right back to him. Tridane, who immediately looked up at the game clock, brought the ball up across half court in a hurry with no one guarding him. Once Tridane got across half court, he looked at Duane Jones who was standing in front of him in a defensive stance. Tridane squinted his eyes before backing up and looking up at the clock again. He leaned forward as he started dribbling toward Duane with his left, he then faked a crossover and stepped right past him using little effort. Tridane next went and pulled up for an uncontested 15-foot 'stop and pop' jumper that fell straight down.

"*Damn*!" Randy said cringing after he saw Duane standing in the same spot looking like he was in awe. "You think he might wanna start playin' defense now?" Tooch looked at Randy with his lips turned up and could only shake his head.

"*Timeout*!" Tech's head coach, a wired Black man in his early 40's named Cal, called out in a panic. He almost pushed a ref down that he didn't see coming up on him as he turned around.

"That was not supposed to happen," Khalil said as both he and Taj looked at each other shaking their heads. Tridane walked pass Chuck with a grin on his face as the two teams headed for their benches. The game clock was now showing only nine seconds and New Jersey was ahead 98-96.

"Close the door! Let's close the *fuckin'* door on this overrated pack of bitches!" Stacey Curtis yelled as he received high fives from his teammates who came partially out on the court to applaud them.

"Yo, *chill*, yo..." one of his teammates said after seeing how a referee glanced at him, looking like he was getting ready to call him for a technical foul for unsportsmanlike conduct.

"Man, fuck these dudes!" Stacey insisted. Tridane walked over to his team's bench and sat down, not saying a word or cracking a smile, took a cup of water from his team's water girl, and started nodding his head as he listened to his coach talking to him.

Randy watched Tridane's behavior carefully and couldn't help but notice his reaction to all of the commotion was very similar to his own earlier. Tridane looked down the sideline at Tech huddled around their coach, who was now drawing up a play on a clipboard. Coach Cal drew up a play for Duane Jones to take the last shot, but once the horn sounded for the two teams to come back on the court, Cal didn't appear all that happy with what he had just drawn up. He looked at Coach Davis, flailing his eyes as if to say, "Oh boy, here goes nothing," then exhaled.

The teams ran back out onto the floor and Tech did exactly as they were told, getting the ball into Duane's hands with nine seconds still remaining on the game clock. Because New Jersey, like Tech, played mostly man to man defense, Tridane was left guarding him. As soon as Duane started dribbling, Tridane immediately moved close to him, placing his left forearm into Duane's right hip. Even though Tridane was using physical contact to guard Duane, it still wasn't enough to ward a personal foul call. Duane, without even bothering to attempt a move, charged toward the basket with a full head of steam and pressed back against Tridane's arm. Tridane then stepped back and away from him, putting both of his hands up in the air and watched as Duane lost his balance and went crashing hard to the floor. Duane lost his footing and slid into the lane, going into an airplane-like slide with both of his arms extended outward. New Jersey's point guard kindly slid over scooping up the ball and passed it ahead to Tridane who had already started down court. Tridane caught the pass, stopped and flung the ball up as high as he could in the air yelling, "*Yeah*!"

"Yeah, Baby!" Stacey Curtis yelled, screaming in Chuck's ear as he ran pass him with his hands held up high in the air and as the final horn sounded. The game was over and the favored Tech team had fallen to New Jersey 98-96 on their home court.

"*I told you*! *I told you*!" was all Tooch could say as he looked at Randy, who was standing in shock. "*Fuckin' whore…*" Tooch said as he looked down at Duane who was still lying on the court where he came to the end of his slide.

Tech went to try and shake New Jersey's hands but New Jersey was too busy celebrating. They had all climbed on top of each other dancing at center court until the whole crowd fell to the floor.

"Never mind!" Coach Cal said waving his team back and sending them to their locker room. No one from Tech's team even bothered to try and pick up Duane Jones. Those whose way he was blocking just stepped over him. Sean, however, didn't feel like leaving the court just yet and pulled away from everyone who tried to console him. He sat at center court staring up into the crowd, away from the New Jersey team's celebration. Sean watched as the crowd quickly cleared the arena after the heartbreaking lost. He placed both of his hands behind his head and leaned back, staring up at the ceiling which was decorated with burgundy, gold and ivory colored championship banners that were won many years ago. This was Sean's third year at Tech, and for the second straight year in a row, he had made it this far and came up short.

"Come on, man. Let's get the fuck out of here," Zac said turning and starting the boys toward the door. All six boys headed for the doors, leaving Randy, who sat down and started staring down at Sean behind.

"Yo, we'll be out in the parking lot," Omar said without looking down at Randy as he passed by him.

Sean sat up and started looking around the arena. He noticed Randy was still sitting in the stands and looking down at him. The two of them made eye contact but never said a word or moved a muscle. It almost looked like they were communicating without saying anything to each other. Sean dropped his head and looked down at the floor, in between his legs, after seeing Randy stand up and put both his hands in his jacket pockets, appearing ready to leave. As Randy turned from his aisle, he spotted two New Jersey assistants who slammed the visitor's looker room door open and went in, both yucking up it. Randy looked at them and then back at Sean, who was still looking up at him with a long face, and turned and walked out the doors.

CHAPTER 59

Over at the house, Mr. Shan was sitting in his living room on the couch listening to oldies, as he fanned through some of his old photos of him and Zac's mother, Carmen. He stared at each picture as he sipped from his glass of Belvi, then closed his eyes and started to think back about some of the romantic dialogue that he and his childhood sweetheart had shared in the past. There isn't a series of words in the English dictionary that could describe the pain in his heart for what he allowed to happen to her. Mr. Shan stood up, holding a close-up photo of her in his left hand and his glass in his right, and began dancing as he thought back to when they were at their senior prom. Before long, the dreadful and dark thoughts of everything that happened the night that she was murdered played out in his mind, and like in all heartfelt or touching moments, something presented itself and disrupted the setting. The phone started ringing. Mr. Shan slowly opened his eyes and glared across the living room at the black cordless telephone that was sitting on its charge. He watched as it rang for about ten seconds before he crabbily went over and answered it.

"Hello?" he slurred in a groaning voice.

"Hey, Shan, what's up big guy?" Diego said happily, which caused Mr. Shan to lower his eyes to the floor, exhaling. "I tried giving you a call earlier, but the telephone just kept ringing," Diego said jokingly and was left listening to nothing but the sound of Mr. Shan breathing into the telephone. "Do you have a minute?" Diego asked now trying to speed things up a bit.

"No, not really," Mr. Shan said calmly.

"Well, do you want me to give you a call back later?"

"Nah, that's alright. I'll give a call you back."

"Ok. Around what time, so I can…" Diego was cut short by Mr. Shan hanging the telephone up in his ear. "I…I could stop…" Diego's face went pale. His cousin, Blanko, who was sitting on the arm of a broken old couch in front of him, could clearly tell that he had just been hung up on.

Diego and Blanko were in what looked like one of their offices, but in reality it was nothing more than a room inside one of Diego's crack houses. The only furniture in the room was an old couch, a lamp that had no shade on it, which was providing the only light in the room, and an office desk that looked like it never had much of a purpose.

Diego closed his cell phone and pressed the hand that he was holding it in up underneath his chin. "You know, we really don't need this fuckin' guy," Blanko said giggling slightly to himself as he shook his head. "We have enough contacts to pull our own weight around here." Diego quickly looked up from the desk at Blanko with a sharp look. "Me, personally, I'm saying this guy is nothing more than just another old man who has been in the game far too long; he's clearly worn out his welcome. We don't need this moyo to make any money. All that should be left now is for him to just get the fuck out of our way. I mean, say the word, and I'm saying I'll personally go move this *fuck*."

"*Patience*, Blanko. Patience. We have to see this thing through first," Diego said patting the top of the desk with his right hand in a calming motion.

"See *what* through? The message is *clear*. You can't see it?" Blanko got up and stood on Diego's right side, looking down at him with both his of hands pressed down on the wood in front of him. "And *Patience*? *Papi*, *Patience* was the little girl that lived down the street when we were younger. We both shared her…*remember*? But now, it's time for us to deal with this. It's time for us to take care of our business as grown men." Diego cut his eyes away from the floor and started staring at his cousin thinking to himself.

CHAPTER 60

In South Philly, Randy made his way across the crowded but silent parking lot over to Kendra's small navy blue car where Inez, Kendra and Billy sat waiting.

"Yo," Randy said as he walked up to the driver's window where Inez was sitting. "Y'all alright?"

"Yeah, we're cool," Inez answered, glancing at Kendra, who was sitting next to her in the front passenger seat. "Are *you* alright?" Inez asked looking up at Randy with her eyebrows slightly raised. "I saw you sitting over there after the game. You looked like you took it harder than we did." Randy looked down at Inez, a bit shocked to hear that she noticed.

"Yeah, I'm good. It ain't shit," Randy replied in a cool, relaxed tone that brought an instant smile to Kendra's face. "You know how that goes, that's a part of what we do..." Inez noticed Kendra smiling and did a double take, but she tried her best to ignore it so Randy wouldn't see her.

"So what're you doing after this?" Inez asked.

"I don't know, we'll probably go back to my man's house and chill for the night," as Randy spoke Zac's gold SUV with black tinted windows pulled up on the other side of the street, behind him, with the music blaring, and parked, facing in the opposite direction of the girls' car. Randy looked back at Zac who was sitting behind the wheel then at Inez who was now saying, "But hey, I forgot to tell you inside—*congratulations*."

Randy looked at her strangely then asked, "For what?"

"You guys won earlier today, right?"

"Ah, yeah. Thanks," Randy started nodding his head slowly as he looked down at her surprised again. "Why does it seem like you're so wrapped up in sports? You know somebody who plays or something?"

"Uh, yeah..." she groaned lightly as she nodded her head. "My brother... he plays in college."

"Really? Where?" Randy asked.

"In Florida."

"Ah..."

"Aren't your friends over there waitn' for you?" Inez asked lifting her nose up at the boys.

"Nah, they're good. It's cool," Randy said quickly, glancing back over his left shoulder at them. A few minutes passed before Randy said, "But, yo, I'm gonna get over here with them anyway and let you ladies get over the bridge before it gets late, alright?"

"Alright," Inez answered smiling back.

"But you drive careful and I'll talk to you later...alright?" Inez nodded her head as Randy gently touched her left arm and turned to walk away.

"Bye, bye," Inez said smiling even bigger once he turned his back to her. The girls watched as Randy climbed into the front passenger seat of the SUV and pulled off with smiles on their faces. Inez turned and looked at Kendra with a look on her face that said, 'Yeah, I know, he looks good," before she put the car in gear and took off.

CHAPTER 61

Exactly nine days later on a late Sunday afternoon, Prescott and Shadewood high schools were duke'n it out for the Public League crown. The high scoring slugfest took place at the same collegiate venue as the semifinals game. This time there were more than twelve thousand fans in attendance, including Tooch, Zac, Omar, Inez, Kendra, Billy, agents Smith and Rapth, and Mr. Wyble. Mr. Wyble attended but didn't want Randy to know he was there. He and agents Smith and Rapth sat high above the court, but just below the second level where Randy could not see him. Inez, Kendra and Billy were 20 rows up from the floor and on the opposite side of the court from Zac, Tooch and Omar. The boys were just four rows from the action and sitting exactly behind the scores tables at midcourt.

Prescott trailed 37-32 with one minute and ten seconds remaining before the half. Pooh slung a one-handed pass over to the left wing to Khalil. Khalil, standing just inside the bend of the three-point line, gave his defender a quick right-footed jab step toward the middle of the lane. Khalil saw his defender had rocked back on his heels and he lowered his shoulder attempting to dribble around him. Khalil went to the basket with the defender trailing closely and missed a tough lay-up. Fortunately for Prescott, Randy flew in and ripped the ball down out of the air from amongst a crowd of players from both teams. Randy's midair collision caused him to stumble as he dribbled back out to the three-point line collecting himself. A defender started to come out to Randy and he took one quick dribble, causing him to pause. Randy then stepped back, launching up a three-pointer that fell straight through. The crowd erupted and Zac shouted "*Booom*!" in Tooch's direction.

Omar was sitting between Zac and Tooch, attempting to serve as some sort of bumper for their trash talking. But it didn't help because every time

Prescott did something good, their fans would cheer so loud that they shook the arena. Shadewood quickly inbounded the ball, forcing Prescott to scurry back on defense. Because Shadewood was aware of Prescott's offensive firepower, they wanted to make them use a large part of their energy on defense. Shadewood's 6-feet-8 leading rebounder and second star player received a pass, as he was cutting through the lane, and was fouled by Taj going for a lay-up. He missed the lay-up then missed the first of his two free throws. He stepped back from the line trying to calm himself, then loaded up and clanked the second one as well. The crowd responded with boos and cheers as Khalil corralled the ball. Khalil passed the ball to Pooh, who took three dribbles and tossed it up court to Randy. Randy was already on the other side of the court and immediately went into a triple threat position, squaring up at his defender. As soon as the other four players on Randy's team came down court, Randy gave the defender a quick right-footed jab step then exploded pass him. Randy got to the top of the key and stopped, firing up yet another healthy three-ball that fell straight through again. Zac and Omar stood to their feet along with the rest of the crowd both yelling at the ref and cheering.

"The boy is bad!" Zac shouted again, aiming his remarks at Tooch. Randy's shot not only drew a big response from the crowd because of its timing, but because the defender hit his arm, fouling him. But the foul was not called. Shadewood inbounded the ball quickly and raced up the floor, causing Prescott to hustle back again. Their star player dribbled to the three-point line where he saw an opening to the basket and attacked it at full speed. But he too would miss the shot after being fouled. He then went to the foul line and missed both free throws; the same as his teammate had just done. Randy pulled the ball down out of the air and took his time dribbling up court. He stepped across half court, watching the time on the game clock expire in the first half, then placed the ball on the floor and walked away from it to an array of applause. At the end of the first half, Prescott now lead 38-37 and Randy had 18 points.

Minutes later, Mr. Wyble and agents Smith and Rapth were laughing and joking loudly as they left their seating section to head toward the concession areas. But their jokes came to an almost immediate halt when they were met by a surprise.

"*Inez...*" Smith said with his smile drying up. "What're *you* doing here?" The sound of Smith's voice captured Inez's attention instantly and the sight of them made her nearly go into shock. Smith then reached out and gave her a hug and she quickly calmed down.

"Oh, umm…I'm here with my friends. We came to see someone play," she said looking at Kendra and Billy who were standing with their eyebrows raised in shock also. Kendra and Billy both knew exactly what was going on.

"Oh, yeah? What team does he play for? Prescott?" Mr. Wyble asked.

Inez turned to Kendra, looking like she was asking, "What should I say next?" and Kendra answered, "No, the other team…uh, Shadewood…" Inez turned back to Mr. Wyble nodding her head agreeing.

"Oh, ok. Well, enjoy the rest of the game. We aren't going to hold you ladies up then. Plus I'm starving…" Smith said stepping pass them and heading down the concourse.

"Tell your father I'll call him," Rapth said as he and Mr. Wyble followed.

After watching the three gentlemen walk away, Inez turned back to Kendra and Billy breathing a sigh of relief.

The second half went almost exactly like the first—a tight-fisted battle heading into the forth quarter. Prescott played man to man defense, pressuring Shadewood's perimeter players, while Shadewood played a three-two zone. The score was now 61-58 in Prescott's favor.

Shadewood trapped Randy, Khalil, and Pooh every time they went to the basket, forcing them to pass the ball. Randy now had 24 points, followed by Khalil with 22, and Pooh with 11. Early in the forth quarter was when the three boys went on a tirade for Prescott. They knocked down six three-point baskets on six out of nine trips down the floor, causing Shadewood's head coach to signal for his final timeout.

"Here we go again," he exhaled. The crowd noise was already at full tilt, but once the timeout was called it went to almost deafening. Inez, Kendra and Billy all stood to their feet, with the rest of the crowd applauding. They were looking at each other with smiles on their faces and their eyebrows once again raised. They were now experiencing the pure '*majesty*' of a public league championship game. Since Shadewood had missed some of their shots, they now trailed 79-65 with just under six minutes left in the game. Randy, Khalil, Pooh, Taj and the fifth player on the floor for Prescott gave each other midair side bumps, as the reserves charged halfway out on the court to meet them. Randy looked up in the stands at Inez and tooted his nose up at her like "what's up," causing her to smile.

"You're gonna learn not to go against the grain," Zac yelled at Tooch, leaning across Omar as all three boys were now standing. Tooch, of course, wasn't really against Randy but he liked to nitpick from time to time.

"Think it's over yet?" Rapth asked Smith and Mr. Wyble.

"I don't know, but I sure hope so," Mr. Wyble answered.

"They're gonna have to come out of that zone," Smith added. "I know that for damn sure!"

When Shadewood went on defense, they were playing man to man. That played right into Prescott's hands as Randy and Khalil went nuts. They set screens for each other, ran pick and roll plays and even tossed up a few alley hoops to each other. When time ran out, the Prescott fans stormed the floor and Randy, who finished with 35 points and Khalil with 34, were jumping around hugging each other at midcourt.

"*Aah*...that's my man's an 'em!" Tooch shouted, beating Zac and Omar out on the court to go celebrate. Randy was hoisted into the air by the crowd before being carried to the ladder for the cutting down of the nets. He finished his junior year averaging 30.1 points a game.

Inez, Kendra and Billy were still standing up in the stands in front of their seats when Kendra turned to Inez and asked, "So, have you made up your mind yet on what you want to do?"

But Inez was in a deep stargaze watching Randy as he stood on the ladder pumping up the crowd with the net in his hand.

"*Inez*!" Kendra repeated nudging her.

Inez took a moment then answered, "Huh, oh...um...yeah...I'm gonna talk to him, see what he's *really* about," taking her eyes off of Randy. Kendra and Billy looked at each other, smiling with their eyebrows scrunched.

Kendra answered, "*Uuh, Inez,* that's *good*. I'm glad for you, but that's *not* what I was asking." Inez then snapped out of it looking at her. "I was asking if you wanted to go down on the court and join the celebration." Billy snickered then started shaking her head as she turned away.

"*Uh*, yeah, *um*, *sure*. We can go down..."

Hold dat...